99 YEARS ON
DEVIL'S ISLAND

That was just for treason. For murder Silvera drew a second century-minus-one stretch. It didn't matter that he was innocent—most of the inhabitants of the planet of Barafunda's penal colony were. Devil's Island was escape proof—but Silvera knew where he could lay his hands on a store of sneezing powder and some whoopie cushions. . . .

THEY BLEW THE
BUTLER AWAY

Worse than that, they'd stolen the secret files —the ones that could put Dunjer's boss in jail and Dunjer out of a job.

There was only one thing to do—follow their trail to Hatesville, to Puritanburg . . . wherever it led. The one thing he didn't count on was the damned time warp. . . .

BINARY STAR NO .3

DR. SCOFFLAW
Ron Goulart

OUTERWORLD
Isidore Haiblum

A Dell Book

Published by
Dell Publishing Co., Inc.
1 Dag Hammarskjold Plaza
New York, New York 10017

ISBN: 0-440-10526-9

Printed in the United States of America
First printing—August 1979

DR. SCOFFLAW

Ron Goulart

Jose Silvera came pushing his way through the crowded foyer of the flying house. A big wide-shouldered man in his early thirties, he nudged into the afternoon cocktail party which filled the vast glass-walled living room. He refused a drink from one of the roving barobots, dodged a stunning green-skinned authoress of selfhelp books, stepped over a well-known lizard man police procedural novelist who was sprawled on the seethrough floor and grabbed the arm of a hefty toadman in a blue sudasilk suit.

". . . coincidence my Aunt Dejah!" the toad-headed green man was saying to three small fearful humans. "That dingblasted gargoyle bears an uncanny resemblance to me."

"Only because it's melting, Mr. Oozman," offered one of the tiny fearful humans.

"We'll ask this total stranger." Oozman turned to Silvera. "Sir, do you see that gargoyle sitting on the food and refreshment table yonder? The one carved from honey-based carob-flavored ice cream."

"You mean the one that's a spitting image of you, Oozman?" Silvera increased the pressure of his grip on the publisher's arm.

The three small fearful humans groaned. "There goes a brilliant career in public relations," murmured one forlornly.

"Aha!" gloated Oozman. "I told you the dogbusted thing was intended as a sendup of me. Me, the most successful publisher on the planet Barafunda. The

7

man who brings you Oozman & Son hardcovers, Ooz-
buk Paperbacks, Oozflik Movies, Ooz—"

"Where is he?" interrupted Silvera.

"Young man, you've been, especially since you are
a complete and total stranger to me and more than
likely a gatecrasher in the bargain, most helpful in
confirming my worst suspicions," said the toad publisher. "Now, however, I must ask you to—"

"I wrote the book."

"No time to look at unsolicited submissions, my
boy. Bring your manuscript to our offices on—"

"I mean this book, the one the party is for." Silvera
pointed at the largest and nearest poster which dec-
orated the cocktail area. "I ghosted it."

"You penned *Gargoyle Power*?" Oozman's green
eyelids flickered. "Then you must be . . . Jose Silvera."

The trio of tiny fearful human public relations
men moaned. "Shall we attempt to give him the old
heave-ho, Mr. Oozman?" one inquired in a very small
voice.

"Jose Silvera," continued the green publisher, "one
of the most formidable freelance writers in the
Barnum System of planets, indeed in the entire
known universe. A man who is not only incredibly
fast but is the master of any style from that of teenage-
girl horse stories to multisexual how-to manuals. Yes,
I've heard a good deal about you, Silvera."

"Did you hear I always collect?"

Oozman blinked more rapidly. "You are no doubt
aware of my reputation in the publishing field. Oozman may well be a cutthroat and an egomaniac, but
he always pays on time."

"You paid Gillis Logan the final money due on *Gargoyle Power* prior to publication, didn't you?"

"Of course."

"Of course," echoed the three small humans.

Oozman went on, "Logan's check for $5000 went out to him several weeks ago. A small amount admittedly, since we didn't realize how many people here in Camposanto Territory would take *Gargoyle Power* to their hearts, begin to learn the ancient secrets hidden in the facades of cathedrals and—"

"Logan owes me $2500." Silvera was scanning the crowd of a hundred or more.

"A matter to be settled between you and Logan," Oozman told him. "One which should have been settled weeks since."

"I was over in Vigilanza Territory ghosting a book for a girl who had a vision," the big author explained. "Got back here yesterday, to find no money waiting."

"A vision? What sort of vision? Something uplifting?" Oozman nodded at his three small human associates. "We might be able to use a book like that on our list. Who's the publisher?"

"Lederer, Street & Zeus. Is Logan here yet?"

"What exactly did this girl see?"

"A goat." Silvera let go of Oozman. He'd spotted Gillis Logan across the room signing a copy of *Gargoyle Power* for a pudgy seven-year-old boy editor who specialized in series books about daredevil robots. "Excuse me."

"A goat?" Oozman frowned at his tiny humans. "What do you think?"

"Goats are sacred in some parts of that territory," said one of the smallish humans. "Around here, though, we might not find an audience . . ."

Silvera avoided a six-armed drinkserving robot, eluded a catgirl who mistook him for Archbishop Fairfield and shoved to within ten feet of the dog-faced Logan. Then someone grabbed his crotch.

"Oof," said Silvera.

"Joe, did I fondle you too briskly again? Darn, I'm really and truly sorry. You're the absolutely last person I want to—"

"Lotti," said Silvera to the lovely redhaired girl who was clutching his private parts, "I'm enroute to collect some money from Gillis Logan so—"

"Did you ghost *Gargoyle Power* for him?" Lotti Waxer's lovely green eyes went wide.

"Yeah, and he still owes me . . . oof!"

"There I go again. My sisters are always chiding me for my enthusiasm. I figure if you're fond of someone, which I am of you, manifest it." She caught the hand Silvera was sending down to rescue his groin, lifted it up to cup one of her smooth warm breasts. "I wish you'd write for Waxer Sisters again, Joe. You did promise me, as I recall, that the next time you hit our territory, you'd get in touch. Do you know the *Yurt Repair Manual* you did for us is still continuing to sell marvelously?"

"Your royalty statements don't indicate such a state of affairs." Absently he rubbed his palm over the girl's lovely breast, while scowling over her shoulder at the unaware Logan.

"Would I cheat you, Joe? Would any of the Waxer Sisters cheat you? After all you mean to—"

"There's another thing, Lotti. This trip I don't want all four of you barging into my—"

"There are five of us, Joe. Surely the man who wrote a hotselling *Yurt Repair Manual* and a guide to carnivorous shrubs for the Waxer Sisters publishing house can remember how many of—"

"Four, five. I'll talk to you later, Lotti."

"You're toying with my kazaba as though you cared some for me. Am I still your favorite Waxer?"

"Kazaba? Since when did you start referring to breasts as—"

Crash!

Tinkle!

Wamp!

"You ought not to do that, clucko!"

"It ain't proper at all, clucko!"

Across the room, quite near the lengthy food table, four young men in two-piece neogold sparklesuits had picked up a baldheaded man of thirty-three and tossed him.

The man, who wore several cameras dangling round his neck, hit the table and slid across it, bowling the ice-cream gargoyle off onto the seethrough floor. He then landed upon it with a mushy thunk.

The fifth gold-suited person was a young woman. Tall, large-breasted, platinum-haired. She was giggling while massaging her chest. "Playing grabbo with a novelist ain't nice at all."

"Whoa now," said the bald man as he arose from behind the table. "You invited me to grasp your kazabas prior to immortalizing them on film for *Momentary Fame Magazine*." Shedding fragments of gargoyle, he came back around the long table.

One of the gold-clothed lads glowered at the assaulted girl. "Did you up and do that, Gussie?"

"Well, I did perhaps say as how I had a handsome set and he might like to—"

"Don't you see that kind of stuff's going to ruin our literary rep?"

Close to Silvera's ear Lotti whispered, "I'm still at the same beach house, Joe. I'd better go control this frumus; it's one of our novelists."

"Which one of them?"

"All five, it's the Murdstone Writers Group. Haven't you heard of them? Their *I Wandered Lonely As A Cloud* is a smash bestseller on six planets, eight satellites and an asteroid. We published it only last week here in Camposanto, yet already—"

"I'll give Palma a hand." Silvera started in the direction of the squabble.

"That's Palma the photog, is it?"

"It is he."

"He's rumored to be one of the horniest men in the Barnum System." Lotti pushed after him.

"Justifiably so," said Silvera. "Hey, Palma!"

The bald man was twisting his moustache back into a satisfying position. "Can it be Jose Silvera, the prince of hacks, the prolific champion of—"

"He didn't get smeared there," one of the Murdstone Writers Group told Gussie.

The platinum-haired girl, using a swatch she'd torn from the neodamask tablecloth, was wiping gargoyle ice cream off Palma's garments.

Silvera made it to the photographer's side, shook hands. "Is your partner Jack Summer on Barafunda with you?"

"Nope, Summer got sent to Murdstone to cover a presidential corruption scandal, a routine assignment," replied Palma. "Me, they shipped here to do a photo essay on minimum-security dungeons. This party is merely a diversion, although I've been getting some

12

splendid shots of yonkers and kazabas. You wouldn't think literary-type ladies would be so amply endowed, yet the pickings have been fantastic. I encountered a girl who authors obscene crossword puzzles whose set of chawammos could, and nearly did, knock my eye out. See, I was bending near to examine a fascinating pendant worn in the vicinity of—"

"Do me a favor," requested Silvera.

"You want me to stop talking about tits? I know it's an obsession with me, I tend to get repetitious about it. I've even gone so far as to consult therapists about the problem. One lady psychiatrist with offices in a satellite orbiting Jupiter turned out to be gifted with the most poignant set of boopies I had, up to that time, ever viewed. By poignant I mean they shared a quality with certain puppy dogs and pretty toddlers. Seeing them you were moved to exclaim, 'Ooh, ah,' while overcome with an irresistible desire to pet them. Which is how I came to be orbiting Jupiter for a short time without benefit of satellite. Fortunately—"

"Go over and take a picture of Logan."

"That dog-faced simp? I couldn't even fit him into *Fringe*, the magazine for almost celebs, Jose," said the bald photographer. "The last dogman author I tried to capture on film insisted on posing with his favorite bone. Well, the goddamn thing was buried in his yard and by the time—"

"Logan owes me $2500."

"Ah." Palma's fuzzy moustache curled upward as he grinned. "Still living up to your reputation for always collecting your fees."

"You've freelanced, you know what it's like," said

13

Silvera. "You can't ever let them think they can get away with stiffing you."

"I'll be your stalking horse, huh? Divert him while you stealthily approach."

"Yep."

"Sure, I'll aid the cause of letters. Fall in behind me, try not to appear so gigantic. Gussie, farewell. I'll see to it your mambos gain interplanetary fame very shortly."

"I'd truly appreciate that, Mr. Palma."

Palma swiftly insinuated himself through the publishing-world crowd. "Gillis Logan," he called, "is it true about the Mishkin Prize?"

The dog-headed author turned to stare at the approaching photographer. His tongue rested on his lower lip as he gave a few surprised pants. "The Mishkin Prize?"

"Oops, looks like I let the snerg out of the bag." Palma was readying a camera. "You didn't know yet? Well, allow me to be the first to congratulate you and let me snap a picture for *Living Immortals Magazine*."

Straightening his plastic ascot, Logan asked, "Don't they award the Mishkin only to works of fiction?"

"Isn't *Gargoyle Power* fiction?" Palma was studying the dog author through his viewfinder.

"Most certainly not, it's a sincere work of mystical philosophy based on my insights into the nature of cathedrals, churches, chapels and similar sacred structures," explained Logan, his bluish tongue now and then lolling out of the side of his furry mouth. "You see, young man, the gargoyles we find decorating the sides of our lofty churches were not put there simply to be decorative. Ah, no, those gargoyles, if one under-

14

stands them and then carefully measures them are . . . awk!"

"Awk?" Palma lowered his camera. "What do you mean by awk, Mr. Logan?"

Silvera had been able to reach the distinguished mystical dog-faced author unnoticed. He had hold of his shoulder. "Twenty-five hundred dollars," he said in a level voice.

"Joey Silvera," exclaimed Logan. "I've been trying to reach you. You can let go . . . Did anyone ever tell you how much you resemble a gargoyle?"

"No one told me that and survived."

"Ah ha ha ha," said the panting Logan. "Always that Silvera sense of humor. I had to edit several quips out of the section of the book you helped me on, Joey."

"Section? Page one through page four hundred in a four hundred and six page book."

"A large section," admitted the author of *Gargoyle Power*, "making it all the more difficult to cut out the frivolous remarks you stuck in."

"A guy who thinks you can tell the future by measuring a stone gargoyle oughtn't to call people frivolous," suggested Palma, who'd hung his camera back around his neck with the others.

"My theories involve considerably more than the measuring of—"

"Twenty-five hundred dollars," repeated Silvera. "In cash, no checks or money orders."

"Joey, I honestly do not owe you the full $2500. After all, I had to rewrite a goodly portion—"

"Three paragraphs."

"Three lengthy paragraphs," said Logan. "I'm wondering if perhaps, Joey, your check hasn't been lost in the mail."

"You didn't send it."

Logan nodded sadly and slowly. He lowered his head to look down between his feet and through the neoglass floor. The flying house was circling, some five hundred feet up, a bright stretch of yellow afternoon beach and blue frothy water. Several lizard adolescents were skinny dipping far below. "Joey, I am burdened with a great many expenses," he said at last. "Last year for tape measures alone my accountant tells me we spent—"

Wump!

Thap!

Whamp!

Palma was the first to glance up. "More ladies," he said, grinning.

Six large young women had landed on the see-through roof, having dropped out of a skycar which was now hovering above the flying house. Each wore a black one-piece flightsuit and gold-trimmed suctionboots.

"Get those dingblasted bimbos off my roof," Oozman ordered his tiny human minions.

"Holy smokes!" gasped Logan. "You know who those dames are?"

"They look, from this angle," said Silvera, "to be members of the Sisterhood of Ofego over in Vigilanza Territory."

"They are, they are!" Logan caught hold of Silvera's arm. "The very order which has been plaguing me since *Gargoyle Power* hit the bestseller lists."

"Why?" inquired Palma, watching the girls very effectively laser-saw an opening in the roof.

"They claim I profaned their Chapel of Ofego in my book," explained the anxious author. "They maintain my mentioning their gargoyles and that ugly idol Ofego is a sacrilege, a major insult to their goofy order."

"Here they come," announced Palma, as a circular section of ceiling came falling a few seconds ahead of the first Sister of Ofego. "Check the bombos on the Mother Superior."

"Don't go fondling any religious fanatics," cautioned Silvera. "Summer told me about the time on Peregrine when you—"

"I don't know why they got so mad. They believe tits are sacred and, lord knows, so do I."

"Infidel!"

"Blasphemer!"

"Swish!"

Logan growled. "I am not gay!"

The members of the Sisterhood landed, wide-legged, all around them. Every one of the large girls carried a blaster pistol, a stunrod and a foot-high image of Ofego.

"My dear ladies," said Logan, a trace of a yowl in his voice, "I must confess something to you."

"Confessions on Fridays and Saturdays only," said a large blonde Sister.

"Get the security 'bots!" Oozman was shouting. "Handle this situation, for pete's sake!"

"Listen, I didn't write the book!" cried Logan, attempting to back into the crowd. "It was ghosted. Yes, yes, I didn't do anything. Even the measurements are the work of another, an agile youth I hired from the Young Agnostics Day Camp." He aimed a paw at Silvera. "Here is the real infidel, the true author of

Gargoyle Power! Joey Silvera, he wrote every offensive word. All I did was improve on his shabby punctuation. He's the man you want!"

The Mother Superior said, "Nerts! Try not to fool us with your cunning literary tricks, Gillis Logan. Your very own name appears on the title page of the horrible book, your unflattering photograph adorns the dust jacket."

"I can take you some better shots, Logan," offered Palma. "Reasonable fee."

"It is you, Gillis Logan," said the blonde Sister, "we are taking to the Shrine of Ofego for chastisement."

"I don't care to visit any more shrines, thank you," Logan told the circling Sisterhood. "That's all behind me. I'm at work on a new book, dealing with knitting for the four-armed races. So no more shrines for me." He pushed at Silvera with a paw. "This is the man for you."

Two of the Sisters gathered up the struggling and protesting Logan, went charging across the crowded room carrying him somewhat like a battering ram. The howling author was dragged out onto a balcony. The other Sisters followed, knocking literary figures and publishing notables out of their way.

While one of the six Sisters was disabling the force screen which protected the balcony, Logan screamed, "Silvera, help me! Rescue me!"

"Twenty-five hundred dollars."

"I have money, lots of it, in my hip pocket!"

"Why aren't those dadblasted security robots here?" Oozman was demanding. "Get them!"

"They're waiters at the moment," explained one of

the tiny humans. "We converted them when the crowd grew so—"

"What a daddangled idiotic situation!"

Silvera was on the threshold of the balcony. "Ladies," he said.

The Sisterhood of Ofego skycar, with the glowing portrait of the ugly Ofego on its belly, was swinging down to the level of the balcony so the wailing and thrashing dog author could be tossed in.

"Our quarrel isn't with you," the blonde Sister told him. "Even though you associate with infidels."

Stepping out onto the balcony, getting a much better view of the beach country far below, Silvera asked, "What are you planning to do with Logan?"

"He'll be taken to the Shrine and chastised," answered the Mother Superior.

"You're not going to kill him?"

"We never shed blood."

"And when you're through chastising him?"

"He will be released."

Nodding, Silvera eased nearer to the struggling Logan. "Could you turn him over for a minute?"

"No reason not to," said the blonde, obliging.

Silvera slid a large hand into the author's hip pocket. Locating the grout-skin wallet, he extracted $2500 and then poked it back into the pocket.

"Some collaborator you're shaping up to be," snarled Logan.

"Proceed, ladies." Silvera folded the money into his own pocket and went back into the party.

Chapter 2

The orange sun dropped into the sea. Twilight spread along the wide soft beach outside.

Silvera removed his trousers.

". . . should have been at the auction for *My Life As A Cannibal And The Famous People I Ate,*" lovely Lotti Waxer was saying from the exact center of her circular floating bed. "The bidding was the fiercest I've ever witnessed during my entire three years in publishing."

Silvera draped the trousers over a grouthide sling chair, watching the girl's lovely reflection in the one-way neoglass wall of her large circular bedchamber.

". . . Oozman himself was there in person and you know he hasn't been at a paperback rights auction since Klassy Books sold off the reprint rights to *Electronic Embroidery,*" Lotti continued, while pulling her dress up over her head. "It was really and truly raucous. Old Zeus turned up, waving all four of his arms and cursing like a starship trooper. Potzenjammer came from over in Trapanza Territory. He's an owlman you know, and when Oozman got especially excited and happened to flick cigar ashes into his feathers, well, Potzenjammer gave him a spop on the snoot that sent him arse over teakettle into Brother Anmar of the Barafunda Paperback Sodality. I tell you, Joe, there was fur flying, feathers burning, quills all over. Quite exciting, and a real coup for Waxer Sisters."

"Coup." Silvera dropped his allseason shorts to the

21

seethrough floor. The darkening ocean was sliding in and out beneath the girl's beachfront stilthouse.

With a languid quirk of one lovely arm Lotti managed to fling her dress over the side of the immense bed and onto the decorative antlers of a floating grouthead light fixture. "Did I tell you we had six on the list last month?"

"What list?" Silvera hopped, yanked off one all-season sock. Hopping on his newly bare foot, he removed the other sock.

"You know the only list I'm interested in. The bestseller list in the *Barafunda Times Literary Supplement.* Do you realize what that means, Joe? It means all over this planet, from the icecapped hills of Camposanto, millions of people are reading Waxer Sister books. Not merely humanoid types, mind you, but lizard people, catpeople, dogpeople, toad people and even a few of your more sophisticated androids and robots. Only the other day we got a touching faxgram letter from a pizza-making robot over in Jelado about our . . . What's wrong?"

Silvera had been in the act of lowering his unclothed backside to the bed edge when he suddenly leaped up to run to a one-way window. Head to one side, he stood frowning out into the dusk. "Somebody over there by that decorative flotsam display on the beach," he said. "Watching this place."

"Nobody can see in, Joe. There's no need to—"

"Willowy sort of silhouette. Better not be one of your nitwit sisters figuring to barge—"

"They're all away on company business, I told you. Which is why I attended Oozman's dreadful party alone this afternoon." She unseamed her bra, releasing her lovely breasts. "Although it wasn't that dreadful, since I met you again. Do you think those hefty Sisters will chop Gillis Logan up into chunks or anything?"

"They promised they wouldn't." Silvera was still watching the gathering darkness. "It's not a woman out there, it's a skinny guy. He just went skulking off."

"Let's forget him. Never bring your worries to bed, is one of my maxims." She spread her arms wide, inviting him, with an expectant smile, to join her. "Not an original thought, actually. It's culled from Professor Steffanson's latest Waxer bestseller, *You Ain't So Goofy*. Have you read it? We got a nice serialization in the *Grout Herders Bazaar*. Although exactly why grout herders would . . . Aren't you going to come over here, Joe?"

"Was waiting for you to wind down." He crossed the room, sat beside the nearly naked girl.

"Excuse my euphoria," said Lotti, her lips close against his naked shoulder. "I really and honestly am excited by our chance encounter, Joe. We haven't seen each other for . . . how long has it been?"

"Three royalty periods." Silvera stroked her warm supple back.

"Well, ever since then I've maintained a deep and abiding interest in you and your work," Lotti sighed. "You may not have given a thought to plain little Lotti Waxer as you rocketed from planet to planet in hot pursuit of your freelance writing career, but here in my heart I—"

"Your heart's over here." He touched a different spot than the girl had.

"Wherever it is, Joe, it's been thinking of you. Every single time there's a mention of you in *Galactic Publishers Weekly*, I snip it out," the girl told him.

"I have faithfully read every darned godawful book you've produced. I read those gothics you did under the penname of Josephine Paradise-Lost, that encyclopedia of beer in six hefty volumes, the series about the Boy Snerghunters . . . and I'm not even certain what a snerg is."

"Somewhat like a rabbit."

"A rabbit?"

"Only green, blue sometimes, with more teeth."

"I don't see how they can be very ferocious." She shook her lovely head, her silken hair burnishing his shoulder. "Your powers of description are waning, Joe. I didn't get that image at all. I envisioned snergs, making my way through your clunky prose, as being big devils."

"They are. On the planet Peregrine your average snerg is over six feet tall if it's on its hind legs, which it often is."

"You just told me they were like rabbits."

"Somewhat like," corrected Silvera, inserting his fingers under the waistband of her plyopanties. "And don't try to get to me by knocking my work. I'm the best writer of prose in this planet system."

"You've never had a bestseller under your own name, have you?"

"Not as Jose Silvera, no."

"Seems to me the best prose writer in the Barnum System ought to have at least one or two chart toppers under his own name."

Gently, or relatively so, Silvera tipped the girl over, removed the undergarment and stretched her out beside him. "No more shoptalk."

"Okay, I promise." Turning slightly, she locked her arms around his neck and thrust her tongue into his most reachable ear. "Oh, but I did very much want to tell you about our latest coup."

"Coup again."

"This will be a big one, Joe, and you must promise to keep absolutely silent about it. Already too many rumors have been circulating, and I'm fearful scoundrels like Oozman will try to undermine our deal."

Silvera said nothing.

"There hasn't been an event like this in publishing since Oozman brought out *Who I Screwed* last season," Lotti went on. "This book is so sensational that once the manuscript is—"

"Hold it." Silvera stood upright on the bed, causing it to twang and sway. "He's up on the roof now."

"Much like those chunky Sisters this afternoon." Lotti sat up, staring at the seethrough ceiling.

A dark figure rolled down the roof, tumbled through the shrubbery in the side patio and went running off into the night.

By the time the naked Silvera reached the switch for the outdoor lights and illuminated the areas around the beach house, the lurker was long gone. "Anybody been watching you lately, following you?"

"I really don't pay much attention, Joe. You know how it is in publishing; somebody's always snooping around." She touched a hand to her lips. "Golly, I hope nobody's got wind of our new autobiog."

Silvera flicked off the lights, returned to the bed. After easing Lotti into a supine position, he placed himself atop her.

"I'd like to finish telling you about the autobiog before we move on to the romantic stuff," said Lotti. 'Because this book is going to be a real blockbuster."

"Okay, tell me about the book, Lotti."

"It's the life story of one of the most notorious criminals in the Barnum System. At one time he controlled the major portion of organized crime here on Barafunda. Two years ago, though, he disappeared from sight, and it was hinted he'd been rubbed out by rival criminals," the girl said up at Silvera.

The hair was rising on the back of his neck. "Wait now, Lotti. Is this guy 90% machine, a sort of android with a real human brain encased in a tin skull?"

"How did you hear about this deal?" She made a pouting face. "Do you know Dr. Scofflaw?"

Silvera got off her. "That son of a bitch owes me $10,000."

Chapter 3

Whap!

"Little bastard, that does it for you!" The plump catwoman flicked the fresh-killed cockroach off the top of their table with one furry paw. "No cockroaches in your chow when you dine at Moms Buckshot's Home Cooking Café. Now what'll you gents—"

"Something's burning, Moms," Palma informed her, inclining his hairless head in the direction of the old-fashioned neowood-burning stove which stood against one wall of the small restaurant.

"My damn popovers!" Moms Buckshot bolted, leaping tables and patrons when necessary, to the smoking oven.

"Your taste in restaurants hasn't changed," said Silvera.

"The food here is very good, Jose," the photographer assured him, "and . . ."

Whap!

". . . wish I could stun them as deftly as Moms does. I always dine here when I'm on-planet in this territory."

Silvera asked, "How often is that?"

"Once every two or three years."

"That's about the right frequency. Have you—"

Thunk!

A long twist of sticky paper had fallen to their table from directly above.

Palma sidehanded it to the floor. "Fly paper," he said. "Pleasant homey touch, especially since they

27

don't have flies on Barafunda. My grandmother used to . . . Have you noticed the boppos on that blue-haired girl at the table over there with the obviously gay lizard? One points east whilst the other—"

"You were supposed to dig up some information on Dr. Scofflaw for me," Silvera reminded his lunch partner.

Palmer was still distracted by the girl three tables away. "Tits such as those could cause you a lot of anxiety, making you feel you were continually at a crossroads in—"

"Dr. Scofflaw?"

Palma turned to face his friend. "It's a hoax."

"Which?"

"The whole damn autobiography."

Silvera said, "I checked into the business end of it. The guy who's handling the sale of the book to Lotti is a legitimate literary agent, if there can be such a thing, over in Jelado Territory. Fellow named Carlos Pigg, with a reputation for relative honesty in his dealings with publishers."

"So mayhap Carlos Pigg was hoaxed, too. I contacted a couple of our publisher's stringers in the territory, and since Coult is the largest magazine publisher in the Barnum System, we can afford the best-informed stringers," said Palma. "Dr. Scofflaw is definitely dead and done for. Hence his so-called autobiography is a fake."

"Lotti Waxer isn't easy to fool."

Palma grinned. "I always get those sisters mixed up. Is she the one with a little bitty azalea tattooed right about here?"

"I can't tell an azalea from a gladiola."

"Didn't you write a gardening book once on Venus?"

"I've written eighteen gardening books, plus one entire book on compost, but once a book is over and paid for, I try to forget it," replied Silvera. "Did you pick up anything on who's behind the hoax?"

"Carlos Pigg's client is rumored to be a young lady named Tammany Kloister . . . There's a catchy name. Suggests a girl with yonkers of the upthrust variety."

"You mean the autobiography is supposed to be one of these as-told-to jobs?"

"Exactly, and Tammany Kloister is the one who claims Scofflaw is telling all to her."

"Where is she?"

"Across the border in Jelado's capital, same as her agent. I hate climates that cold; tend to make knockers . . . what's that smell?"

"Moms is spraying the bugs under the stove."

"Another very homey touch." Palma lifted up his menu, smacked at the greenish cockroach who'd been dozing beneath it and grinned. "How much did you say Scofflaw owed you?"

"Owes, not owed, he continues to owe me $10,000. He or his heirs."

"You actually wrote a book for a guy like that?"

"Three and a half years ago, when I was out here doing a series of grout stories for teenage girls, I was approached by a representative of his and asked to ghost Dr. Scofflaw's *My Six Greatest Capers*. I worked eight months with that human-brained robot and only got half the dough the contract promised."

"You'll write for anybody, huh?"

"Nearly," answered Silvera. "Especially when they offer me $20,000."

"So far you've collected only $10,000?"

"So far."

Palma asked, "What was Scofflaw like?"

"Made of metal."

"Can you tell, isn't he an android?"

"Parts of him simulate human flesh, other parts are raw unadorned metal. His head, although it has human features, doesn't have a synskin coating."

"All that's left of the original Dr. Scofflaw is his brain," mused Palma. "That would be spooky, your brain riding around in a metal carcass. Imagine trying to cop a feel with tin fingers or . . . Darn, I swear that girl's left honker is staring at me."

Silvera continued, "Scofflaw's people stalled me on the final payment. By the time I got back to Barafunda, they'd vanished, and the word was the doctor himself was dead."

Palma hunched slightly. "One of our stringers told me a funny thing, Jose," he said, voice lowering. "Which is why I advise you to forget maybe collecting the money from anybody. Seems there's a strong possibility the Barnum Crime Combine, which as you know is the biggest damn criminal syndicate in our corner of the universe, decided they couldn't trust Dr. Scofflaw. Possibly the book you did for him convinced them he was a little too vain."

"He's a whole lot too vain."

"The BCC, therefore, had Dr. Scofflaw taken care of."

"Yeah, I've heard those rumors, too," acknowledged the big author. "I've tangled with the BCC many times before, done nine books exposing them on various planets and twenty-seven books for publishing houses they control. The Barnum Crime Combine isn't going to stop me from collecting my $10,000."

Palma was twisting an end of his bushy moustache between thumb and forefinger. "One version of what happened to Dr. Scofflaw has it that he was dismantled," he said. "Hate to see that happen to you."

"Dismantled?"

"They allegedly took him all apart and scattered the sections across Barafunda, sort of like turning the old boy into a human jigsaw puzzle. Except there's no intention of ever putting him together again."

"It could be, though, he is back together and writing his life story with the help of that Kloister girl," said Silvera. "If he is, he's sure as hell going to pay up."

Palma shook his head. "Interesting the different things which drive people. With me it's tits, with you . . . Did you hear a click?"

"Nope."

"Yeah, it was a camera clicking." Palma pushed out of his chair and went dashing straight for the girl whose breasts had earlier fascinated him. "I never look good in candid shots, miss." His hand closed over her left breast.

"What gives, you skinheaded oaf?" The large lizard man who was sharing the table rose up. He snatched up a bottle of green wine and conked Palma over the skull.

Wong!

Palma wobbled, swayed and slumped down on his knees. Clutched in his fist was the tiny spy camera he'd yanked from the girl's bosom.

Silvera caught the teetering photographer before he tipped completely over. While he was returning Palma to an upright position, the girl and her lizard escort departed the restaurant.

"Just like home," murmured Palma. "Didn't I tell you?"

Chapter 4

The robot snowplow came whooshing down the lane, tossing great cascades of slush up onto the walkway and muttering to itself. "Endless, an endless task. Snow, and more snow. Day in, day out . . ."

Silvera left the brownstone wall he'd thrown himself against to avoid the flying wave of snow. The wind was whistling across the tile roofs, scattering snow, ripping holes in the raging blizzard. He turned up the collar of his greatcoat, resumed walking.

At the next corner an enormous gust of wind took hold of him, spinning him around, ballooning his coat. Silvera bicycled back, found his balance and pushed into the wind and snow in the direction he wanted to go.

"Snowshoes! Snowshoes! Now's the time to buy 'em! Two pairs for six bucks!" An albino catman, wrapped in a large blanket, was stationed in mid-block beside a cart loaded with snowshoes. "All handmade, elegant craftmanship. How about you, guv?"

Silvera gave a negative shake of his head. "I'm not going to be in Jelado Territory that long."

"Exactly what I thought," said the vendor, clutching his blanket tighter around himself. "Came over here six years back to attend a Porncon, and I've been here ever since. My wives always warned porn would be the ruin of me, but what can one do when . . . oops!"

A great burst of wind blew several snowshoes off

his cart, sent them flapping up into the snow-thick air.

While the catman chased his wares, Silvera continued on toward Carlos Pigg's office. After a moment he halted, looked back over his broad shoulder.

A lizard man was traveling in his wake, a large fellow in a synskin zoot suit. When he became aware Silvera was watching him, he trotted out into the new-plowed lane to help the vendor gather up snowshoes.

Silvera proceeded. After yesterday's tangle at Moms Buckshot's he'd been watchful. So far he hadn't been aware of anyone tailing him. He had noticed no one at the Jelado skyport.

Whap!

A few yards ahead of him a door popped open. Two burly humans, the skirts of their heavy greatcoats flapping, dived out into the blizzard. Their huge gloved hands were held over their earmuffed ears, their thick necks were tucked in tight.

"Snowshoes do your stuff," one of the men urged his extremities.

"My fans must treat me with *respect*, you lop-eared goony!" A very sizable catwoman appeared in the doorway, a blaster pistol in each fist. "Hit the road!"

The two men ran, narrowly avoiding a collision with Silvera, swiftly away from there.

"Are you another one, you mahogany-hued dago?" the large catwoman asked, not lowering her guns.

"This confusion is always coming up," Silvera said, approaching her. "See, my people, centuries ago, came from a place on the planet Earth known as Portugal. Therefore when you refer to me as a dago, you're—"

"Oh, can the baloney, I recognize you now." She dropped the pistols into pockets of her synfur coat. "Jose Silvera, the horny hack writer."

"You've got me mixed up with Palma, the horny photographer." Silvera came up to the doorway. "But I am Silvera."

"Don't try to hand me a line of crapola, Jose. I've heard of your non-literary exploits . . . how you've cut a romantic swath across the universe, loving with fierce abandon and unbridled passion girls of both high and low station, and leaving them to contemplate the fact that once you'd burned a fiery passage through their until then dull and quiet lives, they were merely girls but you had left them *women*. Yes, Jose Silvera, broad of shoulder, handsome of—"

"I know who you must be," he cut in. "You're Dame Agatha Firebird."

"You bet your snookie I am, Jose," said Dame Agatha, lunging forward to give him an enthusiastic hug. "Come on in, warm your bones. Do you read my books?"

"That's how I recognized you, from your style." Silvera entered the reception room of the Carlos Pigg Literary Agency. "I've read them, admired them and written imitations of them on several planets."

"You are a prolific rascal, Jose." She chuckled and bestowed an admiring and hefty slap on his back. "My own favorite of all my books is *Love's Boiling Frenzy*, though there are those, especially in the Solar System, who'd put *Frequent Fevered Love* at the top of the heap."

"Well, I like *Burning Bridges* best. Is Carlos Pigg in?"

ODBERT

"Are they departed?" someone inquired from beneath a substantial orange metal desk.

"They didn't want you, Carlos. They were your typical overzealous Dame Aggie fans." The authoress strode across to the desk and tugged a portly polar-bear man from beneath it.

"Your fans, Aggie, are, I admit, fervid, yet I hardly think, if you'll forgive my so saying, they'd have much interest in looting my files."

"Souvenir hunters," Dame Agatha assured the agent. "Some of them swipe my garments, others make off with chunks of one of the several palatial mansions my literary labors have won for me, while there are other—"

"No, this is something different," Pigg insisted, "When we heard them snooping about out here, you assumed, for possibly logical reasons, from your point of view, they were eager, or rather overeager, fans of your novels." The agent shook his white furry head. "This, however, is not the first instance of . . . ah, excuse me, sir, I didn't notice you standing there. Are you perhaps an editor seeking talent? Allow me, as soon as I overcome the slight dizziness provoked by hunkering under a desk, to provide you with a copy of my client list."

"I'm a writer, not an editor," Silvera told him. "I'm looking for—"

"Drop off some samples of your published work with my secretary, who has momentarily gone into hiding because of the wave of—"

"Don't be a wall-eyed goop, Carlos," advised Dame Agatha. "This is Jose Silvera."

Pigg's fur-trimmed eyes blinked. "Jose Silvera, the interplanetary hack?"

"The same," the catwoman said, chuckling.

"Jose Silvera," said the literary agent. "Exactly the man I want to see."

"I have similar feelings about you," said Silvera.

"Basically," explained Carlos Pigg, paws drumming on his wide desk, "this job calls for a writer who's handy with his fists."

"What's it pay?" asked Silvera.

The two of them were seated in the polar bear agent's private office. Snow had been replaced by the sleet that was now pelting the pastel skylight. The wind howled, rubbing at the neoglass.

"I should be able to get you . . . $4000," said Pigg. "Plus some medical expenses."

Silvera shifted in his blue chair. "Who's going to do me violence?"

"Conditions in Jelado have changed some since your last visit, which was, I believe you mentioned, a year ago," said Pigg. "King Billy has been deposed, replaced by a somewhat repressive junta. These things seem, the way I see it at any rate, to go in cycles. A tyrant comes, a dictator goes, with perhaps an enlightened despot in between. Of late the new regime has been very critical of the press, and the book trade and the more liberal of our publishers have had run-ins with the Federal Police. These run-ins, I might add, now and then involve the smashing of presses and the burning of warehouses."

"Who do you want me to ghost a book for?"

"Have you heard of Dotheboy Rampling?"

"Nope."

"Not enough people have, though I honestly believe, and used to tell the critics as much before the new regime discouraged open-sympathy for radical philosophers, he's one of our most gifted polemical writers."

"How's anybody going to come up with 4000 bucks if the government is smashing presses and riding down liberals?"

"I've arranged, operating a bit more furtively than usual, for a very well-funded underground publisher to bring out Dotheboy's next book," replied Pigg. "He's come up with a very marketable idea and I truly feel . . . ," he said, pausing to lock eyes with Silvera, ". . . though the book will have to be distributed somewhat slyly, it will do well." He steepled his paws. "Dotheboy is intent on presenting his political ideas in a more mass-appeal mainstream sort of way. Which is why the new book is to be called *The Violent Overthrow Of The Government Cookbook*."

Silvera sank slightly lower in his chair. "Catchy title," he said. "Why can't Rampling write it himself?"

"In addition to a newfound interest in gourmet cooking," said the shaggy agent, "he's grown fond, obsessively so if you ask me, of bomb throwing. He's also keen on the making of the things. I don't know if you've ever manufactured or thrown a bomb, Jose, but it's time-consuming."

"A few times," said Silvera. "Most recently on Peregrine when I was researching for *The Compleat Guerilla Encyclopedia*."

"Did you write that book?" Pigg nodded approvingly. "I couldn't put it down, which can be difficult with a book weighing twelve pounds. Little did I realize you were masquerading behind the name Wing Commander Estling."

"I can probably take on this cookbook thing for you," said Silvera. "First, though, I have to talk to one of your clients."

"No reason why my clients can't fraternize. Whom did you wish to meet? You've already encountered Dame Aggie, who's one of my most—"

"Tammany Kloister."

Pigg clenched his paws. "Tammany?"

"Yeah."

"Why exactly," Pigg asked in a low voice, "if you don't mind my asking, do you want to meet her?"

"Because she's supposed to be working with Dr. Scofflaw on his life story," said Silvera. "And Scofflaw owes me $10,000."

"Jose, I'll be frank with you," said Pigg. "When you arrived here today, you saw me, I'm almost ashamed to recall, hiding under a desk. My life, which was moderately tranquil and funfilled until a few scant weeks ago, has turned into a nightmare. Why? Because of that . . . that autobiography."

Silvera asked, "Are you sure it is an autobiography? Have you seen Scofflaw?"

Pigg ran his tongue across his furry muzzle. "No, I haven't actually seen the man, or the machine if you prefer. But Tammany is a reliable girl, and if she says she has access to this notorious fellow, well, I believe her."

Silvera's left eye narrowed. "And why has your life become a nightmare? People been bothering you?"

"Horrible people, yes," said the agent. "They lurk around my offices, prowl about my estate and worry my lovely wife and three sturdy sons. They call me on the pixphone at all hours, asking me rude questions and making dire threats. It's been a veritable nightmare, or have I already said that?"

"What do they want to know? Why are they bothering you?"

"They want to learn the location, the present whereabouts, of this Dr. Scofflaw person," said Pigg. "I've explained over and over, to little avail I fear, that part of my agreement with Tammany involved my not knowing where the creature was hiding out."

"Is that true? You don't know where Scofflaw is?"

"Haven't, I assure you, Jose, the foggiest notion. Tammany has ways of contacting him, but she has never, as I explained, confided in me as to how she does any of it."

Nodding, Silvera said, "Okay, then how can I contact the Kloister girl herself?"

"I do not know," said Pigg. "I haven't been able to get in touch with Tammany for three days."

Chapter 6

Night fell and the sleet turned back to snow.

Silvera left the yurt-style cottage he was renting in one of the quieter suburbs of the Jelado capital. He walked two blocks, the night wind shoving at his back, to an underground tram station. He took a tram to the Civic Square, disembarked and switched to a sky-bus which carried him to the nearest skyport. From there he caught a landbus which deposited him at the Respected Junta Hotel. On the third below-ground level of the hotel he got aboard another tram and rode to within four blocks of Tammany Kloister's apartment building.

Music was flowing out of the place, the hugely am-plified sounds of a sitar-tabla group, an electrified string quartet and a full size Venusian swing band. As Silvera neared the arched entrance to Mecca Flats, an oval window high up on its front popped briefly open and a bucket of yellow paint was splashed out.

"Beautiful, beautiful!" hollered someone two floors below the slowly spreading yellow dribble.

"Old hat," yelled another tenant. "Typical unin-spired facade-smear style of activist painting."

Silvera crossed the foyer and placed himself on an up-ramp. He was conveyed up to the second level.

The thick door of flat 2B was scarred, and when Silvera touched it lightly, the door swung inward. Light bloomed from a crosshatch of lightstrips in the high ceiling of Tammany Kloister's living room.

"Moan, moan, moan." A murmuring complaint was

drifting out of an alcove to the left of the large room.

Silvera, cautious and alert, moved for there.

"Moan, moan, moan. Groan, groan, groan."

A robot typewriter, fallen over on its side.

Silvera got the mechanism back on its wheels, clicked off its bitchbox. It was a relatively inexpensive model, with a simple talk-control and not much of a memory. So it wouldn't know anything about what had happened to the girl or even what had knocked it over.

Silver noticed his hand. There were small flecks of red on his fingers. Crouching he examined the side of the robot typer and found a smear of dried blood.

He left the alcove, circled the living room. An orange sling chair was lying with legs in the air, a broken lightball was on the thermocarpet beside it. No blood here.

Silvera was heading for the sleep area when a deep voice behind him suggested, "Halt in your tracks!"

"Who would you be?" Silvera asked the bearded young man who stood on the threshold with a stungun in his fist.

"Might I not ask the same question of you? And also what have you done with Tammany?"

"I'm Jose Silvera," Silvera told him. "I want to find Tammany Kloister so I—"

"*The* Jose Silvera?"

"Don't think there's more than one in this particular planet system."

"Jose Silvera, the gifted hack, the champion mercenary penman, the renowned writer-for-hire, the crass—"

"Yeah, I'm Jose Silvera. Who are you?"

"Oh, I'm Trumbull Gish. Possibly you've never heard of me or my work."

"I haven't. Why did you barge in here with a gun?"

"Trumbull Gish, the Bard of Barafunda? You're certain you've never encountered even one of my poems? Golly, and here I am one of the brightest lights in the—"

"You a friend of Tammany Kloister's?"

"Friend and neighbor," replied Gish, returning his stungun to a belt holster. "Matter of fact, Jose, I've been quite a bit guilt-ridden since they carried Tammany off kicking and screaming three nights ago. Therefore, when I heard you rattling around in here, I decided I must—"

"You saw somebody carry the girl off?"

"Didn't actually see, Jose. What I mostly did was hear. Well, I saw something, as I'll explain. The thing is, when I'm in the middle of a poem, I can't let anything distract me. On the night in question I was wrestling with *My Pink Mailbox*. You may not be aware, since you aren't familiar with the body of my work, that I specialize in the celebration of the common everyday little—"

"This common everyday kidnapping of Tammany Kloister," cut in Silvera. "Give me some details."

Gish fiddled with his beard. "It was three nights ago. I know that because I'd just completed the first stanza of *My Pink Mailbox*. Did you happen to notice the mailboxes when you came in? They're pink. They used to be blue, which is what inspired my award-winning *My Blue Mailbox*. Then about a month back I noted that management of Mecca Flats had—"

45

"The girl!" Silvera crossed to him, took hold of the poet by his shoulders. "Who grabbed her?"

"It wasn't the local cops or the Federal Police goons," said Gish. "Because, even though I was in the clutches of my muse, I did manage to take the time to glance out my window. I noticed Tammany being dragged into a landvan by three husky fellows in civilian garb while a fourth man looked on. I didn't get a very good look because Zambini up on eight decided to do another of his activist paintings at just that moment, and green paint came slurping down and obscured my view. It did give me an idea for a poem, which I'll be calling *My Temporarily Green Window*. You'd be surprised how poetic ideas are just about every—"

"The men who took her," said Silvera. "Can you describe them at all?"

"I'm really not so hot at describing people. Had Tammany been kidnapped by a mailbox or a stove, I—"

"Try," urged Silvera.

"Two of them were polar-bear men, the third hefty one was a human, I think. All bundled up in heavy overcoats they were." Gish shut his eyes, remembering. "The fourth man was small, yes, a small lizard man who wore a pair of sunglasses. That struck me as an odd thing to do in the middle of a blizzard. I'd guess he was the boss of the operation, a very nervous, bouncy sort of little fellow."

"What about the landvan?"

"Sleek and low, ebon in color as the blackest night of the soul. Poised on the snow-swept curb, eager to push into the kaleidescoping swirl of whiteness," said Gish, eyes opening. "Notice how much better I am at describing *things*? Let me tell you about the tires on—"

"How about its ID number?"

"Oh, that I didn't notice."

"Sit over here." Silvera lifted Gish, carried him by the shoulders to a purple sling chair and deposited him. "Now . . . Did you report this to the authorities?"

Gish sighed. "I meant to, Jose, but on my way to the pixphone I passed my workbench and *My Pink Mailbox* just cried out to be completed," he said. "I am pretty guilt-ridden about the whole business."

Silvera asked him, "Did Tammany tell you about any . . . fears she might have had? Name anyone who might have been responsible for grabbing her?"

"All I know is, Jose, since word of that darned autobiography leaked out, she's been bothered by all sorts of odd occurrences," Gish replied. "Crank calls, strangers hanging around in the lobby, that sort of thing. I advised her to consult the police, even though our present rulers aren't too highly fond of artists. Even so they're supposed to be dedicated to protecting all citizens from cranks and loiterers."

"And did she call in the cops?"

"She refused. Tammany explained to me that her situation was very complex and the police would only make it more so."

"Do you think this book was legit?"

Gish tugged at his beard. "I have my doubts. I never saw Dr. Scofflaw or any of his representatives come here, and I really don't think Tammany ever visited him anyplace else, although it is possible that such things occurred when I was in the middle of one of my poems."

"When she was taken the other night, did you hear anything specific? Beyond the scuffle I mean . . . words, names, anything?"

Rocking slightly in the chair, Gish said, "As I recall, Tammany did shout something like, 'I don't know where he is, I really don't!' Could she have been alluding to Dr. Scofflaw?"

"When I find her," promised Silvera, "I'll ask her."

Chapter 7

Silvera dived into a snowdrift.

"Ho ho!"

"Aha! Aha!"

The six mounted Federal Police officers went galloping on down the late-night street.

Silvera had been crossing the road when the six blue and gold uniformed men came riding hard around a corner and straight at him. He emerged from the pile of snow and, when his fists stopped clenching, wiped snow off his greatcoat, head and face.

In a long career of freelancing on numerous planets he'd learned several things. One of these was never to mess with the army or the police . . . unless it was absolutely necessary in order to collect your fee.

The blizzard had slacked off to a heavy fall of snow. The white flakes dropped down through the blackness in gobs.

Through it Silvera made out the illuminated sign he was seeking. A block ahead, throbbing crimson. An enormous fist floating above a wide doorway.

The six horses which had nearly trampled him were tethered at a hitching rail in front of the Iron Fist Ballroom. There were also several restless grouts and one evil-looking hairy mount Silvera couldn't identify.

Across the wide swinging doors was painted the message MEN IN UNIFORM WELCOME!

Silvera went in.

The noise of the dancing was impressive. The dozen glaz chandeliers shook and rattled, the floor bounced underfoot, the plaz walls of the dance hall vibrated. Nearly a hundred couples were executing the steps of the latest Jelado craze, some sort of stomping and hopping dance. Up on a floating dais eleven bare-chested lizard men played loud brassy music.

"Dance, captain?" A massive redhaired girl detached herself from the nearest wall to come smiling toward him.

"I'm a civilian," he told her as she slipped an arm around him. "And I'm looking for Taxico."

"Plenty of time for that." Her other arm encircled him. "Ah, you're a well-structured fellow under that voluminous garment, aren't you? Come along, let's do the Esteemed Junta Clog."

"That's the name of what everybody's doing, huh?"

"Named in honor of our own Esteemed Junta. Some feel you can't blend politics and the arts, but it's not a bad dance. Good for your heart muscles, too."

"Suppose we stomp over to the vicinity of Taxico?" suggested Silvera when they commenced the Clog. "He works at the snack bar, doesn't he?"

"Yes, but why think of food at a time like this?"

"It's because I promised to pick up some food for an ailing friend of mine."

Medals and military hardware were jiggling and jangling all around them. Silvera spotted the snack alcove far across the dance floor and guided his partner in that direction.

"You're a very good dancer," she remarked. "You hop very gracefully."

"Yes, it's one of my better accomplishments." Three more stomping spins and he was in front of the snack counter, which was ringed by anxious and impatient customers. "I'll return to you shortly." He detached himself from the disappointed redhead.

Trying not to rattle any of the uniformed men, Silvera worked his way up to the long food counter. His man, judging by the photo Carlos Pigg had shown him, was at the left side. A small fluffy catman who was busily spreading green mustard on slices of soybread.

With a few subtle elbow nudges Silvera reached Taxico. "I came to pick up the grout-cheese and snerg-sausage pizza for Mrs. Erb," he shouted at the little catman.

"Yikes!" Taxico dropped his spreader, picked it up, tapped his furry chin with it, resumed spreading mustard. "Um . . . that is, oh yes. How is dear old Mrs. Erb?"

"Sinking fast."

"Grout-cheese pizza with snerg-sausage," murmured a large Federal Police officer who was wedged near Silvera. "That sounds very yummy. I'll take it."

"It's for poor old ailing Mrs. Erb," explained Silvera, wishing the literary agent had provided him with a different identifying phrase. "Her final hours among the living will be brightened—"

"Stuff the old squiff up your cob," advised the FP officer. "I want that yummy-sounding pizza for myself. I'll coldcock any—"

"Perhaps," put in Taxico, "the gentleman would like to step into the kitchen to see if there isn't some alternate delicacy he can take to the old lady?"

"That's okay by me," said Silvera. "This gentleman can have the pizza."

"Nix nix," Taxico tried to whisper.

"Okay, hand it over," ordered the Federal Policeman. "Grout-cheese and snerg-sausage. That's lipsmacking good in—"

"Ah, I was about to explain to this gent that we're all out of grout-cheese. In fact—"

"Out of grout-cheese! What kind of tantalizing scam are—"

"If you'll both excuse me." Silvera ducked behind the counter, pushed through the swinging door into the kitchen.

Nothing but robots and cook stoves in the long, narrow silver-walled room. Silvera began to walk its length, glancing from side to side.

The door of a built-in oven opened and a hand emerged, beckoning. "You're late."

"I stopped to dance."

"Push the quick-roast button, if the coast is clear."

Silvera pushed the button and a section of wall swung open. He entered a dim corridor.

A large shaggy man of forty or so greeted him. "I'm Dotheboy Rampling, welcome to my hideout."

Closing the secret panel behind him, Silvera shook hands with the political writer. "Isn't it risky hiding out in a place that's a haunt of police and soldiers?"

Rampling started down the twisting corridor. "That's where my cleverness comes in," he explained. "This is the last place they'd think to look for a notorious anti-government person. Strategy." They came to a nearwood door and he shoved it open. "Though lately I've been wondering if it might occur to them to hunt for me in the least likely place. In which case they could come directly here. Calls for more thinking." He raised his massive arms, let them fall. "I hate the moving, though. I've so many books and—"

"Let's talk about the book you want me to ghost," suggested Silvera.

Rampling settled in a sling chair in front of his wall-high bookcases. "The last time I had to do a quick skip, I left my library behind. A damn shame, but it was either abandon the books or go off to Devil's Island."

"Devil's Island?"

"Built since you were last here," said Rampling. "The junta's idea. It's located in the only warm sector of Jelado. Wouldn't build a resort there, oh, no. Build a maximum security prison for political radicals, habitual murderers and the like. Grim place, despite the pleasant climate. But you needn't worry. They probably won't put you there simply for lending a hand on my cookbook."

"That's comforting," said Silvera.

Chapter 8

"Is it supposed to do that?" his stove asked him.

Donning a potholder mitten, Silvera snatched the smoking kettle off the front burner. "This recipe doesn't work either." He crossed the small kitchen of his rented yurt-cottage, handed the kettle to the garbage unit.

Two of its many-jointed arms took the pot, emptied the contents within itself. "What was this one supposed to be?"

"Grout Stew A La Barricades," Silvera informed the servo.

"Grout. Uck," remarked the garbage unit while it compressed the contents of the kettle. "No true revolutionary can thrive on a meat diet. My advice to you is to switch to an all veget—"

"I'm not a revolutionary." Silvera set the kettle aside and backed out of the smoky kitchen.

"You never will be if you try to get along on grout meat," put in the stove. "And what was that other junk you had me cooking? The stuff which exploded during the gently simmer stage. Snerg Pie Guerilla Style. More meat."

"Blame Rampling. Those are his alleged recipes I'm testing." Silvera made a circuit of the parlor. "He's probably not much of a revolutionary either."

He hadn't been able to find Tammany Kloister as yet, though he'd devoted two full days to it. She'd been carried off five days ago, and that was all he could learn. Quite possibly the girl had faked the entire Scofflaw autobiography. The doctor was no doubt scattered across the length and breadth of the planet. And yet . . . if he were alive, then Silvera would collect the $10,000 owed him.

Tap! Tap!

Tap!

Above the yowling of the night wind and the pelting of the hail on the yurt roof Silvera became aware of a tapping at his front door.

He eased over to it, activated the spyhole.

A gaunt man in a shaggy peacoat stood on the doorstep, clutching a paper-wrapped parcel to his narrow chest. "Silvera?" he asked, aware he was being observed. "You busy?"

"Just puttering in the kitchen. What is it?"

A burst of wind pushed the man against the door. "Got something for you."

Silvera opened the door. "Okay, come on in."

"Thought you might give . . . give me . . ." He collapsed across the threshold, his sharp knees smacking the floor.

"What the hell's wrong?" Silvera caught hold of the man's arm.

"Brought you . . . thought you . . ." He moved further into the room, stumping on his knees. "This thing . . ."

Wind threw spatters of hail in at them out of the darkness.

Silvera kicked the door shut. Then he noticed the man's back. There were three coin-size holes burned through the peacoat, and blood was coming out and trailing down across the frosted cloth. "Stay right there," he said. "I'll phone a doc—"

"Money," gasped the wounded man. "Heard

you . . . buy this . . . give money . . ." He, hands quivering, held out the package. The effort caused him to lose his balance and fall face-down out of Silvera's grasp.

The package rolled and tumbled across the round rug, hit against the leg of a table and made a clanking sound.

Silvera knelt beside the man. "Who used the blaster pistol on you?"

"Doesn't . . . doesn't matter . . . figured if I got this . . . to you . . ." His head was ticking slowly from side to side. "Smart enough to highjack . . . dodge 'em . . . got here . . . how much . . ."

Silvera dived toward the pixphone alcove.

"Scofflaw . . ." murmured the dying man.

Spinning, Silvera returned to his side. "What do you know about Dr. Scofflaw?"

"I brought you . . . I brought you . . ." He stopped living.

Silvera stood, watching the dead man. "Better call the law," he said to himself. "But first."

The package consisted of several layers of spotty brown paper, tied with grouthide cord. After Silvera tore the cord away and peeled off the paper, he found an object some eighteen inches long bandaged in strips of syncot. When he got that unwound, he found he was holding the lower left leg, from the knee connection down, and foot of an android. There was a smear of loamy dirt stuck to the metallic ankle, and a few tiny white worms were writhing in it.

"This must be," Silvera decided, setting the leg on the table, "part of Dr. Scofflaw." He gathered up the wrappings, examined them closely.

Nothing in the way of identifying marks on the

cloth or the paper. The knots used on the cord were simple ones, didn't tell him anything about who tied them. After putting the wrappings aside, he picked up the leg again.

He rotated it in his hands. "Been buried for a while," he said. "Actually this hunk of Scofflaw doesn't do me much good. I need the part that can sign checks. And why exactly did—"

Bam!

Kabam!

His front door came bouncing into the parlor. It landed smack atop the corpse, covering it. Hail, wind and three uniformed Federal Police came in after the door.

"Jose Silvera?" inquired one, a thickset polar-bear man.

"Sorry I didn't hear you knock or I'd have—"

"Are you Jose Silvera, the notorious hack writer?"

Silvera nodded. "The same."

Another policeman, a bearded human one, told him, "We'll be taking you in now, Silvera."

"In? Why exactly?"

"The charges," announced the polar bear, "are treason and sedition. You are accused of writing and/or conspiring to write a cookbook critical of the junta."

"We got that weasel Dotheboy Rampling," said the third officer, a lean catman with part of the gold trim missing from his overcoat. "He told all, before the torture had barely commenced."

"Then he must have told you I have no political convictions whatsoever," said Silvera. "I was merely hired to do a job which—"

"Aiding a traitor, even it it's only helping him with

his spelling, makes you a traitor," explained the polar bear. "You'll have to come along with us now, so get your snowgear on."

"I have a cake in the oven," he said. "Called the Coup d'Etat Chocolate Ripple Cake. Could we wait until—"

"Now," ordered the polar bear.

"You'll get ninety-nine years on Devil's Island for this kind of treason." The catman came further into the room, bent to pick up the fallen door.

"Might as well leave it there." Silvera took his greatcoat, carefully, off its peg. "Since I won't be coming back here for ninety-nine years, there's—"

"Zowie!" The catman had ignored him and lifted up the door. He flung it against the wall, stood staring down at the corpse.

"Murder," the polar-bear man cop assured Silvera, "is good for at least another ninety-nine years."

Chapter 9

The blazing morning sunlight came knifing in through the unscreened windows of the barracks.

The flimsy door was booted open, and three hefty guards came stomping across the plank floor, sending green rodents and orange spiders scurrying for cover. They stopped beside Silvera's lopsided bunk, circled it and grabbed the awakening writer.

"Warden Tolkien wants to see you, Silvera!" announced one of the gray-clad guards as he shook him by the arm.

The remaining guards were yanking at other limbs.

"Come along, don't resist."

"I'm still," Silvera pointed out, "chained to the bed."

"I'm still chained to the bed, sir," the largest guard corrected, cuffing Silvera across the side of the face.

Another guard unshackled him, then the three of them dragged him out of the crowded barracks room. None of the other prisoners spoke.

The ground around the barrack compound was hard and gritty, supporting only a few dying palm trees. The rising sun bleached everything a pale yellow.

"I could walk," said Silvera, "and save us all some effort."

"I could walk and save us some effort, sir."

"Screw you, sir."

Whap!

Smap!

Slunk!

The three guards cuffed him in turn. Silvera slumped, let them drag him, feet scraping the gritty ground, across to the palatial home of the warden of Devil's Island. As Silvera went bumping and banging up the veranda steps, voices came spilling out of the big house.

"Oh, 'tis a fate far worse than death," cried a piping female voice. "Anything, kind sir, but this. Pray, do not deflower me for I would retain my virtue for—"

"Save your blathering, wench! I would have me way with you!"

"Another nerfing show," remarked one of the guards.

"None of our affair," said another, opening the screen door. "Ready now. One—two—three. Toss!"

They heaved the slightly groggy Silvera into a cool shadowy parlor. He landed hard on an oval rug, stretched out and remained there.

"Oh, pray, don't thrust that awful thing into my intimate recesses!"

"Gar, I'll slip you ten inches of the old liverwurst or me name ain't . . . Is that you out there, Silvera?"

"More or less." He managed to rise to his knees.

"You certainly haven't been a model prisoner." Warden Tolkien came waddling into the parlor. He was a huge orange lizard man, wearing a blue kimono and with a puppet over each hand.

One of the hand puppets was a naked blonde girl with substantial breasts, the other a foul-looking pirate with a bristling beard and prominent penis.

"Oh, kind sir, have you come to deliver me from this vile lustful seadog?" the blonde puppet asked Silvera.

DR. SCOFFLAW

Silvera stood up. "You sent for me?" he asked the warden.

"Don't like puppets, eh?"

"Puppets are okay. It's being dumped into strange parlors that pisses me off."

"Har yar," said the pirate captain, "here's a lad after me own heart."

Warden Tokien removed the hand puppets, placed them gently atop the upright piano. "You've been with us on Devil's Island for a week, Silvera."

"Eight days."

"During that time you have behaved in a very surly manner."

"Well, you've got less than a model prison."

"The junta has strived to make this a tiptop prison, modeled as much as it can be considering the differences of climate and location after a famous prison in the Solar System. Perhaps you've heard of the original Devil's Island?"

"Wrote a book about it once."

"Which brings us to the point of this interview." The warden settled into a wicker loveseat, crossed his thick orange legs. "We've tried you out as a chopper in the cane fields, a spindler in the jute mill, a tromper in the wine presses. What you've done on each of these jobs is make trouble."

"I was railroaded into this place," said Silvera. "Back in the capital they didn't even allow me to have an attorney or—"

"Yes, yes, all the prisoners here try to tell the same story. No lawyer, civil rights violated, innocent in the first place," said the warden. "All very tiresome, dull. Which is why I turned to puppets, to relieve the tedium."

61

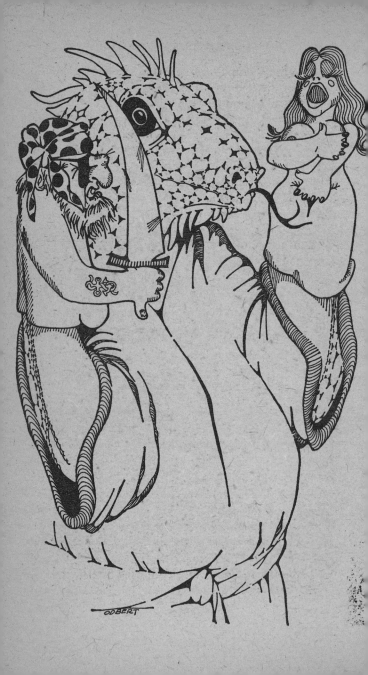

"I didn't claim I was innocent," Silvera told him. "The murder I didn't commit, but I did consort with a radical. The sentence, though, is ridic—"

"Ninety-nine years is your standard treason sentence. Usually it works out, with time off for good behavior, to eighty-eight years. Or so we anticipate, this being a relatively new facility."

"I want to be allowed to contact my—"

"You don't get any extra favors, Silvera, until you settle into some sort of job here on Devil's Island," Warden Tolkien said. "You must learn to be patient, which a man serving ninety-nine years should be able to do." He recrossed his legs, smoothed his kimono. "We have a vacancy on the prison newspaper. In fact, we have three vacancies. The editor, the managing editor and the circulation manager attempted to escape last evening and as a result are no longer alive. Can you edit a newspaper?"

"I've edited several."

Tolkien's orange head bobbed up and down. "It's a shame to see a man with your obvious ability turn to crime," he said. "I would guess it's a combination of faulty upbringing and food allergies. A splendid book entitled *Crime And Sneezing: A New Look At Penology* quite brilliantly links allergic reactions to major—"

"I know. I wrote it."

"You did? Under the alias Dr. Guzman Tipperary?"

"There really is a Dr. Tipperary. But he can't write. He turned in a bushel basket full of six hundred and fifty-six pages of undecipherable scribbles to Thugee & Sons back on Barnum. They called me in."

"Well, if you can improve on Dr. Tipperary, you

should certainly be able to pep up the *Devil's Island Sun-Times*."

"That's the name of your paper?"

"We merged our morning and evening papers a few months ago, after the entire staff of the *Times* perished in an ill-conceived escape try," said Warden Tolkien. "A man of your obvious ability, Silvera, should be able to do wonders with the *Sun-Times*." He stroked a scaly knee. "One area in need of immediate improvement is the comics page. The gags in *Solitary Confinement* are flat, the stories in *Star Cops* take too long to unfold and *Trixie & Hapgood* is a total flop. I'd expected a strip about a homosexual marriage would appeal to many of our men, since as Dr. Tipperary points out . . . oh, but since you're Dr. Tipperary, you already know. At any rate the men complain that Trixie is too much your stereotyped Nellie and Hapgood an outrageous caricature of the traditional Butch figure. Well, it's all in your hands." He rose from the loveseat. "You'll also have to be careful that the Fun & Puzzle Page doesn't print any more escape plans. We had to execute the last feature editor on account of that. I really do think you'll enjoy the job."

"It sounds better than the jute mill," said Silvera.

Chapter 10

"Another of our immediate problems, Mr. Silvera, is the Woman's Page," said Joel Frollo.

"Woman's Page?" Silvera got up from behind his editorial desk and strolled around the *Devil's Island Sun-Times* office. "Why do we need one of those?"

Frollo was a medium-size young man with considerable curly hair. He was huddled behind a large drawing board, watching the pacing Silvera. "It's a special favorite of the women prisoners over in—"

"I didn't know we had any women prisoners."

"An editor can't keep up with everything," said the staff cartoonist. "Editor before last didn't even know which way was south. Which is what seriously fouled up his escape attempt." Frollo eyed him. "You're not planning an immediate escape, are you? Since you're the first editor we've had in a while with any sort of journalistic background, I was sort of hoping—"

"What's the problem with the Woman's Page?" Silvera stopped to gaze out a barred window of their bungalow.

"It's tough to come up with material to fill it," explained Frollo. "We tried a fashion column, but that started a lot of the lady prisoners to complaining their uniforms weren't modish. We've had better luck with a gossip column, but you have to be very careful there. The editor three editors back spilled part of the Wing 4 girls' escape plan in the darn column."

Silvera said, "I'm going to let you handle the page, Frollo."

"But I'm already weighted down revising the comic strips," complained the cartoonist. "We only have a two-person staff after all."

"Double what you had yesterday."

"True." Frollo began to pat the clutter of pictures and notes on his taboret. "I was thinking we might do something with the Koister girl, but now they tell me we can't even see her or—"

"Whoa!" Silvera sprinted over to the drawing board, snatched the glossy photo Frollo had picked up. "Is this Tammany Kloister?"

"You've heard of her, too? Well, then she's obviously newsworthy."

The publicity photo showed a smiling blonde girl, slender, slightly fragile-looking. "She's here? Right here on Devil's Island?"

"Gee, you certainly are excited, Mr. Silvera. If Tammany Kloister's that important, we can maybe give the whole Woman's Page over to her. New Arrival Held Incommunicado On Our Island! Famed Penwoman Detained In Interrogation Wing! Couple heads like that and a nice blowup of the pic—"

"She's not a regular prisoner?"

"No, they're holding her here as a favor to certain important people."

"Such as?"

Frollo rubbed his foot across some memos fallen to the plank floor, watched the foot. "Oh, you know. But you can't print any of this. The Island is always doing favors for . . . you know, organized crime."

Silvera nodded, asking, "How'd you find out the girl was here? And where'd you get this photo?"

"Warden Tolkien is very publicity conscious. He provided me with the information."

"If she's being kept under wraps, why do they want the news in the paper?"

"Oh, no one off the Island ever sees the *Sun-Times*," replied the cartoonist. "A shame in a way, meaning my best work never reaches the influential publishers and—"

"The Interrogation Wing, where is it?"

Frollo pointed furtively. "Over on the other end of the Island, Mr. Silvera, beyond the warehouses and docking area," he said in a very low voice. "They won't let us near her, so any kind of interview is going to—"

"Nevertheless, I've got to talk to that girl."

"Sneaking around isn't a capital crime on the Island, but it's sure to add another ninety-nine years to your sentence."

"So I'll serve two hundred and ninety-seven years instead of one hundred and ninety-eight." Silvera returned to his desk. "We'll put the *Sun-Times* together first, then I'll figure out a way to get to Tammany Kloister." He began opening desk drawers.

"Probably won't find any copy paper in your desk," said Frollo. "Your predecessor had a scheme for building a glider out of yellow paper and—"

"Where's the supply closet?" Silvera stood, opened the door of the nearest closet.

"No, that's where Warden Tolkien stores his surplus stuff."

The closet was jammed with small cartons, boxes and plaz containers. Silvera hefted a small carton. "Sneeze Powder, 1 doz. family-size packs."

"This is what's left of the warden's earlier hobby. Before he went in for puppets, he had a brief fling with practical jokes. The Interplanetary Penal Overseeing Committee didn't take too kindly to his playing pranks on the prisoners so—"

"Two doz. Sure-Laff Woopie Cushions," Silvera read from the gaudy label of a larger box. He stooped, investigating other cartons. "Here's a dozen and a half joke hands. Tolkien went at his hobby on a grand scale."

"Well, if you're a government facility, you get a discount for buying in quantity."

Silvera stood back from the open closet, stroking his chin. "Prof Emerson used the lift-raft gimmick when he escaped from the Barnum Prison for Habitual Loonies," he mused. "I wrote about that in *The Bedside Book Of Nifty Escapes.* Sure, with enough whoopie cushions I could probably—"

"Remember, Mr. Silvera, that a whoopie cushion is so named because when you sit on one or even apply pressure, it makes a loud raucous whoopie sound."

"The common denominator in all great escapes," Silvera told him, "is an ability to improvise." He returned to scrutinizing the contents of the closet. "Wonder if he has joke feet, too. Otherwise we can get by with the fake hands. Evil Eye Anmar did a similar trick when he broke out of the Contrary Persons Prison Farm on Murdstone. Sure, it could be managed."

"Before you do anything suicidal," requested the cartoonist, "could you give me some editorial advice on how to improve the comic page?"

Chapter 11

When the snoring reached a sufficient density, Silvera eased out of his bunk. The shackles which usually held him to the bed were grasping a pair of the warden's leftover plastic joke feet tonight. Silvera had arranged his trouser cuffs around the fake feet and had been able to fool the guard who was in charge of chaining the prisoners. The guard had made a remark about how cold the feet were, but Silvera had been able to convince him he had a circulation problem.

"Here, feel my hand, it's just as chill," he'd invited, thrusting a joke hand out from under his blanket.

"More hard labor and less sitting on your duff in editor's chairs is what you need, buddy."

Now, with pale moonlight coming in through the barred windows, Silvera made his way to the door.

Kneeling, he took out a paper clip he'd borrowed from the *Sun-Times* and went to work on the lock. When he ghosted *Fifty Years A Lawbreaker,* he'd learned a good bit about lockpicking, and the information, unlike that acquired on some of his less interesting assignments, had stuck with him.

The lock yielded in less than three minutes. Silvera, very gently, turned the knob and pushed the door a few inches open.

"Mr. Silvera!"

He stopped still, looked back into the barracks.

In the bed nearest the door a figure, a curly haired figure, was sitting up. "Mr. Silvera," repeated Joel

Frollo in the same anxious whisper, "are you doing a flit?"

"A what?"

"A midnight creep, a . . . you know, an escape. Are you?"

"Hush up, go to sleep."

"But I left the revised *Trixie & Hapgood* strips on your desk, three complete dailies and six in pencil. If you get knocked off before you can approve them, I'll have—"

"They're terrific, Joel. Run 'em on page one."

"Oh, you haven't even looked at them, Mr. Silvera. You're simply patronizing me now because—"

"I'll go read them right now. You, meantime, shut up and lie down."

"But . . ."

Silvera ducked out into the night, shut the barracks door behind him. He sprinted to a sickly palm tree, pressed against its trunk. He'd learned during his week-plus on Devil's Island what the guard schedules were. Two armed men would be marching by this dorm in roughly six minutes.

He remained in the shadow of the palm, listening. Night birds warbled in the jungle, insects twitted and hummed. Silvera, head tucked in, ran. He executed a zigzag pattern and reached the *Sun-Times* bungalow unobserved. Behind the office, hidden in a clump of spikey brush, were three large cartons.

He hefted up the boxes, went trotting across a gray stretch of open ground and toward the woods fifty yards beyond.

Whoopie!

Whoopie!

Whoopie!

"Damn it." Silvera slowed his pace.

Whoopie!

The jiggling of his flight was making some of the whoopie cushions in the cartons exclaim.

"Did you detect a festive sound over yonder, Russell?"

"No, I didn't, Charles."

Silvera sped up, ran as fast as he could for the shelter of the dark woodlands, hoping to reach there before the as yet unseen guards materialized.

Whoopie!

Whoopie! Whoopie!

Whoopie!

"Say, I think I do hear it, Charles. Odd to encounter jubilant outcries here in the heart of Devil's Island."

"We'd best investigate, Russell."

By the time the pair of guards came tromping into the moonlit clearing, Silvera was concealed among the tall trees. He needed the inflatable neorubber cushions in his overall escape plan, but he abandoned them for the moment and pushed deeper into the woods.

Fortunately he also remembered a good deal of what he'd learned when he posed as Colonel Dan Barks and wrote *The Boy Commando's Book Of Woodsy Lore.* Part of that lore involved eluding your enemies in forest and jungle.

In less than a half hour Silvera was approaching the Interrogation Wing. Ducked behind flowering shrubs at the wood's edge, he scanned the large two-story building. Several lights were on and in a guard hut fifteen feet in front of the main entrance a chunky catman sat reading an old copy of *Galactic Dime Detective.*

"I think I wrote the lead novelet in that particular

issue," Silvera said to himself. "But this guy may not be impressed by meeting a real pulp author."

The lower half of the hut was solid neowood, the upper half was glaz.

Silvera reached into his tunic, extracted a packet of sneezing powder. Keeping in a nearly flat-out position, he inched across the open ground between the woods and the guard hut. He made it to the side of the hut unobserved. Near the ground was the backside of the ventilating unit. Using his bent paper clip once again, Silvera opened the unit up and poured the entire packet of sneeze powder into the circulating mechanism.

In a moment the catman guard began fidgeting in his chair. Another half minute and he was sneezing and snorting violently, slapping at his knees with the rolled up pulp magazine.

Silvera rose and ran for the entrance of the Interrogation Wing. "That stuff never used to work that well when I fooled with it as a kid."

He got through the glaz doors, found himself in a long empty blue corridor. Tammany Kloister was supposed to be in this building someplace. Silvera wasn't sure exactly where.

A door halfway down the blue corridor was partially open. Silvera made his cautious way toward it.

". . . really a very stubborn young woman," someone was saying on the other side of the door.

"You're the stubborn one," replied a girl's voice. "I've been absolutely candid with you. The whole thing is a hoax. Dr. Scofflaw is dead, dismantled and defunct. I made the whole autobiography up."

"Shit," said Silvera, "there goes my 10,000 bucks."

Chapter 12

"Don't you pay attention to what I yell at you during our sessions?"

"It's difficult not to, but I try."

Smack!

"Listen to me, Tammany! Dr. Scofflaw is not dead, he's not dismantled."

"That may well be, Kirkus. The real point, though, is that the alleged autobiog I'm doing is a fake."

Bogg Kirkus. One of the kingpins of the Barnum Crime Combine. Silvera was familiar with the name.

"They've put him back together again. Or, if they haven't quite completed him, they're in the process."

"Even so, I'm only an opportunist."

"Don't you realize the Barnum Crime Combine has checked, double checked and triple checked, for that matter, the places where Dr. Scofflaw's scattered parts were scattered? Yes, and the parts are not there."

"So you've told me, Kirkus."

"And what you have to tell me is where the parts were taken. Where did Dr. Scofflaw go after they put him together again?"

"I don't know. I absolutely and honestly don't know."

Smack!

Silvera did a potentially foolhardy thing. The sound of Tammany Kloister being slapped angered him. So he kicked the partially open door all the way open, went charging into the room. He had no idea how many people or what kind of weapons he'd encounter in there. He should have been more cautious.

There were three men and two guns showing. The small nervous lizard man in the dark glasses held a stungun in his left hand. A large human stationed behind the girl's chair had a blaster pistol in one fist. The third man, who apparently did the slapping, was an empty-handed birdhead.

Silvera left the floor, tackled Bogg Kirkus and knocked him over. He grabbed the stungun away from him, somersaulted clear of the sprawled Crime Combine leader and fired the stungun at the birdman, who was in the act of charging him.

"Urk!" The bird hood's arms flapped, his beak clicked, he stumbled and fell down.

"Dumb bimbo!" The human with the lethal gun was hopping around on one foot.

Tammany had caused her chair to jump back, and one of its legs had jabbed down on the gunman's foot.

Silvera used the stungun again, catching the big man in midhop. As the gunman was dropping, Silvera pivoted and fired at Bogg Kirkus.

The crime boss had been in the process of yanking a needlegun out of his vest holster. The blast of the stungun froze him and timbered him back into the wall; his dark glasses went popping up over his lumpy green forehead.

"What branch of the law are you?" inquired Tammany. Although her face had two bruises on it and several red spots, she was still quite pretty.

"You're not as fragile-looking in person." Silvera undid the grouthide bonds which held her to the chair.

"You must have seen the photo on my last book

jacket. I was striving to look gothic," said the blonde. "Who did you say you were?"

"Jose Silvera, I'm not a lawman."

"Silvera the hack?"

"That's me." He helped her up out of the chair.

"Did you come out here to Devil's Island to rescue me?"

He took her arm. "Not exactly, but I have been looking for you."

"Why?"

"So I can find Dr. Scofflaw."

"You, too? Look, I really don't know where the old gentleman is. This Kirkus has devoted over a week to trying to get me to admit I do," she said. "When the electronic gadgets and the drugs didn't force any answers out of me, they resorted to the punch-in-the-face approach. Which didn't get anywhere either."

Silvera hesitated on the threshold. "We can talk about the whole Scofflaw situation later." He glanced out into the corridor. "First, we have to get the hell off this Island."

"Everybody's favorite ambition," said Tammany as they stepped free of the questioning room. "Why did you want Scofflaw, by the way?"

"He owes me $10,000."

"Yes, I've heard about you, Silvera. Silvera always collects. Do you?"

"Yep, always."

"Doesn't that detract from your writing time, chasing after back pay?"

"I write fast." They had reached the doorway leading outside. The guard was back in his chair, tilted and intent on *Galactic Dime Detective*.

"Myself, I'm a very slow writer, and I never get by

on less than three or four drafts," said the girl. "How do you figure to leave this Island, Silvera?"

"On a raft."

"Might work, since the currents aren't too terrible. What do we use for a raft? Do you have one?"

"We build one."

"Out of logs? That'll take time."

Silvera said, "You'll have to trust me. Don't laugh. We're going to use whoopie cushions."

The girl laughed. "Sorry. I wasn't supposed to do that."

"I've got several dozen of the damn things. With any luck we can do it," he said. "But before we tackle that problem, I've got to distract the guard out there so we can sprint into the woods."

"How do you propose to do that, Silvera?"

"With sneezing powder."

Tammany laughed again. "This promises to be one of the most fun-filled prison breaks I've ever been in on," she said.

Chapter 13

Silvera and the girl stole through the night woods in nearly silent single file.

"How much time, do you think," asked Tammany, "before someone notices our absence?"

"Hopefully they won't realize anything until morning."

Their whispered conversation lagged again.

After a few quiet moments Tammany said, "You say you didn't come to Devil's Island specifically to spring me, Silvera?"

"Didn't even know you were here, Kloister."

"Were you sentenced to the Island, then?"

"Ninety-nine years for treason, ninety-nine additional for murder."

The blonde girl nodded. "Who'd you murder?"

"Nobody."

"Who'd they accuse you of knocking off?"

"They never did establish his real name. A fringe crook who tried to highjack his superiors."

"Who did kill him?"

"I figured at first it was the Barnum Crime Combine, but now I'm not exactly sure," answered Silvera as he stepped over a fallen log.

"Is the BCC interested in you, too?"

"It all ties in with Dr. Scofflaw."

"Oh . . ."

"The murdered man was delivering me a part of the illustrious doctor," explained Silvera. "Word must have circulated that I was trying to find Scofflaw, and this nitwit assumed I'd pay cash money for even a part of him."

"Then what Bogg Kirkus has been hollering about for the past week or more is true. They are reassembling Scofflaw."

"Right, and it's got to be some BCC splinter group that's doing it."

"Means my position is going to continue being difficult."

"You put yourself there."

"Come on, Silvera," said the girl. "We're both free-lance writers. You know what a tough business it is. I saw a chance to make some money, so I took it. There's no big crime involved."

"Outside of lying."

"Everybody lies."

"Not always on such a grand scale."

"I heard you ghosted that bestseller called *I Slept With A Watermelon*."

"I did."

"So don't go giving me lectures on morality, Silvera."

"Sleeping with—"

"Tee hee! Hee hee!"

Silvera halted, held out an arm to stop the girl. Strange sounds were emanating from the woods ahead.

"Don't wiggle so much, Claudia."

"Hee hee! Tee hee hee! It's . . . it's your silly moustache."

"I can't scrutinize your kaboopies without taking a close look."

"Tee hee . . . I don't understand how you can photograph them at all in this dismal light."

"With an artist of my ability yonkers can be shot in any light."

"Palma!" exclaimed Silvera, starting to run toward the woodland glade.

"Is that Palma, the breast-fetish cameraman?" inquired Tammany, following.

A bald head rose up from the underbrush. The moonlight seeping down through the intricate interlacing of branches bleached the skin to a pale glowing blue. "It's just as they say," said Palma. "If you hunch down in the middle of a jungle on a wretched penal colony in the middle of nowhere with a prison nurse who has a strikingly monumental set of hangers, sooner or later everybody you know will pass by. What are you doing hereabouts, Jose?"

Silvera stopped at the edge of the small clearing. A lovely girl was seated on the moss, reseaming her uniform tunic. "I'm in the process of escaping from Devil's Island."

"Oh, so?" Palma returned his camera to its case. "I didn't even know you were here. I should have kept better tabs on you but after we parted in Camposanto Territory, I jaunted on to photograph dungeons and—"

"Um um," the nurse was saying, standing up. "I don't want to act like a company person, but this man is a dangerous murderer and pamphleteer and I really ought to—"

"No, no, Claudia, you aren't completely backgrounded on the situation. Jose Silvera here is an undercover agent for the Penal Ombudsman Association. He came here to gather facts about . . . Oh, good evening, miss." He noticed Tammany now, gave

79

her a casual salute. "You're obviously Tammany Kloister."

"Yes, I am."

"I could tell, because you have exactly the sort of . . . Well, let's turn our thoughts to immediate departure, shall we."

"Um um."

"Yes, Claudia?"

"She's another one. A very significant political prisoner of some sort. Don't tell me she's also with this Ombudsman thing."

"Not at all." Palma slipped an arm around the nurse's shoulders. "This young lady is a well-known anthropologist who—"

"He's not a killer, he's an ombudsman; she's not a dangerous radical, she's an anthropologist. And what are you supposed to be in real life?"

Palma shook his bald head, sadly. "I was hoping you wouldn't penetrate my disguise, Claudia. Since my work is the most secret and—"

"Flim flam!" The nurse made fists. "You come swaggering into my hospital, bald dome asweat with horniness and ogling every lass in sight. You give me a line about wanting to immortalize my mammies in some alleged publication known as *Intergalactic Girlie Gags* and you expect—"

"Claudia, a nurse ought to know better than to ridicule someone's handicaps," said Palma. "Merely because a man is afflicted with extreme randiness is no reas—"

"I ought to yell bloody murder. I ought to summon every burly guard on this Island," said the angry Claudia. "In fact, I believe I will."

"Nope." Silvera aimed his borrowed stungun at her.

"Diplomacy has gone as far as it can, Palma. You yell even a smidgen, miss, and I'll use this gun on you."

"Um," said the nurse, shrinking some.

"Do you have a way to get off this damn island, Palma?"

"Sure, my publisher provided me with a handsome motor launch," replied the hairless photographer. "It's moored down at Dock number six this very minute. See, I came here to continue gathering material for my pictorial essay on prisons and dungeons. Little did I dream I'd encounter you and the fabled Tammany Kloister while pursuing my art."

"Art," said Claudia with a sneer.

"You have a terrific sneer," complimented Palma. "When you use it, your left kazootie tilts upward whilest your right points groundward. Symbolic in a way of both the sacred and profane nature of—"

"Palma," cut in Silvera, "it's an ideal time to depart."

"Right you are." He removed his arm from around the girl. "Claudia, I must bid you a reluctant farewell."

"As soon as you scram, skinhead, I'll get our entire staff of guards on your tail!" promised the disgruntled nurse.

"Tut," said Palma. "I really don't enjoy these sentimental partings. But, at any rate, you aren't going to holler for anyone." From one of his dangling cases he produced a knife.

"Um!"

Palma reached up and sliced a long length of vine. "I learned a good deal about tying up young ladies while employed, early in my meteoric career, as a staff photographer for a bondage magazine." After he'd selected and cut down two more hunks of sturdy vine, he added to Silvera, "We'll be ready to embark in scant minutes, Jose. And I trust you appreciate the sacrifices I'm making to aid you like this."

Chapter 14

Palma whipped off his synfur hat and the incredibly beautiful girl behind the counter said, "Oh, my goodness, your poor head."

Reaching up to pat his scalp, the photographer said, "Spare me your pity, miss. We baldies don't ask for—"

"I wasn't alluding to your baldness, sir. I was rather expressing concern and sympathy because your poor little head is all pale and goosebumpy from the cold without."

Nodding, Palma moved across the government office toward the amazingly pretty girl clerk. "I must confess I'm used to warmer climes than Jelado," he said. "That storm out there unsettles me."

"Well, the snow and sleet aren't so bad this afternoon," the girl said, resting her handsome bare elbows on the counter top. "It's the iceballs."

"Iceballs?"

"Big round things composed of ice? Some appear to have smacked your greatcoat, there and there."

"I assumed some prankish youths had pelted me."

"Oh, no. I forget the meteorological explanation, but we get iceballs about once a week. I had one come whizzing down my front only this morning, right down into here."

Palma watched her hand trace the path of the iceball. "Quite an experience. And now to business." He executed a brief stomping dance in front of the counter, slapping his arms across his chest and shedding most of the snow and ice he'd accumulated walking from the hideaway to the Federal Police Lost & Found Division. He removed his thermmittens, rubbed his hands together.

The stunningly beautiful girl clerk reached across, took hold of one of his hands. "Allow me to help you stimulate the return of circulation to your poor little hands, sir."

"I appreciate that. In my line of work fingers are very important."

"You're probably an artist."

"An artist with a camera." He took back one of his hands, unseamed his greatcoat to give her a glimpse of his dangling cameras. "You know, from the moment I saw you . . . what is your name?" He squinted at the nameplate which rested near her left elbow. "Ramona Gospel, that's a splendid name for—"

"No, that's Ramona's nameplate, not mine. I actually haven't been laboring here long enough to have earned a plate of my own. Indeed, if poor Ramona hadn't been chased up a flagpole by a berserk snow-plow, I wouldn't even be on duty out front like this."

"How fortunate, for us if not for poor little Ramona."

"My name is Natalie Vivarium."

"Natalie Vivarium. Has a definite lilt and will look excellent in a caption to . . . but first." He assumed a more serious expression. "Let me inform you of my reason for calling on the lost & found."

"I am eager to hear it."

"My respected great-aunt has misplaced her left leg," he confided. "You know how old people are, forgetful."

"That is certainly true. My grandfather can never

find his nose. You see, due to an unfortunate mining accident on the third moon of—"

"Exactly. Now then, Natalie, is it possible my poor little great-aunt's lost limb is reposing here?"

The stunning girl drummed slim, beautiful fingers on the counter. "It's funny you should mention a leg," she said. "Because I gave out one the very day I took over for poor Ramona."

"You handed it out?"

"Yes, a false leg, made of metal, not in very great shape if you ask me. I had the impression it had been buried in someone's yard for a great long while. So it couldn't have belonged to your poor—"

"Let's not rule it out. My aunt is a shade eccentric, has been know to play a rather macabre game of hide and seek with her detachable limbs."

"Limbs? You mean there's more than one piece of her—"

"It pains me to detail the various replacement parts she . . ." Palma paused to stroke his brow. "I was hoping her absent member would turn up here at the Federal Police's L & F."

"The people who claimed this particular leg were quite positive it was their leg," said Natalie, a look of concern touching her amazingly lovely face. "They described it in minutest detail and certainly seemed intimately familiar with it." She moved her beautiful head closer to his. "There's an odd thing about this leg. Do you know where it came from?"

"Not from my aunt?"

"From the Homicide Squad," the girl confided. "Yes, Homicide. They thought it might be an important clue in a brutal murder case, but it turned out not to be, and so they dumped it on us."

"That's truly fascinating," said Palma, staring into the girl's lovely green eyes. "My aunt will be delighted when she hears the odyssey her limb has undergone."

"I really don't think it can be hers. Because the movie people were positive it was theirs. They identified it very thoroughly, and I gave it to them."

"This whole matter can be cleared up quite simply," said Palma, giving her a pat on the elbow. "I'll drop in on these people, scan the leg in question and if it is indeed my aunt's, make all the necessary arrangements. Movie people did they say?"

Natalie said, "Actually they didn't. But I recognized them. I didn't comment on it, since I imagine persons of a certain level of celebrity don't like to be singled out in public. The thing is I'm a former movie buff."

"You mean some actors came for the leg?"

"Not actors, but on the staff of one of the large studios. I recognized them as being from Cliffhanger Productions, Inc."

"I'll pop in on them and get a—"

"You'll have quite a trip. Cliffhanger is over in Trapaza Territory."

"Trapaza, good. They don't extradite," murmured Palma. "Silvera will be safe there."

"Beg pardon? I didn't quite catch—"

"I was praying," explained Palma. "Praying that one day soon again I'll meet a girl I can spend more than nine or ten minutes with."

"Cozy," observed Tammany from the groutskin rug in front of the large fireplace. "A roaring blaze and the sound of snow, sleet and iceballs on the roof."

"You're going to have to get used to a new climate," Silvera said from a nearby sling chair. "Jelado isn't safe anymore."

"I suppose not," acknowledged the girl, hugging her knees. "Not only am I a conperson, I'm a fugitive from Devil's Island."

"Would you mind," said the third inhabitant of the room, a thin nervous catman, "not dwelling on the illegal aspects of this situation?"

"I'm sorry, Mr. Mamlish," said Tammany. "You've been very kind, allowing us to hide out here in your—"

"See, you're doing it again. The only people who *hide out* are criminals."

"You're absolutely right, but what I'm trying to convey is how much we appreciate your helping us."

"I have to," said Mamlish, leaving his chair and taking another look out an oval window. "A whole career in journalism is at stake. A man can't live entirely on the salary they pay me at *Igloo & Garden Magazine*. I have to supplement my income with what being a stringer for Coult Publications pays, and thus when Palma shows up with you two fugitives . . . that is, you two wayfarers, I have to put you up. For a limited time anyway."

"Even so, we appreciate it, don't we, Jose?"

Silvera was watching the anxious catman. "Why don't you go into your study and do something?"

"Who can work under these conditions? I'm harboring you people, Palma is off trying to pull the snergfur over the eyes of the police, the Federal Police mind you. How can any—"

"I don't care whether you work or simply sit and cringe," Silvera told him. "Just so you leave us alone for a while."

"Well, you certainly have a nice way of asking," said Mamlish, edging for a doorway. "Here I am in my own bought and paid for house and you—"

"Go," urged Silvera.

Mamlish left them.

"You weren't very cordial to him," said Tammany.

"I'm probably going to have to stay here in Jelado for a while," Silvera said to her. "Until I find out where Scofflaw is being reassembled. You, though, we can smuggle across the border into—"

"I don't want to be smuggled, Silvera."

"They're going to hunt you. Not only the Crime Combine, but the law. You—"

"What I want to do is salvage as much as I can out of this Scofflaw project," said the girl. "Carlos got some damn big advances out of publishers all over this planet for the autobiography. I don't intend to give that dough back."

."That much of your motive I can appreciate," he said. "But there's very little chance you can do any sort of auto—"

."Who says? Scofflaw is alive, or at least on his way to being alive." She stood, faced him with hands on hips. "You're going to find him to collect what he

owes you. Okay, after you finish with him, I come in and make a deal."

"You can't deal with a guy like Dr. Scofflaw. He's likely to steal what dough you've already got, sell you to slavers, have his goons break all your bones and—"

"You don't know me," said Tammany. "By your own admission you've never even read a single one of my books."

"You've only written three."

"Three *good* ones! Not a whole stack of garbage ground out simply for a fast—"

"Hooey!" said Silvera. "The con you tried to pull with this Scofflaw book proves you're as crass as—"

"Crass as you?" She shook her head. "I don't think you have any idea, Silvera, what it's like to be a good writer. I mean really *good*. I'm good and yet I haven't been able to earn any kind of comfortable life. There are, as you know, all sorts of solutions to the problems. I chose not to become a mindless hack. Instead I decided to make a tremendous amount on one big blockbuster of a book. I was scared when I first came up with this Scofflaw idea, but the more I went over it in my mind, the better it looked. Scofflaw wasn't about to surface and say the book really wasn't his life story. I did a hell of a lot of research; I knew I could fake it. With the money I've made already on this, I can live really well for years. I can write exactly what I want to after this, which is more than you can say."

"What I can say is, you're not going to tag along with me."

"Yes, I am. We're going to find Dr. Scofflaw together," said Tammany, defiant. "Try not to work with me, Silvera, and I'll do everything I can to screw you up and sabotage you."

He grinned at her. "You have the dedication of a true hack, Tammany." Silvera turned his back on her, shrugged. "All right, we'll try it together, as a team. But you do what I say and you keep in mind that the main objective of the quest is getting $10,000 out of Scofflaw."

"I won't stand in the way of your collecting your money." She moved to a chair and sat. "If you did a real bestseller, you'd be able to give up this pattern of life. Don't you see that?"

"I like living this way," said Silvera.

Chapter 16

Splop!

"Again? Cut!"

"I told you and I told you, Mr. Zantz, this here scene wouldn't hardly play."

"The scene is brilliant, Buddy!"

"If it's so here now brilliant, how come everybody keeps falling on their butts, Mr. Zantz?"

"It is because," replied Hugo Zantz, slapping his riding crop against his thigh, "you are a bunch of thick-witted and clumsy twits!"

"You keep calling me and Miss Flaming dirty names, and I'm going to pop you one, Mr. Zantz."

"Thick-witted twit is not a dirty name," the catman director explained.

"Then how about flat-footed boobie? Which is what you called us last time I inadvertently fell on my butt because this scene ain't no good."

"The scene is brilliant!" repeated Zantz. "Is it not, Jose?"

Silvera, who had written it, agreed. "Absolutely."

Buddy Cream stalked across the set, stood at its edge glaring out at Silvera. "I'd like to see you wrestle six mudmen, cousin, and keep from slipping and falling on your butt."

"The problem," Silvera told the handsome, blond, muddy actor, "is not in the writing or the direction but with the makeup. Your mudmen are too gooey."

"Oh, here it comes," sighed the waspish lizard man

in charge of makeup. "When in doubt, drop a load of crapola on poor Prez's shoulders."

"That's a brilliant insight, Jose!" Zantz stepped onto the simulated desert and approached the half-dozen idle mudmen.

Slop! Kaplop!

"See! You took a flop, too." Buddy Cream snickered and hugged himself, his raygun belt jiggling.

"Which proves once and for all, you cockeyed ninny, that the fault is with the mudmen and not the script," said Zantz from where he was sprawled in a puddle of mud.

"Oughtn't Buddy," said the redhaired actress who portrayed his sweetheart, "to know what constitutes a good Streak Chandler, Planeteer, script and what does not? I mean to say, he's starred in five of these dippy serials already. To the vast thrill-seeking movie fandom of Barafunda Buddy Cream, after all, *is* Streak Chandler. From the time he appeared in *Streak Chandler Takes On The Universe,* he—"

"Shut up!" suggested the furry director as he extricated himself from the surface of the planet Xink. "Only I know what's good and what is not good. All you have to worry about, you moon-faced goopy, is—"

"Hold off now, Mr. Zantz, I won't have you address Miss Flaming as a goon-faced muppy or—"

"Moon-faced goopy! Moon-faced goopy! Can't you remember any lines at all?"

"Miss Flaming has been playing Elsie in all my serials and I'll punch any—"

Sploop! Splatz!

While attempting to poke the director, Buddy Cream missed, slipped and crashed down in another spill of mudman makeup.

"A few more of these nasty falls," observed Olympia Flaming, "and Buddy'll do permanent damage to some vital part of himself."

"We could have avoided all this," Prez whispered to Silvera, "had you come up with something other than mudmen."

"Mudmen are very effective," said Silvera. "You can't really have a first-rate science-fiction serial without mudmen or their equivalent."

The makeup man sighed once more. "I suppose you're all too right. In *Streak Chandler Blows Up Jupiter* it was slime men and in *Streak Chandler Against Several Planets* I had to do swampmen," he said. "I spent many a sleepless night, as my male secretary and longtime companion will attest, getting slime of just the right consistency. It has to be slurpy enough to look spooky and yet not so slurpy that it'll slide right off the actors."

"I think if you thicken this mud just a shade, you'll be okay," advised Silvera.

"Perhaps you're—"

Sputch!

Olympia Flaming, while attempting to get Buddy Cream upright, had slipped. She went scooting, backside down, across the desert and bowled over Zantz.

Thump!

"Silvera!" the director cried.

"Yes?"

"I think we'll rewrite this scene after all," Zantz said. "Get rid of these nitwit mudmen."

"Haven't I been telling you that all along?" said Buddy Cream, chuckling.

* * *

From his cubicle window Silvera could see the dry red surface of the planet Xink, the dusty main street of Devil's Doorknob and roughly an acre of prehistoric jungle. After staring out the window for a moment longer, tapping the mike of his talkwriter on his knee, he started to leave his chair.

"Back on your wazoo, buster."

"Have to go to the jakes."

"You did that already."

"It bears repeating."

"Stick in your chair," advised the voice of the typing machine, "or you get a goofoff slip. Six of them things and you get a can tied to your tail."

Silvera couldn't afford to be fired from Cliffhanger Productions yet. He'd had to pay $1000 to the writer who'd preceded him on this job in order to inspire the man to come down with a sudden attack of idiopathic hypogeusia and suggest Silvera as a substitute on the script of *Streak Chandler's Double Trouble*. In his two days on the Cliffhanger lot Silvera hadn't been able to find a trace of the metal leg which had been claimed over in Jelado Territory by someone from this outfit.

"Come on, come on, we're not paying you to day-dream."

"What's the fine for stepping on a talkwriter?"

"Six and out."

Silvera shifted in his chair. "Not worth it."

"That's what Beany decided."

"Who?"

"Beany DeLucca, the miserable hack you replaced. Your allegedly close friend Beany DeLucca."

"We call him Lucky, his close friends."

"So what's going to happen in this revised scene? You got the foggiest notion?"

"Okay, here's what comes next. Elsie puts her hand to her breast, gazes—"

"Which breast?"

"I like to let the director decide these technical questions. Elsie, putting her hand to her breast—"

"Zantz doesn't go for loose ends. He's not the most imaginative gazabo in the world."

"Elsie, pressing her hand to her right breast, exclaims, 'Streak, over there! Look!' Cut to close-up of Streak reacting to something horrible. 'Keep calm, my dearest.' Elsie says, 'Whatever are those dreadful creatures?' 'They may be friendly, Elsie. Let me see if I can converse with them.' 'But they're made of fungus, Streak, and hardly likely to be your intellectual equals.' Cut to medium shot of fungus men as they come lunbering toward—"

"Yang," commented the talkwriter as it paused in its typing.

"Beg pardon? Are you having a mechanical malfunction?"

"Merely making an editorial comment, to preserve my sanity."

Gazing out the window, Silvera noticed a small barbarian strolling by. There was something familiar about him, something which suggested Silvera ought to follow. He snapped his fingers. "Sanity," he said. "That's terrific."

"What's terrific?"

"I'll have to check with Zantz right away, see if we

can do it." He bounced out of his chair. "Polish up what you just took down. Be back soon as I can."

"You better not be trying to con me by . . ."

Silvera went out the door.

Chapter 17

Silvera was right about the barbarian.

The shaggy man in the animal skin wasn't an actor at all. He was a moderately notorious criminal named Denton Bowers. Silvera remembered him from a *Jumbo Crook Calendar* he'd done copy for during an earlier visit to the planet.

You don't see too many barbarians who are only five feet two, especially in Cliffhanger serials. That was what had made Silvera suspicious when he'd seen Bowers go by his cubicle window.

Twilight was spreading across the ten-acre movie lot, a warm humid twilight. Bowers went trotting down a lane between two sound stages, cut across the ruins of a lost city and insinuated himself into the high weeds around an abandoned prop warehouse.

Silvera waited behind a ruined column, watching the spot where Bowers had disappeared. Thus far in his search of the lot Silvera hadn't checked out this particular building.

The twilight thickened, everything grew grayer and grayer and then turned black.

Silvera eased across the ruins and approached the old warehouse. There was an opening visible in the brambles, large enough for a small barbarian to get through. Silvera had to hunch considerably to squeeze up to the doorway in the side of the neowood building. He pried the door a few inches open, waited and listened.

DR. SCOFFLAW

After a moment he ventured inside. A musty blackness surrounded him.

"Denton Bowers could be the guy in charge of the
Crime Combine splinter group," mused Silvera as he
took a few tentative steps across the warehouse floor.
"He and Bogg Kirkus are supposed to be rivals. Spot-
ting him here, running around in a disguise, indicates
he's up to something."

Far across the place light showed, a narrow circle of
pale yellow. Two figures were standing in that circle,
Bowers and a thickset catman. And seated in a canvas
chair was about two thirds of Dr. Scofflaw. He was shy
his head and one arm, but Silvera had no difficulty
recognizing the cyborg who owed him money.

"What do you mean, *flea market*?" Bowers, tossing
his barbarian locks angrily, was asking his furry henchman.

"I mean a flea market, boss."

"How in blue blazes did Scofflaw's right arm get to a
flea market in Camposanto?"

"I guess after Big Phil lost it, somebody else found
it and sold the thing, boss."

"Sold it to whom?"

"That's the very question we're working on, boss,"
said the catman, eyes on the partial Dr. Scofflaw. "We
think it either went to Don & Maggie's Nostalgia
Boutique in Vigilanza or—"

"What's his damn arm got to do with nostalgia?"

The catman shrugged. "This Don and Maggie
maybe collect old robots, boss," he said. "We aren't
too exactly sure. It is also possible a pansy, name of—"

"Just get me the damn arm. Don't tell me any more
stories."

"You'll maybe excuse my saying this, boss, but why

99

doesn't the Doc just buy a brand new arm. We got most of him back to—"

"It's a matter of *pride*," said Bowers, glancing away from the lighted area into the surrounding darkness. "Dr. Scofflaw won't help us on the caper unless we get all his original parts."

"That six-million-dollar dingus isn't going to wait forever, boss. We ought to—"

"Maybe you'd like to go over there and talk to his head, over to Vigilanza Territory and tell Dr. Scofflaw's head you got better ideas than—"

"Aw, I'm not especially scared of just his head."

"Scofflaw is one of the brainiest, nastiest men you'll ever encounter," Bowers assured him. "He's snide, too, capable of—"

"Maybe we could fake the arm, boss. With all these movie ginks around we could make an arm exactly like the one he—"

"Wouldn't you know your own right arm?"

"I would, but mine isn't metal. A metal arm I might not, especially if I'd been all apart for a spell. If I'd been scattered all over Barafunda for a few years, I might accept a reasonable facsimile."

"You might, which is why you're not a criminal mastermind."

"Oh, I don't know. In high school I always did very well in—"

"We won't debate," Bowers informed him. "When we have *all* the parts, we take them over to Vigilanza to reunite with the head."

"Think Scofflaw will throw a reunion party? It's a sort of sentimental occ—"

"Dr. Scofflaw isn't sentimental. Once he is back together, he'll start masterminding the caper for us."

"He better succeed," said the henchman. "We're defying the Barnum Crime Combine and—"

"Scofflaw always succeeds. Didn't you read *My Six Greatest Capers?*"

"Not the entire book, only excerpts in *Woman's Day.*"

Bowers paced around the dim circle of light. "I don't want to stick here much longer," he said. "Where the blue blazes is Venusian Slim?"

"Right here," said a voice immediately behind Silvera.

Silvera started to turn.

Thunk!

Tammany opened the apartment door, eyes widening. "You look as though you fell into a waffle iron," she said sympathetically as she took Silvera by the hand.

"I did," he said. "Also a pancake grill and three kinds of processor. Cliffhanger stores all the old props from their domestic comedy days in the particular warehouse where I got waylaid."

The girl guided him to a pinstripe tin chair, settled him into it. "Who did the waylaying?"

"Fellow name of Venusian Slim, in the employ of one Denton Bowers."

"I'll get some first-aid stuff for your face." She moved across the parlor and into the bath area. "I've heard of Bowers; he's prominent in the BCC."

"Not any more," corrected Silvera. "Bowers is now the headman of the splinter group, the group that's putting Scofflaw on his feet again."

Tammany returned. "They conked you on the back of the skull awfully hard."

"Well, hard enough to knock me out for over an hour. Time for them to get clear of Cliffhanger, with a goodly portion of Dr. Scofflaw."

"Scofflaw was there, on the lot?"

"Not entirely," Silvera told the girl, while she patched up his face and head. He filled her in on what he'd learned in the prop warehouse.

"So are we at a dead end?" she asked when he'd concluded.

"This is only a temporary setback," said Silvera. "I have a pretty fair idea of the caper they have in mind."

"You know what they're going to try to swipe?"

"There aren't that many items over in Vigilanza Territory worth $6,000,000," he said. "In fact the only one I know of is—"

"The Eye of Ofego," finished Tammany.

"The Eye of Ofego," croaked the veiled lizard woman, waving a fistful of tri-op postcards in the air. "Fabled jewel set in the mug of a truly unpersonable idol. I offer an assortment of colorful and artistic art shots of this rare treasure. Sir, lady?"

Silvera shook his head. "We'll settle for a firsthand view," he told the old vendor who'd stopped beside their outdoor café table.

"Snerk snerk," said the old lizard, apparently laughing. "You'll never set foot within a thousand feet of Ofego, mister." With her free hand, the one not clutching bright postcards, she gestured at the huge neomarble dome across the sunbright square. "They don't let tourists into the inner shrine. In fact, only last week they gave the bum's rush to the Benevolent Despot of Turbante Territory. Tossed him, his retinue and six of his seven wives out right smack on their tokes. Snerk snerk. It was a sight, surely."

"Tough place to get into, huh?" inquired Tammany after taking a sip of her grouthunter's punch.

"Tough? Snerk snerk. That joint is impregnable, lady." She leaned closer to the girl, held a spread of pictures out to her and tapped the nearest. "That orb of Ofego's is worth in the vicinity of six or seven million bucks. Not only that, it's a sacred object to the thousands of devoted shrabs who worship the ugly bugger. Now if he wasn't traditionally depicted as winking and had both of his googly eyes showing, he'd be worth twice as much. Wouldn't he now? Snerk snerk." She used her handful of cards like a fan, laughed again and went shuffling on and away from them.

"We're in the right place," said Silvera quietly when the old vendor was out of earshot.

"Something the old dear said?"

"That's not an old lady, it's Two-Way Sathis, the best female impersonator the Barnum Crime Combine has," said Silvera, watching the vendor make another pitch a few tables away. "I found out about him when I did *The Coffee Table Book of Transvestites* on Murdstone three, four years back."

"You have one of the most interesting bibliographies of any one I've ever encountered," Tammany said, smiling. "How'd the book do?"

"Pretty well, since there was a big transvestite controversy on the planet at the time," he replied. "A female impersonator had just been elected governor of one of the biggest territories and insisted on being addressed as Madam First Lady. Only trouble was I had a hell of a time getting my royalty checks. The publisher absconded and snuck across the border disguised as a little old lady."

"No doubt inspired by your book," said the girl. "Whose side do you think this Sathis is on now?"

Silvera shrugged. "I'd guess he's working for the splinter boys," he said. "Can't be sure, though, except Bogg Kirkus didn't indicate to you he had any idea where Scofflaw was going to be reassembled."

"We have a difficult time ahead of us. Intercepting

Dr. Scofflaw in the midst of a caper, running the risk of tangling with the BCC as well."

A turbaned catman came slouching up to their table. "Interest you lovely folks in a finely detailed replica of Ofego, captures his extreme ugliness and has a gem worth $3.99 representing the fabulous Eye of Ofego."

"We have our hearts set on a full-scale replica," Silvera told him.

"Typical wiseoff tourist," said the catman, reaching into his wicker basket of wares. "Knows full well the real statue is forty feet high if it's an inch. How about, folks, a copy of that runaway bestseller, *Gargoyle Power*? Personally autographed by the author, containing several touching paragraphs about the Shrine of Ofego. The *Vigilanza Daily Thrust* said of the book, 'I couldn't read it fast enough. I devoured its tingling prose, gobbled up its—' "

"No thanks, we just ate," said Silvera. "Move along."

"May Ofego bless you, despite your churlishness." The vendor moved along.

"You're not really churlish," Tammany told him.

"Actually churlishness isn't—"

"Jose," the girl interrupted. "Take a look at the man who just came rushing through the doors of the Mosque-Ritz Hotel across the plaza."

"You mean the bald guy wearing nothing but a gaudy pair of allseason briefs?"

"That one, yes. He looks, at this distance anyway, a good deal like our friend Palma."

Silvera stood up. "He does," he agreed. "And that fellow chasing him with the flashing scimitar bears

105

an uncanny resemblance to the Benevolent Despot of Turbante Territory."

"Could it be Palma assaulted one of the gentleman's seven wives?"

"One at least." Silvera ran toward his fleeing friend.

Chapter 19

"Come on, you have to ignore her name," insisted Palma.

"How can you ignore a name like Trixie Tattoo?" inquired Silvera.

"Okay, don't ignore it exactly but be liberal minded enough to admit somebody with a whimsical name can be telling the truth." Palma was dressed again and had, with Silvera's help and diplomacy, retrieved all his cameras from the hotel suite shared by the third through seventh wives of the despot. "And, Jose, I'm sure Trixie is telling the absolute truth. Which is one more reason I'm happy I've encountered you once again."

"We don't know each other very well," said Tammany, who was sitting in a sling chair near the wide-view window of their hotel room. "I do think, though, your particular interests are going to get you into trouble, Palma, more serious trouble than today's little skirmish."

"True, all too true, Tammany dear," the bald photographer admitted ruefully. "Obviously I would never in the normal flow of events have turned up cavorting with a quintet of wives belonging to a man whose idea of rational debate involves the violent brandishing of pointy implements. But when I first beheld such an array of . . . well, we all have our burdens to bear."

"Let's get back to Trixie," suggested Silvera, resting his buttocks against a floating whatnot.

"Trixie, by the way, is a fan of yours, Jose," said Palma. "Indeed it was the reading of *Get Your Mind In Gear* by Dr. Rollo Rubarp, as told to Jose Silvera, which helped Trixie to overcome her ingrained shyness and become more outgoing. The result is she's the part-time mistress of Denton Bowers, recent defector from the ranks of the Barnum Crime Combine."

"And also a friend of yours," said Silvera.

"I encountered the young lady quite by accident while climbing out a rear window of a monastery on the outskirts of town," explained Palma. "Here in Vigilanza monasteries are coed and while snapping some shots of their old abandoned dungeon, I met this girl with the most flamboyant set of—"

"Trixie," reminded Silvera.

"Trixie happened to be leaving the monastery chapel wherein she'd been participating in a novena. Did I tell you Trixie is also very religious? Chiefly as a result of having read *There Is, Too, A God And You Better Believe It!* by the Most Reverend Nafaka Kama Ngano, who maintains—"

"I know, I know. I wrote the damn book."

"It's awesome, Jose, the influence you have on people," said Palma with a sigh. "At any rate, Trixie and I struck up a friendship, and she hid me in her landvan until the monastery dogs got tired of sniffing around for me. These robot dogs were originally designed to aid wayfarers lost in blizzards, but since the climate around here is so—"

"She knows, this Trixie Tattoo, what Bowers is up to?"

"Isn't that what I'm trying to tell you?"

"So far," said Silvera, "it's been mostly about tits."

"You can speak freely in front of me," said Tammany.

"Trixie," continued Palma, rubbing at his bare head, "tells me Bowers is the very lad behind the reassembling of Dr. Scofflaw. They actually have the old boy's noggin tucked away in the villa Bowers and his gang have rented on a famous lagoon near here. She complains Scofflaw's head is always making snide remarks, which she tries to ignore since he's disembodied and—"

"He won't be for long. Bowers must have brought all the other parts over here last night. After they scurried off the Cliffhanger lot."

"Bowers is back?"

"Should be."

"There goes my air-tennis date with Trixie."

Silvera commenced roaming the large oval room. "They are planning to steal the Eye of Ofego, aren't they?"

"They are," answered Palma. "Soon as Scofflaw is himself again, they'll move. According to Trixie his cunning old brain is already working out the details of the caper. Do you really think he can bring it off, steal that gem?"

"He's one of the best caper planners in the Barnum System," said Tammany. "I think he will."

Palma looked from the girl to Silvera. "Now that you know about it, you can stop him. We can alert the Sisters at the Shrine."

"Nope," said Silvera, "we'll let him go ahead and steal the Eye."

"Why is that?"

"Because I have a caper of my own in mind."

Chapter 20

"We didn't want a restaurant that was too quiet," said Palma.

Kachow! Kachow!

"That much I'll give you," said Silvera from his side of the booth. "I'll agree Karnivorous Klute's Kafe is not quiet."

Kachow! Blammy Blam!

"For conspiring, or for discussing other people's conspiracies," said the bald photographer, "I find a noisy bistro ideal."

"Has madam made up her mind?" A birdhead waiter scooted along a walkway and up to their table with a weapon case held out to Tammany.

The girl was sitting beside Silvera. "Just a cup of syncaf," she said to the waiter.

"You don't wish to kill anything?"

"Not just yet."

The waiter indicated the assortment of guns and knives resting on thé plush lining of the open case. "Many ladies prefer slaughtering a small zark. For that the number two blaster does nicely, killing the little feller but doing no harm to the flesh. For more hearty fare you may want to bag a boko. Ah, a thick boko steak sizzling on the—"

"Just syncaf, thanks."

All the booths in Karniviorous Klute's were supported on catwalks over a vast jungly pit. Customers, armed by their waiters, moved through the pit hunting down the animals they'd selected for dining on.

DR. SCOFFLAW

Once you felled your entrée, it was whisked to the abatoir, skinned, cleaned and then prepared in the spacious kitchens.

Kachow! Kabam!

Someone directly below them brought down a heavy beast.

The waiter's beak clacked several times. "And for the gentlemen? Perhaps you'd like to stalk a wild onoogo? That's the fearful blue creature you'll notice ducked down behind the ferns surrounding the water hole."

"I'll have the Vegetarian's Delight," said Silvera.

The waiter fluttered. "You can't kill that, sir."

"Nevertheless."

"I could arrange for you to go down into the pit to pick the—"

"No, I'll trust to your staff's good judgment."

After letting out a disappointed twitter, the waiter turned his attention to Palma. "You, sir? I might suggest the quilp. Very tasty, although with a quilp you must tackle it with your bare hands."

Palma said, "Pie a la mode."

"Meat pie?"

"Apple."

"Very well, very well." Shoulders slumped, the waiter departed along a catwalk.

Kachow! Blam!

"Guy down there just shot his waiter," observed Palma.

"What," said Silvera, "have you been able to find out from Trixie Tattoo?"

"Scofflaw is completed," Palma replied. "They ran down his missing arm in a nostalgia boutique someplace."

"What about the caper?" asked Tammany.

"It will occur two nights hence." Palma reached through the dangle of cameras into his tunic and produced a rolled-up document. "This is a floor plan of the Shrine of Ofego. I've been studying it, in the light of the information Trixie's been passing on to me. I can't quite see what Dr. Scofflaw has in mind." He spread the diagram out on top of their seethrough table.

Tammany leaned forward, her shoulder touching Silvera's and her blonde hair brushing at his cheek. "Scofflaw isn't the first one to try for the Eye of Ofego, is he?"

"There have been several attempts," said Silvera. "Most recently Prof Hypno made a try."

"He failed," said Palma, tapping the floor plan. "Although he gave it a nice try. He came right through the main entrance here during a midday worship service. He knew the routine of the place and was able to hypnotize both the Mother Superior and the Associate Mother Superior."

"They're the only ones who know the daily password phrase," said Silvera. "Each knows half of it. And it's the left hand of the Mother Superior and the right hand of the associate you need to operate the 10-hole printlock on the Control Center door."

Tammany moved a fingertip across the chart. "There's Ofego himself right in the center of the dome."

"But under a separate dome of his own," added Palma. "Then inside the invulnerable plaz dome is a force field six feet wide which can knock out the toughest person going. In fact, when Ancient Mariner

113

Metz made his try six years ago it was the force field that did him in, inducing a fatal heart attack right there."

"Metz had a particular wild talent for—"

"I know," said Tammany, interrupting Silvera's explanation. "He could walk through walls. Dr. Scofflaw used him on one of his earliest capers."

"As for Prof Hypno," said Palma, "he got into the control room and forced the two mind-controlled Sisters to turn off the force screen and deactivate the door in the inner dome. He made it through those. When he got to this moat here, though, he discovered he couldn't hypnotize the fish."

Tammany drew a circle around the idol. "That's right, there's a ten-foot-wide moat filled with deadly varanda fish."

"Thousands of the little rascals," said Palma.

Silvera leaned back in the booth. "Who's Scofflaw hired so far?"

"Sounds like a strange crew to me," said Palma. "Trixie tells me he's bringing a guy named Jesus Brown in on this caper."

"I've heard of him," said Silvera. "Guy from the Earth System, specializes in walking on water."

"Okay, then Dr. Scofflaw intends to go across the moat and grab the eye out of the idol," said Palma. "But even if Brown gets across, the gem is electrified. Anybody touches it and two dozen scattered alarm bells go off, and he gets a strong shock."

Silvera bent to study the chart. "Their power all comes from here," he said, pointing to a building just outside the dome.

"It's a completely self-contained generating unit," said Palma. "All the wires and cables run underground from there to the Shrine. There are seven Sisters, fully armed, on guard around the periphery of the power house day and night."

"Be very tough for Scofflaw to cut off their power then," put in Tammany, "and shut off all their security systems."

Absently Silvera took hold of the girl's hand. "Who else has he recruited for this job?"

"He's been in touch with a local guy named Strathmore Benbolt. Know about him?"

"No, what's his specialty?"

"Strathmore Benbolt is rumored to operate a bootleg matter transmitter."

Silvera said, "After Scofflaw gets the Eye, he'll pass it to this Benbolt guy for transmission to his customer. And, let's hope, the payment to Scofflaw will be sent by way of Benbolt, too."

"Payment?" Tammany retrieved her hand. "You mean you intend to allow him to get—"

"The rest of the crew," said Silvera. "Who are they?"

Palma said, "This is what really puzzles me, Jose. Seems somewhat redundant, but he's hired the Maypol Brothers, Bafflebar SanClare, John Holbrook Sheps and the MacQuarrie Quintuplets."

Silvera's brow wrinkled. "They're all teleks, aren't they?"

"Exactly. Each and every one of them has the power to teleport objects from one spot to another. With the exception of Granpappy Fox, who strained himself trying to lift an armored skyvan, Dr. Scofflaw has gathered together just about every major telekinetic thief on the planet."

"Maybe," suggested the girl, "he's going to get them

to pool their teleporting power and move the whole idol out of the Shrine."

"Then he wouldn't need Jesus Brown." Silvera's fingers drummed on the tabletop. "Nope, he's going to do something more audacious. That's the major characteristic of a Scofflaw caper. Audacity."

"What do we do next?" asked Tammany. "Contact the authorities? Or go to Scofflaw and tell him we—"

"We stay absolutely clear of Scofflaw."

"You want to get your money," she said.

"There's a simpler way," Silvera told her.

"I was under the impression we'd eventually see him," Tammany said, angry. "That was the reason for my joining this expedition. I still want to approach him about doing the authorized story of his life. Remember?"

Silvera said, "You'll have to wait until after the theft, Tammany."

"What, exactly, is it you plan to do?"

"Modify his caper slightly," replied Silvera.

Chapter 21

A dozen hefty birdgirls were strutting and kicking on the spotlit stage. A few feathers drifted and spun in the amber light.

"Feathers on yonkers spoil them," observed Palma as he and Silvera moved through the dim backstage area. "Although I suppose to a birdman they—"

"Did you brief this guy thoroughly?"

"Obviously your anxiety on this, the eve of Scofflaw's caper, is getting the better of you, Jose," said the bald photographer. "Otherwise you'd recall I'm nothing if not thorough. Did I ever mention the lass on Jupiter who had a single red hair sprouting right next to her left—"

"Here's his dressing room." Silvera knocked.

"I don't even think I've described Trixie's whammies to you. Since I've been discussing her in the presence of Tammany and have been a bit reluctant to recount the amazing fact that the devils have what amounts to a life of their own. Yes, as incredible as it may seem, each of her hojos can—"

"Where the hell is he?" Silvera knocked again.

"Don't get your yurp in an uproar," suggested a female voice on the other side of the star-marked door.

"His lady," explained Palma. "Very tall. Interestingly enough her kazabas don't move me at all. What is unsettling is I find myself absolutely fascinated by her—"

"Is Bob Phantom in?" Silvera asked the unopened door.

"Keep your nurf in gear. He'll be right back."

"Not even here?" Silvera shook his head. "Palma, the caper is going to take place in less than a half hour."

"Remain calm, Jose. Bob Phantom is an old chum of mine." Palma turned to squint in the direction of the stage and the chorus line of birdgirls. "I've caught his magic act on several planets. Once I photographed him and Altadena for *Almost*, the magazine of near celebrity."

"Who's Altadena?"

Palma tilted a thumb at the door. "Her. Very tall girl, with the most fascinating ass I've ever observed. It's spooky because as a man suffering from a total and obsessive interest in tits, I can't imagine why I am so intrigued with an alternate area of—"

"Boy, I'm sorry." A small man in a dark one-piece suit was coming toward them, carrying a large opaque plyosak. He had prickly dark hair, deep-set eyes, a hawkish nose. "Altadena insisted I run around to the deli and get her a couple of snergburgers on neorye."

Silvera scowled at Palma. "Why's he have to go out for sandwiches? He's supposed to be a telek."

"Oh, I am," answered Bob Phantom, new rings forming under his eyes. "The best in the entire Barnum System, by far. You simply don't know Altadena, Mr. Silvera. She's lovely, very tall and with a most provocative ass. She does, however, have a few little quirks. She insists teleported food has a funny taste, so to pacify her I—"

"If you're going to yak," shouted Altadena on the

other side of the door, "haul your bupps elsewhere. Leave my chow first."

Bob Phantom opened the door a few inches and tossed in the sack. "See you back at the hotel, love."

"Up your gooper."

"Lovely girl," said Bob Phantom, escorting them down the shadowy corridor. "Not too appreciative of me or my god-given talent I'm afraid." He rubbed his small hands together. "Well now, are we all ready for the caper?"

"Are we?" Silvera was dubious.

"Bob is very enthusiastic about this," Palma assured the annoyed author. "It appeals to his sense of fair play."

"I've made it a lifelong policy," said the magician, "to collect every cent owed me by clubs, theaters, vidstations, church groups, summer—"

"Come along now." Silvera took hold of his arm. "I want to get you stationed in the neighborhood of Strathmore Benbolt."

"I'm ready." Bob Phantom rubbed his hands together again.

"And you know what to do?"

"Exactly. Palma and I went over it numerous times," said Bob Phantom. "I wait until the Eye of Ofego is sent off to Dr. Scofflaw's customer over in Polonia Territory. As soon as the $6,000,000 in unmarked bills arrives, I cause it to teleport from the hands of Mr. Benbolt and into our waiting landcar."

"Right, good," said Silvera. "Then I'll take my $10,000 and your fee out of the pile of dough. After which you send the rest on to the Sisterhood of Ofego's Free Hospital."

"I could just as easily teleport the money to the Shrine," offered the magician.

Guiding him to an exit, Silvera said, "The Shrine won't be there."

Silvera, fingers steepled and a moderate smile on his lips, relaxed in the floating lounger. He was alone in the early morning parlor of the hotel suite.

The door made no noise as it swung suddenly open.

"Exactly what I expected," said Tammany as she came striding in. "A smug look on your face."

"Not smugness, merely contentment," he said. "I collected my $10,000."

"Tainted money." She kicked the corridor door shut behind her, shrugged out of her coat.

"All money is tainted, one way or another. I got your note."

"Letting me run over there when you knew that—"

"You were supposed to wait here until I came back, to let you know whether or not we'd second-guessed Scofflaw on his caper."

"I'm an impatient person." Tammany came closer to him. "You knew I wanted to talk to Dr. Scofflaw, try to get him to agree to letting me do his real life story."

"Wasn't he at home?"

"Very whimsical," she said, voice loud and filled with anger. "There were . . . lord, it must have been a good hundred police running around that villa where Scofflaw was holed up."

"Probably there to put a stop to the battle."

Tammany gave an infuriated jerking nod of her pretty head. "Yes, it seems Bogg Kirkus suddenly found out where Dr. Scofflaw was, and he attacked

121

the villa with a large bunch of Barnum Crime Combine thugs. The police arrived in time to grab nearly all of them, both sides and including Scofflaw and Kirkus and that guy Bowers."

"So justice has been served."

She jabbed a finger at the air between them. "You tipped off Kirkus! You told the cops to get over there!"

"Dr. Scofflaw needed something to distract him," said Silvera, grinning. "This way he didn't have to dwell on his six million bucks disappearing."

Tammany folded her arms. "You know what else I had in mind for tonight?"

"Besides sneaking off and trying to hustle Scofflaw?"

"I was really growing fond of you, Silvera. Yes, as ludicrous as that seems now." She circled his floating chair. "We've been through a great deal after all, shared an escape from Devil's Island, worked in close proximity for days and days. Yet we've never been physically intimate."

"So I noticed."

"I, nitwit that I am, was actually thinking that when we both returned here tonight, we'd celebrate. You'd have your damn money and I'd have my signed agreement from Scofflaw to do his life story."

"Too many strings," Silvera said, watching her. "Either you make love or you don't. It's got nothing to do with making money or signing papers."

"What's that, Silvera? Some cockeyed aphorism from one of the dumb selfhelp books you ghosted?"

He didn't reply.

She crossed the room, threw herself into a sling chair. "Have they located the Shrine yet?"

"It's out in the suburbs in the middle of an old soccer field."

"You didn't tie up that end, bring it back or anything."

"Bob Phantom can't move anything that big," said Silvera. "Which is why Scofflaw needed a whole crew of teleporters to get the Shrine of Ofego dome away from there. I'm fairly sure the Sisters will be able to get the thing back together. In fact, Scofflaw's bunch of teleks will probably volunteer to do it, in return for lighter sentences."

The girl said, "It was an audacious caper at that. Instead of lifting the idol out of there, Dr. Scofflaw lifted the rest of the shrine off the idol. Like taking the lid off a box. That disconnected all the security systems and Jesus Brown could walk right in and pluck the Eye out of its socket."

"We did return the Eye to the Sisters," said Silvera.

"Bob Phantom was able to do that?"

"He's a very gifted telek; can work long range."

Tammany ran a hand through her blonde hair. "This whole business I've been through with you," she said, eyes half-closed, "would make an interesting book. Yes, it's got Scofflaw, it's got adventure and excitement. Plus which, I'm an eyewitness to most of it." She stood, smiling. "You'll make an interesting character, too. Hack writer, obsessed with money, big and burly. Darkly handsome. Yes, I can see this shaping into one of the big non-fiction bestsellers of next season. Would you mind if I wrote it up instead of you?"

"Nope." Silvera sat up, his right foot tapping the satchel which held his recently acquired $10,000.

"I'm really excited about this. Yes, I can even

salvage a lot of the material on Scofflaw I've already done." She went to the door of her bedroom. "Jose, I'm sorry I was nasty to you. I think I would like to go to bed with you after all. First, though, I want to call Carlos Pigg and see what he thinks about the sales possibilities of this idea." She opened the door, smiled over her shoulder at him. "You wait."

Silvera rose as she closed herself in the bedroom. Stooping, he picked up the satchel.

He didn't wait.

AFTERWORD to Dr. Scofflaw

by Isidore Haiblum

So, if you're at this stage of the book, ladies and gentlemen, it obviously figures you've concluded act one of Ron Goulart's Great Vaudeville Spectacular. Don't go away, folks, act two follows shortly. It's by that other fellow, Haiblum. (And while modesty might prevent him from saying more than a few words about himself, there is fortunately another Afterword floating around here somewhere which doesn't suffer from that drawback.)

Yes, the curtain has definitely come down on the Great Goulart Spectacular in this volume. But there are the innumerable other volumes where the special blend of Goulart hijinks still goes on. In fact, for a mere pittance at your corner bookstore, it is possible to catch Jose Silvera strutting across the stage time and again. (The only Haiblum character who turns up more than once anywhere is Tom Dunjer of *Interworld* and *Outerworld* notoriety. But then Haiblum hasn't been at this game as long as Goulart.)

Silvera has been called Goulart's alter ego, and while there are some differences between them (Goulart is a bit shorter than his creation and would probably prefer a lawyer to a laser in settling contractual disputes), there are marked similarities. Both are disgustingly prolific and remarkably successful at their trade.

Silvera has the habit of referring to himself as a hack. But a quick perusal of his credits leads one rather to believe that he is some kind of Einstein, for God's sake:

Gargoyle Power (of course)
My Six Greatest Capers (ghosted for Dr. Scofflaw himself)
The Violent Overthrow of the Government Cook Book (unfinished, alas)
The Compleat Guerilla Encyclopedia
Crime and Sneezing: A New Look at Penology.
The Bedside Book of Nifty Escapes
Fifty Years A Lawbreaker
The Boy Commando's Book of Woodsy Lore
I Slept With A Watermelon
The Coffee Table Book of Transvestites
Get Your Mind In Gear
There Is, Too, A God And You Better Believe it!

And these only the tomes mentioned in *Dr. Scofflaw.*

Goulart usually refers to himself as Ron or Mr. Goulart, depending on whom he's talking to. Critically, he should, no doubt, be referred to as The Great Entertainer. Stranded in the Middle Ages, he would've been a wandering minstrel with a penchant for humorous ditties. It is no accident that way back in primitive times when Goulart attended the University of California, he edited the campus humor magazine, *The Pelican.* (Haiblum, too, edited a college humor magazine, the CCNY *Mercury.* This is one of the things he shares with Goulart, besides this volume. There are a couple of others which will be gotten to presently.)

Above all, Goulart delivers the goods:

AFTERWORD

Funny stuff.

Very funny stuff.

Falling down and rolling around on the floor funny stuff.

Sometimes violent. Sometimes suspenseful. And often exhibiting a keen linguistic finesse; i.e., a classy choice of words. Readers of *Dr. Scofflaw* will have no trouble identifying these nifty synonyms:

> yonkers
> chawammos
> whammies
> hojos
> kazabas

Although they may occasionally wonder about:

> "Don't get your *yurp* in an uproar."
> "Keep your *nurf* in gear."

Or:

> "Halt your *bupps* elsewhere."

"Up your *gooper*," however, is probably self-explanatory.

Goulart's deft handling of real-but-special words is also worth a laudatory tip of the hat. Slang and underworld lingo caper through his novels and short stories like a troop of Keystone cops; they add that spiffy something extra.

Nor is he a stranger to the world of publishing. (And, quite frankly, after all these years it would be most peculiar if he were.) Goulart peppers his Jose

Silvera tales with all kinds of inside dope. (Actually, some of it *isn't* satire, folks, but the god-honest truth.) Where else but in a Goulart story can you come across:

Momentary Fame Magazine
Fringe, the magazine for almost celebs.
Living Immortals Magazine
Galactic Publishers Weekly
Solitary Confinement (a prison comic strip, what else?)
Galactic Dime Detective
Intergalactic Girlie Gags (Why do I seem to remember this one from *my* childhood? And how do I go about forgetting it?)
Igloo & Garden Magazine
Almost, the magazine of near celebrity.

Which finally brings us back to Ron Goulart's Great Vaudeville Spectacular. For the nutty magazines, snazzy lingo, whacky books and goofy characters—not to mention the spaced-out plot lines—are all part of the show. Did anyone ever doubt this was a show? Goulart has cooked it up for our amusement (and his profit, of course). We have satire here, gags galore, witticisms, pratfalls and monkeyshines. Occasionally depending on his mood—Goulart will even toss in the kitchen sink. Lord knows, none of this is meant to change the world. (It is doubtful if Goulart believes the world *can* be changed.) It's his aim merely to entertain us as the world tumbles along toward its own ruin.

So the actors dash out on stage, do a quick turn (Goulart's chapters are short, you'll note), and either scoot off into oblivion or pop up again as the plot or Goulart's fancy dictates. Always there are the comic bits, the fast patter, the double-time pace. And while the lizard men, androids and birdgirls are standard SF fare, most of the aforementioned shtick are not. They are, however, not entirely without precedent. A sort of comic tradition does exist in SF, although it has not exactly taken the field by storm.

Henry Kuttner's Gallegher stories are a case in point.

Fredric Brown was responsible for numerous chuckles during his career.

Robert Sheckley can still make you laugh.

Keith Laumer's Retief tales remain jolly fun.

And Isidore Haiblum, in his own demented manner, tries to keep the gags hustling through his novels. (Why Haiblum has never written a short story is a mystery. Maybe they just haven't paid him enough, eh?)

And, of course, there are a small—and perhaps growing—number of comic short stories tossed off by authors who usually devote themselves to more serious stuff.

But taken all in all, this is hardly an overwhelming trend. Why so few comic efforts then in a genre noted for its variety?

Maybe because not enough readers really care. After all, comedy can be found in plentiful supply just about anywhere—from movies to TV sit-coms to the daily and Sunday funny pages.

But *some* readers seem to care. And so do some writers. The versatile Ron Goulart among them.

Versatile?

Well, yes. Goulart *does* write non-funny items as

well—whole mountains of them, in fact. No SF writer specializes solely in comedy. (Not even Haiblum, whose first book, *The Return*, has nary a laugh in it, and whose latest novel, *Nightmare Express*, is equally bereft of smiles.)

And this solemn side of Goulart's craft leads us to uncover yet another element in his work, one that is present, to some extent, in his humorous writings as well:

The tough guy tradition.

It came out of *Black Mask Magazine*, a mystery-detective pulp whose heyday was from the mid-20s to the mid-30s when Joseph T. Shaw held down the editor's chair. Shaw had a knack of bringing out the best in his contributors. Under his tutelage, Dashiell Hammett, the creater of Sam Spade, the Continental Op and the Thin Man, and Raymond Chandler, who gave us Philip Marlowe, produced some of their most enthralling works. These men set the standard, and their styles were enormously influential, not only in books, but also in movies, on radio, TV and even the comics. (See Will Eisner's *The Spirit* for a dandy example of the latter.) But Hammett and Chandler were merely the two foremost practitioners of *Black Mask* mayhem. Some of the other *Black Mask* graduates were:

Lester Dent. We know him better as that writing-machine who produced over two hundred Doc Savage pulp novels.

Erle Stanley Gardner. His hero in those days was Ed Jenkins, a reformed crook.

AFTERWORD

Horace McCoy. Today perhaps best remembered for his *They Shoot Horses, Don't They?* He specialized in the lyrical side of hard-boiled fiction.

George Harmon Coxe. His Casy Crime Photographer was one of the notable radio shows of the 40s and early 50s.

Carroll John Daly. Back in the early 20s he created the primitive prototype of the private eye, a violence-prone character called Race Williams.

And such forgotten authors as Paul Cain, Raoul Whitfield, Norbert Davis and Frederick Nebel, who all deserve to take a bow.

Ron Goulart is an expert on the tough-guy school of writing. Not only did he edit an anthology, *The Hard-Boiled Dicks*, but he weighed in with his own private-eye series a while back featuring a man called Easy.

Tough-guy elements surface periodically in Goulart's SF writing. In this he is almost, but not quite, unique. Keith Laumer has been mining a similar tough-guy vein for years. But Laumer is chiefly in the Raymond Chandler tradition—similes and metaphors abound. While Goulart favors the lean, sparse approach of Dashiell Hammett.

Haiblum, too, has to be placed within this tradition. His Tom Dunjer comes out of both the Hammett-Chandler grab bags. And this is doubtless another reason why Haiblum finds himself sharing this volume with Goulart.

Come to think of it, tough-guy writing is even scarcer in SF than humor. So why do two reasonably sane-looking types like Goulart and Haiblum bother in the first place?

Probably because they *like* writing comic tough-guy science fiction.

And actually there are worse ways of making a living, aren't there?

OUTERWORLD

Isidore Haiblum

Chapter 1

It was a scream, all right, clear as day, come from somewhere up ahead. I stood stock-still, cocked an ear and waited for something more to happen.

There was only wind, darkness and the sounds of crickets tuning up for their nightly songfest.

Some animal probably. I hadn't known there were any in this neck of the woods.

I took a last look at my heap—it seemed safe enough by the main gate—and began hoofing it down the gravel path. Bushes and trees were on both sides of me. A full moon, like a spotlight rented especially for the occasion, shone over my shoulder. Pretty. But wasted on me. Neither my mood nor bank account was likely to profit by this little trip. And both had been taking a licking lately.

I turned a corner. More gravel and green stuff greeted me. I was starting to wonder where Whitney had put his house when something knee-high moved in the bushes.

I jumped back fast, my eyes hunting for a handy tree to climb. The thought of teeth clamping around my leg made me especially spry. Maybe there *was* an animal loose around here.

No teeth came out of the bushes to get me. There was no movement at all. Someone groaned. I didn't like that. Very gingerly I stepped over to the foliage, peeked in.

A man was lying there.

He was an old, white-haired geezer dressed in a

blue chauffeur's uniform. Blood was on his forehead.

"Hey, buddy," I said.

I got my hands under his arms, dragged him out onto the road. He opened his eyes.

"What happened?" I asked.

The chauffeur looked up at me, pointed a feeble finger into the darkness.

"The house . . ." he gurgled; his eyes glazed over and rolled up into their sockets as if more small talk was too terrible even to contemplate.

"Mister," I said.

I might've been chatting with one of the trees for all the good it did. The old galoot was out cold.

"Jeezus," I muttered. This guy weighed a good hundred and eighty. I wasn't about to lug him piggyback to safety; he seemed safe enough right here.

I left my find by the bushes, trotted off down the path. I had no idea what had happened to him. Maybe the guy had taken a spill, cracked his noggin on a rock or something; that might even account for the scream—I hoped. The thing to do now was find help.

I rounded a bend and Cyrus Whitney's mansion, all five floors of it, stood in a clearing. Not quite as imposing as City Hall, but a lot more solid.

His door was wide open.

I stepped in, looked around. No maid, no butler, no nothing. "Hello," I called, "Mr. Whitney?"

I added no answer to my list of noes and started down the hallway. I hit an empty living room, hiked through a half dozen more rooms, peered into the kitchen. Clean as a whistle. All this emptiness was starting to give me the creeps.

I went back the way I'd come, feeling less chipper with each step I took. None of this was right.

Cyrus Whitney had called earlier in the day, just before quitting time. A small matter had come up, one that a man of my talents might polish off in jig time. As Executive Director of Security Plus, Happy City's largest private protection agency, I usually turned thumbs down on extra chores. But Cyrus Whitney was Board Chairman of Security Plus; it made a slight difference.

Only where was he?

I took a deep breath and started up the stairs.

As if on signal, noises sounded from above—running feet, more than one pair.

While I stood there wondering whether to rush up and greet 'em or run for my life, two men rounded a bend in the staircase. They were moving fast. The first guy—a middle-aged party—had on a tuxedo; that probably made him the butler. The guy behind him—a roly-poly character in a peaked cap—had a gun. I wasn't exactly sure what that made him. But I could guess.

I didn't have to wait long for an answer.

The guy raised his gun. A resounding bang shook my eardrums.

The butler spread his arms as if he were going to fly away. The top part of his head fell off, landed at my feet. The rest of the butler went sailing past me, tumbled down the stairs.

I froze as though I were posing for a very touchy painter; I didn't even breathe. If I stood very still, maybe the guy wouldn't notice me.

Peaked Cap had stopped short. He cast a quick

glance at his handiwork near the foot of the stairs, spun around and raced back up the staircase.

I put a shaky hand on the banister and waited for my intestines to stop crawling through my stomach.

I turned my head slowly and looked down at what was left of the butler. Nothing more would befall him.

But what about Cyrus Whitney and the rest of his household—not to mention me? The thing to do—obviously—was dash back to the car, grab my gun. Only one small hitch. I didn't have a gun in the car, hadn't carried one for years. As chief sleuth for Security Plus I had other people do my shooting for me. It'd seemed safer—till now.

More footsteps sounded from above.

I took the stairs three at a time, hit the ground floor, hopped over the butler and ran into a room just off the main corridor.

The lights were out. I didn't mind. I closed the door behind me, leaving a thin sliver to peek through. I wanted to see this crew.

As I watched from my hiding place, five men sprinted by in the hallway. My look-see wasn't all that informative after all. All five had either jacket or coat collars pulled up obscuring their faces, even my pal, Peaked Cap. So much for that.

They came and they went.

I heard the front door slam shut. I figured I could breathe again.

A voice in the darkness behind me whispered, "P-s-s-s-t, Dunjer." I almost dropped my teeth.

Chapter 2

"Hurry up," Cyrus Whitney said.

"Yes, sir," I said. A reasonable enough reply to the Chairman of the Board. Although under the circumstances I didn't think I was going to get too many points for it; maybe even none at all.

"You let them *all* get away?" Whitney asked; he sounded incredulous.

"It didn't quite seem the time for hand-to-hand combat," I explained, working on the last of the ropes which held him.

I got the rope untied, and Cyrus Whitney stood up. Up, in his case, was pretty high.

Whitney was six foot seven and rail thin. His nose was long, pointy. High cheekbones jutted under gray eyes. He had a black pencil moustache over narrow lips. What little hair was left, he combed sideways over his bald pate. Whitney's voice was a smooth basso with a petulant note in it. Over the phone he tended to sound like a man complaining to himself at the bottom of a wall. At least now he had something legitimate to complain about. Me, too, probably.

"Follow me, Dunjer," Whitney said when he was through rubbing the circulation back into his arms and legs.

I followed him.

We hurried by the last remains of the butler, Whitney pausing long enough to murmur, "Poor Slotnick," an indisputable statement if ever there was one.

The speed lift to the left of the stairs whisked us to the fifth floor—Whitney's office. The scene that greeted us when we stepped out was orderly enough, except for two small items: a floor and wall safe, both wide open and empty.

Whitney eyed them disgustedly, shook his head and marched off along the hallway. I tagged along.

"Quite a job," I said. "How'd they get em open, eh?"

"I gave them the combinations," Whitney said. "Do I look like a hero, Dunjer?"

"Uh-uh."

"What good is money if someone shoots you? After all, I do have lots of money."

We turned into a large room. Whitney's house staff—three men and two women—were trussed up like so much beef at the local slaughterhouse. I cut the cook loose with a razor Whitney dug up, and he went to work on the rest of the crew. "The chauffeur's out on the road," I told em when they were all back on their feet. Two of them hustled off to find their co-workers while I followed Whitney to his office.

Motioning me to a seat, he plopped down behind his wide desk: "We are in terrible trouble, Dunjer."

I looked around to see where the other part of this "we" might be. "Meaning what?"

"I've been a fool, Dunjer. And now, inadvertently, I have brought ruin on you, too."

"Now? You mean this very minute? On me? Too?"

"H-m-m-m, scratch the 'too.' After all, I'll still have my millions left. But you, Dunjer, will be out of a job. And no doubt pauperized."

"That's worse. Verging on hideous. What the hell are you talking about, Mr. Whitney?"

Cyrus Whitney leaned over his desk to peer at me. "As you know, Dunjer, a meeting of Security Plus' Board of Directors is due in less than two weeks. The faction which I head, which has until now held a controlling interest in our firm, has supported your stewardship for the last four years."

"Four bountiful, fruitful years, Mr. Whitney. Stock has almost doubled since I took over. Not that I want to brag. But facts are facts."

"Exactly. And has not the Board rewarded your efforts with a series of pay increments as well as various stock options?"

"Sure."

"But in so doing we have incurred the wrath of Reginald Grash."

"Grash," I said, "is a sorehead."

"Assuredly. He has twice tried to wrest control. And twice been beaten back."

"Swamped is more like it. The creep's got eight percent of the stock, and his buddies, maybe, fourteen. That's nothing. This Grash is a millionaire now and knee-deep in business. But before that he used to be an Assistant DA. He thinks that makes him a hotshot sleuth. He's getting bored with finance. What he wants is my job. As a plaything, no less."

"Ludicrous, of course. Everyone knows Grash, as security chief, would be a mere puppet. Were it not for the malicious and libelous lies being spread about me, he would have no chance at all."

"Lies? Chance? He has a chance?"

"That's why I called you, Dunjer. To aid me in exposing these charges as base canards. It would have been in both our interests to do so. Cyrus Whitney Inc. controls only thirty-five percent of Security Plus stock. But a majority of stockholders have always seen fit to follow my lead."

"They made you Chairman of the Board," I pointed out.

"And as such—an all too visible position on the firing line, as it were—I incurred some resentment. Not enough to matter under ordinary circumstances . . ."

"But something's not ordinary, eh?"

"I'm afraid not."

"What are the charges, Mr. Whitney?"

"Conflict of interest. That I own large quantities of stock in firms employing Security Plus services."

"Do you?"

"I own no such stock. Now."

"Now? You used to?"

"My wife, may she rest in peace. She used to. She died last year. I inherited the whole lot, Dunjer."

"Arggg," I said.

"I sold it off, naturally. And made certain that my tracks were covered. To retain the stocks would have revealed that my wife had owned them all along."

"Jeezus," I said.

"There were rumors. Word apparently leaked out. But what could they prove?"

"Nothing, I hope."

"Mere tongue wagging, Dunjer."

"I'm glad to hear that."

"You would have shown them up for the sneaks they were."

"There's something about the drift of all this that I don't like. What do you mean, 'would have'? That's past tense. What is this terrible thing that's happened?"

"Well, it is somewhat embarrassing, Dunjer. I have no one to blame but myself. The sale of my wife's bonds went off without a hitch. Money can buy many things, Dunjer. You may have heard that?"

"Yeah. I heard that. For God's sake, Mr. Whitney, get on with it."

"In this case, Dunjer, it bought fool-proof protection. Those stocks were laundered through third and fourth parties. We were safe, Dunjer."

" 'We' again?"

"Safe. Except for my foolhardy habit of keeping records."

"You keep records, eh?"

"Personal records, for my eyes alone."

"Where," I asked, "do you keep these records?"

"In my bank vault, naturally. However, before my records go to the bank vault, Dunjer, I keep them here." Whitney pointed a long bony finger at the empty floor safe. "Money in the wall safe. Records in the floor safe."

"And among those records, Mr. Whitney, were?"

Cyrus Whitney nodded. "Photostats of my wife's portfolio."

"That figures," I said bitterly.

We sat in stony silence for a while. Cyrus Whitney cleared his throat. "This is clearly the hand of Grash. He aims to destroy us both. To get out of this, my legal fees will be astronomical."

"Maybe," I said, "and maybe not."

"You know a good, cheap lawyer?"

"Uh-uh. The 'maybe' was for the first part. The hand of Grash. Maybe it wasn't."

"But it has to be, Dunjer. Who else would do such a thing."

Isidore Haiblum

"Just about any crook in the business, Mr. Whitney. You had dough in your safe. That's what crooks want, right? Your records were just incidentals. The boys emptied both safes hunting for the green or some facsimile thereof. No time to sort the stuff. When I showed up, they just took it on the lam. Everything went into the sack, including your photostats. They probably haven't got the faintest notion what they landed. I'd lay odds on it."

"But how, Dunjer, can you be so certain?"

"Listen, Mr. Whitney. Grash would've been nuts to bother with the dough. Glom your records and you gotta stay mum: report the theft and you're blowing the whistle on yourself. But run off with the works —all that dough—and two to one you go to the cops."

"You'd lose that bet, Dunjer."

"Maybe. But how would Grash know? Uh-uh, Mr. Whitney, he wouldn't want to make a big thing of this; he'd be afraid of the fuss."

Whitney cocked an eyebrow. "Well, I suppose it *is* a possibility; but where does that leave us?"

"Out in the cold. But not exactly in Grash's clutches. It's like this, Mr. Whitney. All this stock folderol is pretty deep stuff. Run-of-the-mill hoods don't know beans about that. Just maybe, they'll pocket the dough and junk the rest."

Whitney's eyes lighted up. "You really think so, Dunjer?"

"Uh-uh. First off, who says we're dealing with average crooks? These guys may even be able to put two and two together for themselves. But let's say they can't."

"Let's," Whitney said, a touch of hope in his voice.

"Then," I said, "they'll dig up someone who can.

And sooner or later they'll figure out what they got."

"Your job won't be worth a prayer if Grash wins, Dunjer."

"Yeah. But to win he's got to get those photostats. And he hasn't yet. That buys us time."

"Time for *what*?"

"To see if we can run down the desperados, Mr. Whitney. Or make a deal to buy back the stuff. Outbid Grash. It'll cost some. But it might be worth it. Remember we do have all of Security Plus going for us, and that's the biggest protection outfit in Happy City."

"H-m-m-m-m," Cyrus Whitney said.

"Yeah," I said. "We may be on the ropes, Mr. Whitney, but we ain't out yet."

Chapter 3

My headlights cut through the night like a cleaver through butter. The highway unraveled under me like a soiled tissue strip. Trees, fields, bushes, an occasional farmhouse rose out of the landscape like stray pieces from a child's toy box. I needed reassurance, a kindly word, a friendly pat on the noodle. What I had was the dark night, empty highway and nifty memory of Slotnick the butler with his head blown off. I could've done without that memory.

I flashed my buzzer at the mech doorman and went into the building. The lobby was dark and still like a cadaver's insides. I grabbed the speed lift and was whisked up to the ninety-first floor. My key got me into the Security Plus suite. I ambled down a darkened hallway to my office, flicked on the light and let my eyes range over the familiar surroundings: wide desk, a couple of chairs, an intercom system and a lot of computer hardware. Maybe it wasn't the Ritz, but it was all mine, and I aimed to hang on to it.

Going to the computer which made up my west wall, I punched out a question. A spool of paper instantly slid out of the slot. On it were five names. I recognized three: Fingers Malone, Whispering Smith and Baby Face Sampson. They would do. We'd had dealings in the days when I was turning a buck as a licensed gumshoe. Each would've sold out his mother for a song and tossed in any other stray relatives as a bonus.

What I had here was a list of stoolies. I fed the computer another question and got back three addresses and a list of hangouts. I did some more finger work on the computer and a tiny one-inch mike clicked out of the slot. I put it in my pocket. Everything that was said to me, or around my person, would be transmitted back to the computer and recorded. It beat taking notes, and had a couple of other uses, too. In any case, it couldn't hurt. I sighed, turned out the light, locked the hall door behind me and took the speed lift down to the storage basement. The guard mech saluted as I went past.

I moved off up the east corridor till I reached the Security Plus rental. Pressing my thumb against the door's print scanner, I heard a satisfying click, and the door slid open. I stepped in, rummaged in my pocket, dug out the master control cube and used it to activate XX42 and his twin, XX43, two of the best sleuthing mechs on the market. They climbed off their shelves and stood before me.

"Okay, gents," I said. "This is strictly hush-hush. Report directly to me and not a word to anyone, no matter what; got that?"

"Aye-aye, skipper," XX42 said.

"Right-o, chief," XX43 agreed.

"Fine. Have the master computer feed you its file on Reginald Grash; it's got all the dope. Stake out his house, his office; tap his phone. Use as many auxiliary mechs as you need. I want him shadowed at all times. Full details on everyone he meets. Visual and auditory tapes where possible. And for God's sake don't get caught. Disguise yourselves as a tree or fire hydrant or something. Someone may try to peddle Grash a couple of hot photostats. Watch for that. We

147

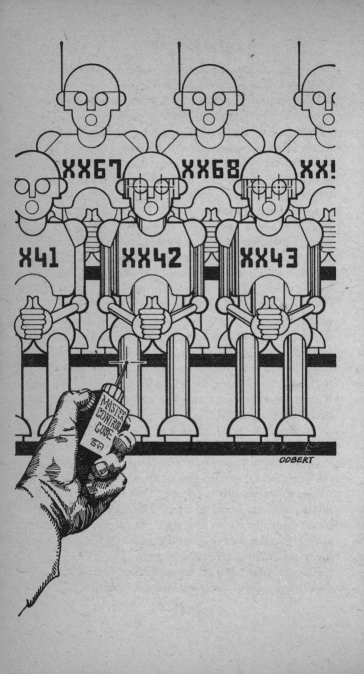

want to get to this someone before the deal's sewed up. On the double, now."

I parked my jalopy next to the No Parking sign. Across the street red and gold neon lights spelled out Calypso Casino. I waited.

Fingers Malone showed up by and by, attired in evening clothes.

I lowered the car window, put out an arm. "Got my message, eh? This way," I said.

He climbed in beside me. Malone was a medium-sized portly guy in his early fifties with slicked-back black hair, a round face and flat nose.

"Sure. What's the good word?" he asked amiably. "Didn't know you were back on the beat."

"I'm not. Not yet, anyway."

"Slumming, ha?"

"Thought I'd throw some business your way, Fingers."

"Thanks. I can always use some business. What is it?"

"Just some information."

"What else is there?"

"Crooked cards. Shaved dice. A gaffed wheel."

"Ah, but not with you, Dunjer; with you it's always information, isn't it?"

"I suppose so. Know the name Cyrus Whitney?"

"Sure. Who doesn't?"

"His home was knocked over." I filled him in on the details.

"And you, Dunjer, no doubt, want the bad guys," Fingers said when I was done."

"Uh-uh. Let the law do its own dirty work."

"Whitney wasn't a client of your outfit?"

149

"If Whitney had been a client, none of this would've happened; we'd've had a mech guard on duty over there. No," I said sadly, "Whitney is just Chairman of the Board."

"Kind of puts you on the spot to do *something,* doesn't it, Dunjer?"

"Yeah. What I've got in mind is to get a few of the items back."

"I see. How?"

"Buy 'em back."

Malone grinned. "Ah!"

"Right. That's where you come in, Fingers."

"How much in?"

"A couple of grand. Maybe more. Depending on how the transaction goes."

"I'll ask around, Dunjer. Quietly. I'd like the transaction to go very well. But I haven't heard a peep on any of this till now. Any specific items you're looking for?"

"Some photostats."

"They get anything else?"

"A lot of money."

"What about that?"

I shrugged. "Let 'em keep it. It's only money, eh, Fingers?"

I tried Baby Face Sampson next. He holed up in Cheery Village, five miles of residential skyscrapers, human and mech shopping centers and a neat series of intertwining elevated walks. The speed lift took me up to the fifty-eighth floor. My thumb pressed Baby Face's doorbell. The door popped open. A platinum blond in a long black evening gown stood there. She raised a languid eyebrow. "Yes?"

I said, "Baby Face in?"

"Baby Face? His name is Lionel."

"Lionel, eh? Well, tell Lionel that Tom Dunjer wants to see him."

"What is it, toots?" a flat voice called from inside.

"There's a Tom Dunjer here," the blond called back.

"Yeah? Let him in."

Baby Face was waiting for me in the living room. His hair was blond, his eyes, lips and nose small. He must've been somewhere in his thirties but his face was completely unlined. He was no bigger than five three. He wore a long green lounging robe. We shook hands.

"Long time no see, Dunjer."

"Uh-huh. Living high on the hog, eh, Lionel?"

Baby Face grimaced. "Don't call me that, Dunjer."

"You like Baby Face better?"

"I like Sampson better."

"Okay, Sampson."

Baby Face grinned, showing small white even teeth. "Sounds good," he said. "What's the occasion?"

"I've got a problem," I told him.

"Who ain't?"

"This one could mean some dough for you, Sampson, maybe five grand."

"Why don't you go powder your nose, toots?"

Toots went. I poured myself a slug of whisky, told Baby Face about the Whitney doings.

"Just the photostats, huh?"

"Just that."

"No names? No rough stuff? No cops?"

"No nothing. This is Whitney's baby. He's the

guy who took the licking, so he gets to call the shots; it's only fair."

I'd saved Whispering Smith for last. He stashed himself in a flophouse a few blocks from skid row. I left my crate parked in a pothole and tramped across the cracked pavement toward a tired row of crumbling tenements. I was sorry now I hadn't tanked up on Baby Face's booze; there was something about facing this neighborhood cold sober that made me want to turn tail and run.

Rusty hinges squeaked as I pushed open the unlocked front door. I groped my way down a dark hallway, got to the first door on the left. I didn't waste time hunting for a bell; I used my knuckles. When that got me nowhere, I banged the door with my foot.

"Watzit . . . ?" a hoarse voice said from inside.

"Open up," I bawled.

"Huh . . . ?"

"Come on," I yelled, rattling the door for good measure. I heard a lot of stumbling around, hoarse mumbling; a chair or something crashed to the floor. The door opened.

Whispering Smith stood in bare feet and grayish, wrinkled long johns, bleary-eyed and unshaven, squinting into the dark hallway. Behind him a small dangling light bulb cast a pale, yellow gleam over crooked floorboards, a lopsided unmade bed, a chair with pants and shirt thrown across it.

"Waddya want?"

"It's Dunjer," I said.

"Who?"

"Dunjer, the private eye with the bankroll, remember? I'm the guy who's always good for a sawbuck, right?"

Whispering Smith stepped back. A shaky hand tried to wipe sleep from his eyes. "What is it, Mr. Dunjer? I ain't done nothin'; honest to God; anyone says I ain't shot square—"

"Can it, Smith. I'm here to do you a big favor."

"A favor?" Whisper blinked at me as though I'd offered him a five-star generalship in the local militia. He didn't look any too steady on his feet.

"Sit down," I told him.

Whisper backed over to his bed, sat down.

"Ever hear of Cyrus Whitney?" I asked.

"Whitney. Yeah, sure. You bet, Mr. Dunjer."

"Who is he?"

"Who?"

"Uh-huh."

"Well, I ain't too sure about no details. I mean . . ."

"Just remember the handle: Cyrus Whitney. He's a big shot and he's loaded. Someone clipped his home tonight, ran off with a bundle of dough and a couple of other items. I want a line on who this someone was. I'm willing to make a deal on the items. That's all I want. Think you can remember that?"

"Remember? Sure, I can remember, Mr. Dunjer, you bet. What're the items?"

"Just items. You get half a yard if you turn up something. Here's a fin on account."

I left Whispering Smith fondling my five bucks as though it had already turned into a bottle of hootch.

Chapter 4

The night seemed to lean against the car window as
if the darkness were trying to seep in through the
cracks and carry me off. My hands turned the wheel
as though they had suddenly become enfeebled by
old age and despair. I had as much bounce as a
punctured beach ball and maybe as much future. My
chats with the three stoolies had done nothing for
my mood. Seeing them in the flesh had reduced whatever confidence I had in their abilities to below zero.
I decided I'd better put in a couple of more hours
trying to save myself.

The Happy Hour was a two-bit dive near the
honky-tonk section of town. I went down five stone
steps, pushed open the wooden doors. The joint was
churning. As fine an assortment of grifters as could be
found outside of the city pen crowded around long
and short tables. There was smoke, chatter, the odor
of booze, the clang of glasses. I made my way to a
small empty table by the north wall, ordered gin
and tonic from a sour-looking waiter. While I waited,
I picked faces out of the crowd. There was Two-Ton
Harris, the strong-arm specialist; Smiley Jenkins, the
con man; Sally Ann Caruso, pickpocket; Gordon
Blinky Nash, bunco artist; Miles Sortie, who was
rumored to've knocked over the First City Bank.
I'd done a lot of dickering with these birds in my
sleuthing days, but since then I'd lost the touch—one
of the few losses I didn't much mind.

The waiter brought my drink. I poured half of it down my throat, got to my feet and went calling.

Three men and two women looked up as I approached their table. They stopped talking as if someone had made off with their vocal chords. I worked a smile, pulled up a chair from an adjoining table and seated myself. I turned to the only one I knew, a small stubby man in his forties called Gimpy Kreeg. "Don't bother introducing me to the rest of the gang, Gimpy. I can only stay a minute. Cyrus Whitney's digs were nicked tonight. A lot of scratch and some personal property was hauled off."

Kreeg shrugged.

"Whitney wants his property back; he's willing to pay for it. No questions asked. Just thought I'd spread the word."

One of the two ladies, a small brunette, said, "You've got the wrong party. We don't know beans about that. Why don't ya go peddle your papers somewhere else?"

"Yeah, why don't you?" Kreeg asked.

"That's okay by me," I said. I got up, nodded and took my drink and myself to another table.

"Hi, Lulu," I said.

"Tom Dunjer, isn't it?"

"Uh-huh."

The blond in the evening dress smiled at me. "Pull up a chair, if you want to."

"Thanks." I sat down.

"This is Paul Regan," the blond introduced her companion.

Regan nodded at me. He was tall and slender with a pointed moustache. Somewhere in his thirties. His skin was tanned, his black hair slicked back and glistening. His teeth were very white. He was said to be shiftless as hell. But who wasn't in this crowd?

Lulu said, "Dunjer runs the Security Plus outfit."

"The protection service," Regan said.

"The same," I admitted.

"Dunjer and I've met professionally," Lulu said.

"I pinched her back in eighty-two," I explained, "but she beat the rap."

Regan grinned. "If the cops did their job, you'd be out of work, pal."

"Along with you," I pointed out. "Kind of puts a different light on things, eh?" I downed some more whisky and told em my story.

Regan thought it over, nodded thoughtfully. "The guy you want to see," he said, "is Oswald Gripus."

"Gripus, eh? That's like using a cannon instead of a fly swatter."

"Maybe," Regan said, "and maybe not."

"No maybes about it. Gripus got his hands full running a crime *empire*; this job was just run-of-the-mill."

"Of course," Lulu said. "But Gripus got connections."

"*Lots* of connections," Regan said.

"Yeah," I said, "but as the guy who's spent the last four years trying to put Gripus in the pen, I might not be the ideal person to brace him on this topic. But that don't mean that you two or someone palled up with Gripus can't pull down a big score. All it takes is the right dope. This is strictly business."

"Okay, buddy," Regan said. "Anything comes my way, I'll pass it along."

"That goes for me, too," Lulu said.

"Right," I said. "Thanks."

I visited a couple of other tables and used more or less the same spiel. No one told me to shut up. No one got up and did a jig either. After a while I figured I'd done my duty. I put the last of my drink down my gullet and went back into the night.

I got to my office bright and early the next morning. Ambition had nothing to do with it; I was too jumpy even to think of work. My home phone wasn't listed and I was hoping that someone—anyone—had gotten my message and would be dying to reach me about a deal. As hopes went, it was nothing to write home about.

I sat around in my swivel chair for a while and looked out the window. Ninety-one floors below I could see the translucent dome of the World's Emporium—Happy City's trade center. Around it, in neon lights, posters, signs and placards urged: DRINK SQUEEZEX AND FEEL GOOD AGAIN. PROTECT YOURSELF WITH AN ALL-GUARD AUTOMATIC LASER. BUY LEGAL AID AT TROUBLE-SHOOTER, INC. CANNED FROLICS TAPES MEAN QUALITY IN YOUR ENTERTANIE SET . . . Maybe what I needed was a good old slug of Squeezex; somehow I doubted it.

I used the swivel chair to swivel toward the window and spent the next twenty minutes staring glumly at Happy City, not exactly an inspiring interlude. After a while I heard noises coming from the anteroom and other offices. The staff was starting to drift in. I turned back to my desk and got out a sheaf of papers; it wouldn't do to be caught lolling, not a week before the stockholders' meeting. Maybe I *was* ruined, but there was no point in hurrying the end along.

The door opened and Miss Follsom stepped into my office. "Good morning, Mr. Dunjer."

Miss Follsom was a curvaceous blond; her hair was long, flowing. She had an ample bosom and nifty legs only partially obscured by the neat blue suit she wore. Miss Follsom was our chief junior exec (a designation I'd have to look up one of these days) and next to my weekly paycheck the nicest thing about Security Plus. "Anything wrong, boss?"

"Wrong? What could be wrong?"

"I don't know. But you haven't tried to grab me yet."

"An oversight. Just give me time. The cares of the day have got me down a bit."

"Would you like a report on our latest doings?"

"Not especially. But go ahead anyway."

For the next ten minutes Miss Follsom regaled me with a list of old and new clients who wanted various things done to protect them or their property. They ranged from bank presidents to local candy-store proprietors. When it got down to protection, the city cops came in a poor third—way behind old-fashioned self-protection and spiffy new-bought protection. Not that self-protection didn't have its points: anyone who longed to shoot it out with a gang of mangy desperados would opt for it without a moment's hesitation. But most folks preferred to have someone else do their shooting. Mechs didn't bleed. And anyone who messed with one got what he deserved. Security Plus specialized in mechs.

"There you are, Mr. Dunjer; any instructions?"

"Not that I can think of, offhand; but then I'm not thinking too well this morning. Feed the lot to

Computer Central and let the old cyborg assign personnel."

"Right you are, boss."

Miss Follsom left.

When no one else barged in, I reached for the communo, punched out XX42's code.

"Greetings, skipper," a metallic voice said through the speaker.

"What's happening?"

"We've been hiding here behind a bush all night. No one's come or gone. Unless you count the milkman."

"Let's not. What abut Grash?"

"He's inside."

"You sure?"

The voice of XX43 interrupted. "I personally tapped his phone, chief."

"And?"

"His bookie called. He lost five hundred on a nag in the fifth yesterday. His ex-wife called; she's going to sue for more alimony. His business manager called; he wants a raise."

"Anything else?"

"No, but it's early yet."

"I suppose so. Okay, keep me posted."

"Roger."

I pulled open the bottom desk drawer, reached for the office bottle and took a healthy swig of the barley juice. Things began to seem brighter right away. Maybe nothing would happen. Maybe the crooks would overlook their find, miss its implications. The thought of betting all my marbles on a couple of maybes began taking the glow off the whisky pronto. Before it was all gone, I pressed one of the buttons on my desk. Hennessy came into my office a minute later.

"What's up, boss?"

Mike Hennessy was a small, dark-haired sleuth with narrow lips, bony cheeks and gray eyes. His gray business suit was custom-made, his white shirt and narrow blue tie came from one of the more expensive men's shops in town. As one of our few human ops, Hennessy pulled down a good-sized paycheck.

"Sit down, Hennessy."

"Thanks, boss."

"We've been friends a long time, Hennessy, haven't we?"

"Sure. About fifteen years, I guess."

"Fifteen *good* years. Years in which we've cracked dozens of capers together, not to mention getting the goods on countless law breakers. Years in which we've guided both men and mechs in a relentless battle against evildoers, eh, Hennessy?"

"If you say so, boss. What do you want, a loan? Things are pretty tight now, but I think I can manage twenty till payday."

"Uh-uh. It's worse than that."

"What could be worse?"

"The evildoers, Mike; they're going to get me."

"*What* evildoers? What are you talking about?"

"The Cyrus Whitney knockover."

"Whitney's been robbed?"

"Last night. They got some dough. And they got the goods on Whitney, too."

"He's done something bad?"

"Who hasn't? Only Whitney put it in writing. If Reginald Grash gets his mitts on the evidence, Security Plus gets a new Board Chairman."

"What's so awful about *that*?"

"With Grash in the driver's seat, I'm out of a job, Hennessy; and as part of my team, so are you."

Hennessy turned white. "That *is* awful."

"Sure. Grash'll put his own guys in all the top jobs, and we'll be out in the cold."

"The cold," Hennessy said, as if he could already feel it. "What's this incriminating evidence?"

"Photostats proving stock fraud."

"How'd it happen?"

I told him. For something that could turn our lives upside down, it didn't take long.

"That's all?" Hennessy asked.

I shrugged. "It's not enough?"

"It's too much. I could use a drink."

I got the bottle out along with two pony glasses and poured us both a shot. "Can't stand to see a man drinking alone. Cheers."

"Cheers." The diminutive op downed his in one gulp, wiped his lips and asked, "So what have you done so far?"

"Nothing brilliant. I put some mechs on Grash and made the stoolie rounds. No word yet."

"How about Whitney?"

"He's sitting tight—thumbs down on the law. It's all in our laps."

"That's big of him. Think someone'll call?"

"I hope so. Half the hoods in town ought to know about it by now."

"Well, maybe I should go inform the other half."

"Maybe you should."

"And then, boss, I think I'll take the rest of the day off and go on a king-sized bender."

"Yeah, that sounds about right."

I lay back in bed. Night came through my bedroom window. Outside I could see a festival of lights: milky white elevated drives curved over giant skyscrapers. I pulled the cord on my reading lamp and the room went dark. I lay there waiting for sleep to take me away. Like everything else, sleep wasn't going to oblige. It just hadn't been a swell day. Reginald Grash had left his home around eleven o'clock with my trusty mechs in hot pursuit. Grash went to his office where he remained all day. The only thing that came through our bugs was a lot of business chatter. An industrial spy would've had a field day. All I got was a headache.

The stoolie department hadn't distinguished itself either, had in fact come up with zilch.

I lay in the darkness and listened to the sound of an occasional copter drifting by my window. I wondered just how bad off I'd be if I *did* lose my job. The stocks I'd shrewdly bought had hit rock bottom. My bank account was down to dimes and nickels, and I owed the finance company on my new car. Aside from that, I was sitting pretty. I turned over on my side and fell asleep.

The phone jarred me awake as though someone had tossed cold water over my face. I groped for the receiver, stuck the phone close to my ear and managed to say hello.

A voice whispered, "Dunjer?"

"I hope so," I mumbled. "I can turn on the light and make sure. Who is this?"

"Smith."

"Smith? What Smith?"

"Whispering Smith, *me*, Mr. Dunjer."

I sat there in bed holding the phone. I turned on the light. That didn't help any. I turned off the light. I said into the phone, "How'd you get my number, Smith?"

"I've got my ways," the voice whispered back.

"You do?" It was a new and startling idea.

"You wanted the dope on the Whitney caper, right, Mr. Dunjer?"

"Right."

"Meet me at my place."

"Your place? When?"

"Now. Bring dough. That's it, Mr. Dunjer; don't be late."

"Not for the world," I told him.

The phone went click. Just in time, too. I was all set to call him "sir."

I hustled out of bed and started getting dressed fast. Old deadbeat Smith coming through with anything would take some getting used to. Maybe he was all tanked up. Maybe he'd gone off his rocker. Maybe it was all a stunt to chisel another sawbuck out of me. Whatever it was, I could hardly afford to pass it up. At this stage of the game I couldn't afford to pass anything up.

I parked my heap between the cracks in the asphalt pavement and walked over to Smith's tenement. Something about this neighborhood at three in the morning made me want to go back for my gun.

I suppressed this almost overpowering urge and knocked on Smith's door.

"Yeah?"

"Dunjer."

The door opened and Smith came shuffling out. He was still unshaven but had put on a pair of wrinkled dungarees and a flannel shirt. "Let's go," he said.

"We're going somewhere?"

"To Swifty's."

We went. I followed Smith out of the building, onto the street, through a mazelike series of back alleys which led to a dirt road. I didn't even know there *was* a dirt road around here. By now I didn't even know where here was. Small wooden shacks were on both sides of us. If this wasn't skid row, it'd do as a perfect stand-in. Smith shuffled over to one of these shacks, glanced around furtively, pushed open the door and motioned for me to join him.

One flickering candle gave off all the light there was. A small, white-haired man lay on a cot. His face was lined, his eyes bleary; he turned his head to stare at us.

"This is Swifty," Whispering Smith said.

He didn't look very swift to me. "He knows about the knockover?" I said.

"He gets around," Smith assured me.

The man on the cot groaned.

"What's wrong with him?" I asked.

"He needs his fix."

"That's what I need," the small man croaked. "My fix. You got it?"

"Jeezus," I said.

"He's the guy with the dough, Swifty. Tell him what you told me. Come on, Swifty."

"I need my fix," Swifty groaned.

165

"One-track mind," I said.

"He worries a lot," Whispering Smith explained.

The old man moved his head, his eyes seemed to focus. "You want the inside track, mister? Gripus got it."

I asked, "*You* know Gripus?"

"Usta be his right bower. Run errands for him now. He don't treat me good, mister."

"Did Gripus turn the trick?"

"Uh-uh."

"Who did?"

"Don't know that either, mister."

"What *do* you know?"

"Heard Gripus talkin'. He *said* he knew."

"He mentioned Whitney by name?"

"Yeah."

"And nothing else?"

"Uh-uh."

I looked at the old man.

Whispering Smith said, "See?"

"See what?"

"He had the dope."

"Some dope," I complained.

"You got anythin' better?"

I sighed, reached for my wallet.

"That's it, skipper," XX43 said. "The works."

I looked at the report again. It'd been compiled by the mech team I'd sigged on Reginald Grash. Just as well—humans would've dozed off on their feet. Grash was a man nothing ever happened to—except business and businessmen. If anyone else had contacted him during the last two days, my mechs had failed to notice.

"Okay XX43," I said, "back on the job."

"I hope this job ends soon," XX43 said and went away.

Mike Hennessy walked into my office.

"Learn anything, Hennessy?" I asked.

"Not to mix gin and whisky, boss. A valuable lesson."

"And aside from that?"

"Nothing."

Hennessy left. I looked at my watch: 11:45. I took a paper bag out of the lower desk drawer, removed a peanut-butter sandwich and began to munch. If anyone decided to call me, I wanted to be on hand.

Miss Follsom came into my office.

"Oh, Mr. Dunjer, sir, I know all about it."

"You do?"

"Hennessy told me. What are you going to do, boss?"

"Lord knows. Wait for something to break. If it doesn't, you get to work for Reginald Grash, I suppose."

"I'd loathe that."

"Who wouldn't? Care for a peanut-butter sandwich?"

"I'm too upset to eat."

"Thank you, Miss Follsom. I appreciate the sentiment. Try to keep all this to yourself, however. We don't want to make the mechs nervous."

"Of course. And whatever happens, I'm behind you one hundred percent, Mr. Dunjer. I want you to know that."

"That's nice, Miss Follsom. I've seen to that raise I promised you."

"Thanks, boss."

She left.

I ate the last morsel of sandwich, brushed the crumbs off my lap, balled up the bag, tossed it into the waste basket, swiveled my chair to face the window and spent the next thirty minutes gazing out at Happy City.

The phone rang.

"Dunjer," I said into the mouthpiece.

"Whitney here."

"What is it, Mr. Whitney; something pop?"

"Not yet, Dunjer, but it's about to."

"It is?"

"Grash has been contacted."

"Impossible. We've got him under surveillance round the clock. His office and home are wired for sound—"

"Listen, I have a man planted in Grash's office."

"You do? Since when?"

"Since years ago, Dunjer. A simple business precaution."

"I can imagine."

"Naturally, I alerted him at once. He called me from a pay phone during his lunch hour. He used a prearranged code word—it seemed safest. I have none of the details yet. Cringly leaves work at five. Can you go to his home?"

"I'll do better than that. Sit tight, I'm on my way."

I stood in a doorway opposite the Grash building and waited for quitting time to roll around. I had a pretty good view of the main entrance. Four forty-five and the street was already starting to fill up. Buses, trolleys, cars and pedestrians clogged the main arteries—exhaust fumes, noise and bustle on the go. I shrank back in my doorway; being here reminded me of the good old days when I used to go on stake-outs; it turned my stomach.

Soon the large revolving door began to spin, two side doors popped open and the Grash building started to empty out. I looked at the sea of faces and knew I wouldn't've been able to spot my own mother, let alone a perfect stranger. But few things are perfect, and Cringly certainly wasn't one of 'em.

"There he goes, skipper," XX38 said through the communo. "Heading west."

"Right," I answered. "Stick with him."

I stepped out of the doorway, headed west.

Grash—as befitted a major stockholder—was a Security Plus client. That made it simple. Our master computer had all the dope on Grash's staff, including photos.

"This way, chief," the voice of XX38 said in my ear. I followed the homing tone, crossed at a traffic jam, waded through a crush of pedestrians and fell

169

abreast of XX38. He wore the disguise of a portly businessman. "The little guy," he told me, "up ahead in the gray jacket."

"Got it," I said. "Anyone taking a special interest in us?"

Five mechs scattered through the crowd chorused no in my ear.

"Okay, men," I said. "You can take off now. Thanks."

XX38 turned on his heel, vanished in the crowd. I put on the steam, caught up with Cringly.

"Mr. Cringly," I said.

Cringly turned to stare at me. He was a small, narrow-faced, balding man with a thin moustache.

"I'm Dunjer," I said.

Cringly glanced around nervously. "What are you doing here? We'll be seen."

"Uh-uh. We're clean. Just keep walking. Tell me what happened."

"A letter. That's what happened."

"What'd it say?"

" 'If you want to buy some interesting items which will make you Chairman of a large, well-known security service, put the following ad in the *Daily Tattler's* personal column: Am willing to spend big. Moneybags.' The very words. I memorized them."

"Handwritten or typed?"

"Typed."

"Any chance you can get that letter to me—either the original or a photocopy?"

"No chance at all. Mr. Grash took it away with him."

"That figures. How'd you get to see it?"

"The letter was lying on his desk this morning. I

read it quite carefully before Mr. Grash returned from the board room. I saw him put it in his pocket."

"No signature, I suppose."

"None."

"Thanks for the dope, Cringly."

Chapter 8

"Have another drink," I said.

Cyrus Whitney poured himself a king-sized jolt, downed it in two gulps. "Tell me again," he said.

"What's to tell? The grapevine's come up empty and so've I. We've got only a few days to do something before Grash clinches the deal."

"You think he'll run the ad?"

"Sure. Why not? What's he got to lose?"

"Perhaps he won't."

"Then they'll try again. They've got a hot item. They'll catch his eye one way or another before that stockholders' meeting, you can bet on it."

Whitney stared at me, his face haggard. "You must double your surveillance."

I got to my feet, went to the window, looked out. The sun was setting. I could see Whitney's garden from where I stood and the trees beyond. In the distance the high stone walls which ringed his estate stretched off toward the horizon. Whitney was fixed for life. But me? I'd be lucky to land a job selling pencils on street corners. I sighed, padded back to my easy chair, slumped down in the soft leather. "I've already put six more mechs on Grash. We could probably nail some of this crew when they turn up for the payoff. But that's not the problem."

"What's the problem?"

"They'll holler murder and your photostats are bound to go public."

"We could bribe them, Dunjer."

"Sure, if we could get em off in a corner before they reach Grash. Well, don't hold your breath, Mr. Whitney. These guys know what they're doing. The job they pulled here was slick as a whistle. And it didn't take em long to figure out what they had, either. They'll be very careful setting up a meet with Grash. I wouldn't lay odds on our being able to intercept em ahead of time. And if we turn up on the site, it'll be touch and go. There's also a pretty good chance that they've copied the photostats, too."

"Good heavens, why?"

I shrugged. "Why not? Grash wouldn't mind, he's going to spotlight em anyway. It just gives the gang an extra ace if something goes wrong."

"Then it's hopeless."

"Uh-uh. Where there's life, there's hope, as they say, eh, Mr. Whitney? H-m-m-m. Actually, that *isn't* very impressive, is it? But what's the worst that could happen to you, eh? Like you once said, Mr. Whitney, you lose some dough. You're unchairmaned at Security Plus. Maybe you even end up in court for a couple days. Big deal. It'll give your lawyers a workout, that's all. No one's gonna send a big shot like you to the hoosegow, right? Half the judges in town owe you a favor and the rest wish they did. And after you've lost that dough, what've you got? Why, a lot more dough left over, that's what, bushels of it. Take it from me, Mr. Whitney, no matter what happens, you're sitting pretty. But me? Why, I'm a lost cause, one step away from being a bona fide charity case.

"Security Plus uses all kinds of methods in uncovering skulduggery, chicanery and just plain cheating; and most of those methods are resented by the bad guys. Like bugging. The bad guys resent that like hell. And because half the time we don't know who the bad guys are, we end up bugging the good guys, too. They don't much care for it, either. Some of em find out eventually and take it personally. Sad to say, but our competition—the other security outfits—will think nothing of blowing the whistle on a colleague. Naturally, *we* perform the same service for *our* clients. To do less would be shirking, right? Well, you'd be surprised, Mr. Whitney, how much resentment this causes with the other agencies. The point I'm trying to make is that I haven't got a prayer trying to land a job with some competing outfit. Why they wouldn't touch me with a ten-foot pole. That's ironclad policy. And as far as a spot outside the industry, that's touchy too. I've been a security op most of my adult life. The plain truth is that while most concerns use security ops, they just hate to employ *ex*-ops themselves. Maybe it's the bad press, eh? Maybe it's all that bugging stuff. Who knows? But there it is, a fact. So maybe we'll nail these birds before they trade the photostats to Grash and that'll be that. But Grash is a big-money guy just like you, Mr. Whitney, and once he gets wind that something's cooking, he won't let up till he finds out what. So I guess what I'm asking is if worse comes to worse, maybe I can land a job with you, eh, Mr. Whitney?"

I'd done it, had my say. In the silence which followed, I squirmed around in my chair wishing I could crawl under it, sighed, and let my gaze drift to the window. Night was falling. Dark shadows were lengthening outdoors. Outdoors was where I wanted to be—far, far away from Cyrus Whitney and this whole rotten mess. I'd done everything but get down on my knees and beg. The only thing left was to break into tears. I'd hold that in reserve. Certainly I wasn't going to stand on dignity. I'd just lost it all.

I glanced at Whitney. He was pouring himself another drink. He looked worse than when I'd begun. The bags under his eyes were so full he could've hauled groceries in em. His hands were shaking as if he'd been mixing martinis all week and forgotten how to stop. Worse yet, his eyes wouldn't meet mine; they were straying all over the joint, as if hunting for a very dark corner in which to hide. I was beginning to get the impression he was going to tell me something I didn't want to hear, something *bad.*

Whitney finally spoke. "It's all over, finished, done for."

"What is, Mr. Whitney?"

"Don't ask, Dunjer."

"I'd better. It sounds like my career."

"Wrong, Dunjer. *Mine.*"

I allowed myself a small, bitter chuckle. "Come, come, Mr. Whitney, it's only money. Think of all the money you'll still have left."

"I'm afraid you don't understand. There can be no job."

"That's what I figured," I said in disgust. "Well, as far as I'm concerned, I'll do anything possible—"

"No job," Whitney said, "because I'll be in jail. I saw my attorney last night. Not Carmichael and Sprung who represent my business interests, but Ben Frazer, my personal lawyer."

"The criminal lawyer?"

"Precisely. We had a long, disheartening talk."

"You've committed some crime?"

"Stock fraud. A major felony."

"Major?"

175

"And they've got me dead to rights. An open and shut case. I'll swing, Dunjer."

"Swing, yet. Have a heart, Mr. Whitney; let's quit the horseplay, eh? No one swings for stock fraud. Calm down, okay?"

Cyrus Whitney wiped his brow with a hanky. A corner of his mouth tried to smile, gave up the effort as too strenuous. "You're right, of course, Dunjer. I was carried away. But in some ways the end would be preferable to a life behind bars. I owned substantial interest in companies which did business with one another, you see. I manipulated the bids."

"Let me get this straight, Mr. Whitney: there were *others* and you made photostats of them, too—"

"Some in my wife's name. A few in my cook's name. Even one in poor Slotnick's name, may he rest in peace. I'm a ruined man, Dunjer."

"You didn't tell me about the other stuff," I complained.

Whitney shrugged. "The less you knew, the better. Once you made contact, I could have bought them all back."

"Nuts. They *will* throw the book at you."

"Of course."

"Better forget about that job. A guy in my racket can't afford to consort with known criminals. And it's just a matter of time before you're known, Mr. Whitney."

"Of course. But as you've pointed out, Dunjer, you won't be in that, er, racket for very long, will you?"

"Yeah, true enough. Maybe since you won't be needing that dough in the can, Mr. Whitney, you could kind of just give me a large handout? I'd be willing to settle for that, and not too proud to take it. In a pinch like this beggars can't be choosers. All you'd have to do is offer, Mr. Whitney. After all, why should we both be ruined, eh? And I'd even visit you in the clink."

"Thank you, Dunjer, I appreciate the thought. But perhaps there's a better way?"

"A better way? What could be better?"

"My not going to jail and you not being ruined."

"Yeah, I suppose that *would* be better, but how do we manage that little thing?"

"Gripus."

"Gripus? I don't get it."

"He's the key, Dunjer. I'm convinced Gripus could save us both."

"Forget it. Gripus wouldn't give me the time of day. And as for you, Mr. Whitney, he'd just as soon rob you as look at you."

"I am acquainted with his reputation, his antipathy toward the wealthy, toward authority."

"Uh-uh. Not mere, mild antipathy. Blazing hate is the word you're looking for."

"Very well." Whitney made a steeple of his fingers, leaned back in his chair. "But Gripus literally controls crime in Happy City, doesn't he? From what you've told me, Dunjer, *he* could locate the photostats if he wished to."

"Sure. Probably. He could also build an orphanage on Main Street and donate the rest of his money to charity. But he isn't going to do that, Mr. Whitney. And he isn't going to dig up your photostats for you, either. All this stuff with Gripus is just a pipe dream."

"He'd do it for you, Dunjer, if you were a criminal

177

on the run, if you had a scheme that might add to his coffers."

"Yeah, and if I had wings, I could fly home. You're not talking sense, Mr. Whitney."

"On the contrary, Dunjer, I am talking about the only chance we have of saving ourselves."

"All I got to do is become a criminal, eh? And on the run, yet."

"Simplicity itself. Steal something."

"Like what?"

Whitney shrugged. "City bonds; the Security Plus vault has a stack of them."

"That would sure put me on the run, all right. Then what?"

Whitney's eyes were gleaming. "You worm your way into Gripus' confidence using the bonds as bait. Then you tell him the significance of the photostats."

"He'll love that."

"I should hope so. Let him coerce the culprits into turning over the photostats to him."

"Look. You really think Gripus goes for every two-bit deal that comes along? For him all this is peanuts."

"You misunderstand, Dunjer. Remember I'm a multimillionaire with vast holdings in the business community. I'm sure Gripus won't overlook the black-mail potential."

"Yeah, he might go for that angle. So what?"

"He'd think he had me over a barrel."

"Oh brother, what's this think business? He'd have you—signed, sealed and delivered. Come on, Mr. Whitney, use your head: once Gripus gets his mitts on those photostats, you're a goner."

"Ah, Dunjer, you forget one thing."

"Just one?"

"*You'll* be there."

That was good for a laugh and got one. "What am I supposed to do, sig him?"

"Why anything you want. There are at least several options open to you. Steal the photostats from Gripus, or destroy them."

"Right. I was afraid you were going to come up with something hard, Mr. Whitney."

"There is no need to be facetious, Dunjer; that was only a suggestion. Or you could always *intercept* the photostats before Gripus claims them. Simply find out when he plans to pick them up and be there first."

"Simply, no less." I got to my feet, began to wear out a groove in Whitney's carpet pacing back and forth. "Have you lost all your marbles, Mr. Whitney? Do you know what you're asking me to do?"

"Certainly. To save us both."

"Worry has blunted your otherwise sharp wits. The odds for pulling off this stunt are almost nil. The only thing's going to happen is that I'll either get nailed by the cops or Gripus. Probably Gripus. You know who that guy is? He's the kingpin crook in Happy City; he'll eat me alive, and you too, Mr. Whitney. Getting tangled up with Gripus is like going for a dip in a shark tank. Count me out."

"Surely there's some way I can convince you."

"Uh-uh."

"What about money?"

"Nope."

"Let's say half a million dollars."

I stopped in my tracks, took a close look at Whitney. "Say it again."

"I'll give you five hundred thousand."

"Just like that?"

"Yes."

"In advance?"

"If you wish."

"That's the silliest thing I ever heard of, Mr. Whitney."

"But you'll do it, Dunjer?"

"Of course. Who wouldn't?"

I staggered into the office at a quarter to nine. I hadn't slept any too well. That I'd slept at all was a miracle. I felt as lively as a cigar-store Indian, but not quite as clearheaded. I closed the office door behind me, leaned up against it, got a hanky out of my pocket and wiped my brow. My hands were doing a quick tango, and my knees were knocking together keeping time. I got to my desk without falling down, lowered myself carefully into my chair as if my skin had turned to rubber and I was trying to avoid a fatal puncture. I sat there trying to catch my breath; it stayed a jump ahead of me. I got the office bottle out of its hiding place in back of the bottom desk drawer. Only a couple of mouthfuls left; I polished em off in nothing flat. They didn't do much good. I wondered what would. Outside in the hallway I could hear the rest of our human crew checking in for the day: footsteps, voices, doors opening and closing. I'd miss em. All this—for me—would soon be a thing of the past—the routine, my co-workers, the paychecks. . . . Of course, the paychecks were kind of academic right now; a guy with a half million bucks in his kick can make do without a paycheck. So why did I hate this turn of events? There was something about setting myself up as a clay pigeon that didn't agree with me. The more I thought about it, the less enthusiastic I became—and I wasn't all that enthusiastic to begin with. Get hold of yourself, Dunjer, I told myself, think of the bright side. The bright side, unfortunately—with the exception of the half million smacks—was playing hard to get. Concentrating on my newfound wealth didn't give me much of a rear, either, since to spend, I'd have to survive the next couple of weeks, a tricky proposition, at best.

I got to my feet, went over to the master control board, punched the talky button. "Well?" I said.

"If you are referring to the lamentable occurrences of the last few days, 'well' is hardly the correct term," the master control board said. "Try horrendous."

"I don't doubt it. Get everything down?"

"Certainly."

"Okay, hand it over."

A three-inch spool clicked into the eject slot. "Thanks," I said, dropping it into my pocket.

"Are you, in fact, attempting the project suggested by Mr. Whitney?"

"If you mean putting my neck in the sling, yeah, it looks that way."

"Then allow me to take this opportunity to say good-bye. It's been pleasant working with you, Mr. Dunjer."

"Actually, I expect to be back."

"Don't we all?"

At my desk I used the intercom. "Miss Follsom, may I see you for a moment?"

Miss Follsom stepped into my office. "What's cooking, boss?"

"Me, I'm afraid."

"Nothing catching, I hope?"

"There's no need to back up, Miss Follsom, it's not a virus. What I'm about to tell you may cause tears and heartbreak. You'd better sit down."

"You've scratched my yearly raise?"

"Relax. This bad news is about me, not you. I may have to go away for a while. Under a cloud, no less. A deep dark one."

"Oh." Miss Follsom sat down. "I can take it if you can, Mr. Dunjer."

"That's just the trouble. I don't know if I can."

"You poor dear."

"Precisely, Miss Folsom; I'd better tell someone just in case I don't get back. Someone who'll clear my name."

"Is the someone me?"

"That was my plan."

"I'm a pushover for sob stories, boss." Miss Follsom crossed one neat leg over the other, folded her arms and looked attentive. "Shoot."

"You remember the tale of woe Hennessy unfolded?"

"About you?"

"About me."

"It all but kept me sleepless, boss."

"Well, things have managed to take a turn for the worse."

"I didn't know there could be a worse."

"Neither did I. Mr. Whitney found one; he's come up with a scheme to save us both. I abscond with some city bonds, become a fugitive, win over Oswald Gripus, have him corral the goons who made off with Whitney's dumb photostats and then swipe em myself."

"And then they put you away for a good long rest cure, right? Because you've obviously blown a fuse."

"I *did* forget to mention one small item."

"Oh?"

184

"The bucks. I'm being paid a half million."

"Wow."

"My thoughts exactly."

"What can I do for you, boss; tell me?"

"You could do *it* for me. But then you'd probably want the half million for yourself, eh?"

"Darn right."

"That's what I figured. In any case, you lack the training, the skill, the wherewithal to pull it off. The trouble is, I may lack it, too."

"You had it once."

"Once was twenty years ago. Once I could run the mile in jig time. But things change."

"Not that much, boss. I've got confidence in you, honest."

"Thank you, Miss Follsom, I appreciate that. Suddenly I've begun to feel quite lonely, you know. May I ask a favor?"

"Anything, Mr. Dunjer."

I took the voice spool out of my pocket, put it on the desk. "Hang on to this for a while."

"What is it?"

"Me. And all the things that happened to me these last couple of days."

"You bugged yourself?"

"A minor precaution. It's always best to keep a record. But this one is really important. There's just the chance if things get balled up that Whitney won't own up to his end of the bargain. Why should he? This way I've got an ace in the hole. Or more properly speaking, you do."

"I'll guard it with my life, Mr. Dunjer."

"That won't be necessary, I hope. No one knows

185

this thing exists. Just put it away somewhere till I get back."

"We'll miss you, boss."

"Not as much as I'll miss you."

The speed lift carried me down to the lobby. I made my way through the lunchtime crowd and out onto the streets. Pedestrians filled the sidewalks. A guy could lose himself in a crowd like this, I thought gloomily. A bit premature, maybe, but in a matter of hours I'd be on the run. I shrugged, headed east. Nothing to do about it now; I was committed. Unless, of course, Whitney didn't hold up his end. I wasn't exactly sure which way I was rooting. I headed east for three crowded blocks, turned north on Linstrom. The Whitney building was halfway down the block. I ducked my head at the robot cop on duty in the lobby, took the speed lift directly to the top floor.

"Mr. Whitney is expecting you, Mr. Dunjer," the pert, brown-eyed receptionist told me.

"Thanks, sweetheart." I hustled into Whitney's office just as if my legs hadn't turned to jelly.

Cyrus Whitney rose from behind a huge desk, extended his lean fingers. I shook em. "Well, Dunjer, the moment is at hand."

"Don't remind me. Got the dough?"

Whitney grinned. "What do you think?"

Whitney handed me a small leather satchel. "Go on, count it, Dunjer."

"You look honest, Mr. Whitney; I'll take your word for it."

"We will keep in touch?"

"I'll phone."

"When?"

I shrugged. "Whenever I can."

Whitney nodded. "I have two private numbers."

"I know. I've got em both. I don't mind going through the switchboard, either."

"But I do."

"Don't sweat it, Mr. Whitney. I'll use the name Dant. It'll be okay."

"Very well. You have my thanks, Dunjer." Whitney put his hand on my shoulder. "I'm counting on you."

"Yeah. Me too. But sometimes I get old and tired. Take care, Mr. Whitney."

I didn't bother stopping off for a snack, not with all that dough on me. I beat it back to the Security Plus building. The speed lift carried me down to the basement vaults. My life of crime was about to begin. I got the master control cube out of my pocket, moved quietly down the corridor. The security mech, I knew, was stationed just around the bend. No guesswork involved—I'd put him there myself. I stopped short of my destination, flicked the cube's cutoff switch. When I turned the corner, no fond greetings issued from the metal contraption standing against the wall—it was just so many nuts and bolts, wires and gears. I'd shut it off. The Security Plus vaults were absolutely crookproof. Unless, of course, the head of Security Plus himself turned out to be a crook.

I almost blushed as I sat on the floor counting my half million. Trust can only go so far; I'd waited a full thirty minutes before checking the dough—too bad Whitney wasn't here to appreciate the compliment. The moolah was all there. I sighed, stuffed it back into the valise, got up, lugged it and myself to an empty safe and deposited half a million smacks in its shiny interior. I left the safe door ajar, strolled down a couple of corridors, turned a few corners, used the master control cube twice, shorting out the mech personnel, and reached the safety vault where the city stored part of its negotiable bonds. Again I used the cube. The safety vault snapped open. I went in. A second cube button sprang the city-owned locker. The bonds were in metal boxes against the wall; each contained a couple hundred grand. One box was all I took. I locked up behind me. My criminal career was starting off nicely.

But if no one knew about my crime, what good would it do? The master control board had a spy-eye set up by the vault. Standing in front of it, I waved, gestured at the strongbox under my arm and went away. Back at the other safe I placed the strongbox next to the satchel, removed the combination slot, slammed the door, twirled the dial. I was done. Theoretically, at least, I'd become part of the annals of crime.

Chapter 11

I went into my office, closed the door behind me. Stepping over to the master control board, I flicked on the talkie button. "I hope you got all that," I said.

"I did, indeed," the control board intoned. "What a disgrace. To think that one of our very own would stoop to such underhanded skulduggery—"

"Cut that out," I said, "I had no choice."

"No choice? What's it to me if you lose your job?"

"Yeah? Well, how'd you like a couple of batteries removed?"

"Only a lunatic would tamper with a master control board," the control board said with dignity.

"Precisely. How do you know who Grash'll put in charge here? Probably Grash himself, a very unstable character."

"Good heavens, what *is* it you want?"

"Ah! That's more like it. Put all background about this case on the back burner under security classified. That's number one."

"For how long?"

"A couple of weeks ought to do it. If I'm not back by then, you can spill the beans; in fact, I'd want you to."

"Mechanicals can't testify in court."

"Yeah, but they can raise a stink. By then I probably won't care one way or the other. But it'll be nice to know in the meantime."

"What's number two."

"You help blow the whistle on me for the bond theft."

"H-m-m-m. Now *that* sounds like fun."

"No doubt. Only do it tomorrow, not today. Sometime around noon. Just say you saw me swiping em. You'll be asked. Can I depend on that?"

"The trusty mechanical stands by your side, at least for a short while."

"Thanks. You're a honey."

I buzzed Hennessy from my desk. He came in a moment later. "What's up, boss?"

"I'm going on the lam," I told him.

"Congratulations. Who's after you?"

"No one. Yet."

"But they will be, huh?"

"Yeah. As soon as you tip 'em."

"Great. Do I get to turn you in, too?"

"Let's not get carried away, Hennessy."

"Sorry, boss; I lost my head. About what do I sound the alarm?"

"I've run off with some city bonds."

"No joke?"

"They're stashed down below. It's better if you don't know exactly where. It'd only make you an accomplice."

"The last thing I'd want is to be an accomplice."

"Fine. You go on a little inspection tour of the safety vault tomorrow. Take along some of the staff; you'll need a witness or two. A city strongbox'll be gone."

"How do I pin it on you?"

"Easy. Ask the master control board."

"It's going to snitch, huh? So why didn't it raise a

holler when you were glomming the stuff? Just in case someone asks."

"It figured I was there on an official visit. How's that?"

"Sounds okay. It knows all this?"

"It does by now. It's been sitting in on our little chat."

"I certainly have," the control board said.

"Nuts," Hennessy complained. "A witness. Won't it squeal on us, boss?"

"Uh-uh. It can't testify against you. Besides, it'll keep its lip buttoned. Also, you haven't done anything. And nothing was really stolen. Am I getting through to you, Hennessy?"

"I guess so."

"Good. There's no reason for both of us to panic. One is more than enough. And I'm the one, unfortunately."

"Better you than me, boss. You've had more practice at it."

"Thanks. Miss Follsom is in on this. But no one else. Any questions?"

"Yep. What's the point of your turning badman, boss? It escapes me."

"The point is, if I get in solid with Gripus, sooner or later I'll get Whitney's stuff back."

"It better be sooner."

"You're telling me?"

I cut out of work early. Before going, I asked the master control board, "You know where the money and bonds are stashed?"

"It's my job to know."

"Just checking. If worse comes to worse and I don't make it back, better tell em about it."

"Have no fear."

"Yeah, I'll try not to. But it won't be easy."

Downstairs I withdrew a wad of money from my bank, headed home. I broiled a steak, baked a couple of potatoes, tossed a salad. I needed a hearty meal. All condemned men get one. Besides I didn't know when I'd have another chance for a leisurely chow. I washed the whole mess down with a couple mugs of beer. I got a laser handgun out of my closet, saw that it was in working order.

I reached for the phone to make a last phone call.

"Is Fingers there?" I asked.

"Hang on a minute." I could hear voices, laughter, music. The Calypso Casino was going full tilt.

"Hello?" a voice said.

"Fingers?"

"Yeah. Who's this?"

"I don't want to give any names over the wire. We had dealings a couple days ago."

"Oh."

"Listen, I need you again."

"If it's about that little matter we discussed earlier, I've hit a brick wall. Absolutely solid. Sorry."

"Don't be sorry," I said. "You get another chance to earn some bread. Only this is something else. I'm in a jam. I'll need a place to lay low."

"You're *serious*?"

"Uh-huh. Dead serious. This'll blow over in time. But till it does, I'm going to be hot. Will you help me?"

"Yeah. If the price is right."

"It'll be perfect."

"Okay. For when?"

"Tomorrow. Things'll start heating up around noon, I figure. I'll want to be all tucked away by then."

"I think I can manage that."

"Swell. How do we get together?"

"Call me in the morning." He gave me a number. "Around nine thirty."

"Thanks. I'll need some contacts, too. I've got stuff to unload."

Fingers lowered his voice. "A fence?"

"Bigger than that."

"Bigger?"

"The top."

"You don't want much."

"I can pay my way. There'll be enough for everyone."

"It's your show. I don't get it. What's gotten into you?"

"Greed."

"That I can understand."

"I figured you might, Fingers."

Chapter 13

It wasn't a nice day.

Rain came down heavy and fast. Tall buildings glistened wetly around me. I wondered what was going on in the office. The mere thought of the office depressed me. I looked at my watch. Ten thirty. Fingers was late. I shifted the umbrella. I was cutting it a bit close. In another couple of hours the fat'd be in the fire. I wanted to be off the streets by then. A cop in a black slicker, walking his beat, passed within a couple of feet. I tilted the umbrella over my face, shrank back against the show window I'd been leaning on. Great. I was developing all the earmarks of a two-bit lamster. In advance, yet. If I was going to bring this off, I'd have to show more class.

A black, shiny coupe curved out of traffic, pulled up to the curb. A hand attached to a body and face I didn't know motioned to me out of a half-opened window. I walked over to the car. "Fingers sent me," the heavyset pug behind the wheel told me. "Get in."

I got in and we drove away. I sat in the backseat and looked at the close-cropped gray hair and large ears of the driver. Neither of us spoke. I glanced out at the tall buildings. In a couple of minutes they were gone. Downtown Happy City was left behind. Along with my innocent past.

My chauffeur chose the highdrive. It just about carried me past my building. A few more feet and I could've stepped back into my very own living room.

I wouldn't've minded one bit. The whole thing was starting to seem screwy, as unlikely as a three-headed moth. What was I doing here? I tried to remember what prompted me to do this nutty thing. The prospect of losing my job? The money? They didn't seem so important now.

We hit ground level again and started working our way through the slums. Dingy buildings seemed to tilt at us as we drove by. Rain beat against car top, windows and windshield. There were few people around, as if the inclement weather had washed them from the neighborhood.

We drove into a side alley, parked beside a two-story wood and shingle building. "In there," my driver gestured with a thumb.

"Fingers inside?"

"Later."

I got out. The car backed up and drove away. I turned the knob on a wooden door, stepped into a narrow, dark hallway. "Anyone home?" I called. No one answered. I went into a living room, snapped on a table lamp, shrugged out of my wet raincoat, tossed it on the couch and went to inspect my new home. It wasn't much. The ground floor consisted of a living room, bedroom, kitchen and bathroom. The furniture was old and worn. Cheap faded linoleum covered the kitchen floor. I looked in the fridge. Half-full. At least someone was expecting me. I climbed rickety stairs to the first floor. It was a repeat of what I'd already seen. I went back to the downstairs living room, settled into an easy chair, and waited for things to happen.

It took a little while.

Around twelve forty-five, I turned on the Tele-

vista. A daytime soap was flailing away at the airways. Turning down the sound, I let the seconds tick away. I was rewarded for my patience some fifteen minutes later. My face popped up on the screen as the first item on the one o'clock Happy City news. I turned up the sound. The story was short and sweet: it told how I—the director of the largest security firm in Happy City—had absconded with an unspecified, but large, amount of city bonds. Miss Follsom was briefly interviewed. "I can't believe it," she told the cameras. Who could? The office was visible in the background. The authorities said something about rounding me up in short order, as if I were a stray herd of cattle. I didn't wish em good luck. The newscast moved on to a bathing-beauty contest, and I clicked off the set.

Fingers Malone showed up a little after two o'clock.

"You really did it, didn't you?" he grinned good-naturedly, taking off his black raincoat and tossing it next to mine.

"Sure," I said smartly.

"You know, somehow I thought you were stringing me, Dunjer."

"Why should I? This is straight—too straight."

"So I see. How much did you get?"

"Plenty. More than two hundred grand."

Fingers whistled. "That's not chicken feed, is it?"

"It's enough," I said modestly.

The round-faced man nodded, looked at me shrewdly. "But there's more to it than the dough, right?"

"Maybe." I didn't have to try sounding evasive: I *was* evasive.

"Come on, don't kid me, Dunjer. You were sitting

pretty at Security Plus. What made you pull a stunt like this?"

"I was all washed up at that place, Fingers. This business with Whitney finished me."

"H-m-m-m. I guess it might."

"Uh-huh. But I know a couple of things too; things I learned on the job. They're worth more than I got now—lots more."

"So you're going to play the angles?"

"That's it, Fingers. But I need help."

"Yeah?" Fingers looked interested.

"You get a piece of the action if you help me connect with Oswald Gripus."

"That won't be easy."

"What is?"

"I'll do what I can."

"That's all I ask."

The rain was still coming down hard some nine hours later. I was back in the coupe, only this time with a new driver. Fingers himself was doing the honors. Thunder crashed overhead like two giants bumping bellies. Lightning lighted up the night sky like a neon light festival. The windshield wipers took long swipes at the splashing rain, made it shimmer as we passed red and green traffic lights. I didn't mind. The rain helped hide me. By now I was Happy City's number-one celebrity. I'd made the afternoon editions of the *Daily Tattler* and all of its rivals. The Tele-vista channels were giving me a big play, too. A couple days more and there'd probably be Dunjer windup dolls in the kiddy stores. Where was all this attention when I needed it?

We drove through the downtown business section, passed within three blocks of the Security Plus building. Cheery Village came and went. We beat a fast retreat through Make-Shift Haven, a collection of clapboard dwellings and wooden shacks housing the indigent. Empty fields told us we'd left the city proper. The moneyed estates came next. Only some of the mansions were visible behind their screens of trees and shrubbery. We turned down a paved, tree-lined path, came to a large gate. Two men stepped from the gatehouse, approached our car. Fingers rolled down his window, exchanged some words with them. The shorter of the two returned to his post. The gates opened; Fingers drove through.

We parked in front of a large four-story house. A butler let us in the front door, took away our coats. A pert redhead led Fingers off for what she promised would be a diverting drink. I followed the butler down another hallway. A small man was at the end of it. He stared at me, turned a corner and was gone. It had looked like Gimpy Kreeg, the hood I'd braced at The Happy Hour. I shrugged mentally; it didn't seem important. Double doors were at the end of the hallway. I went through them.

I was in a huge living room. Plush brown, green and gold easy chairs, couches, drapes sank into a three-inch-thick rug. Paintings lined the walls. Mahogany end tables gleamed in the soft glow of silver-based floor lamps.

A gross figure got up from an easy chair at the far end of the room, stood waiting for me. Its hair was thinning; it had a huge belly and double chin; its nose was wide, lips thin. It wore a lot of rings on its pudgy fingers. It smoked a cigar and was in shirtsleeves and slippers. This short, fat creature was Oswald Gripus, underworld emperor of Happy City.

I went on over. We didn't bother shaking hands.

"So you're Dunjer," he sneered, "the big shot gumshoe-turned-thief."

I admitted it.

"Listen. Your being on my side of the fence don't cut no ice with me. I've had the hatchet out for you, shamus. Only up till now, I've missed." Gripus blew smoke my way. "I was too busy to slap you silly. Now you've saved me the trouble."

"Glad to oblige."

"I don't get it, shamus; no matter how you slice it, it's dumb, real dumb."

"Uh-uh. I can beat the rap."

"You're loco."

"Look Gripus. You really think I'd set myself up so the cops could nail me?"

"Yeah. That's what I think."

"Well, you're wrong. The law's got me pegged for the job because I was the last guy seen in the safety vault before the bonds skedaddled. Nobody saw me pinch the stuff."

Gripus leered at me. "But you did."

"Sure. Only who can prove it?"

"Bah!" Gripus chewed his cigar savagely. "They've got you dead to rights, shamus. You dusted out. You turned tail and ran."

"Uh-uh."

"What uh-uh?"

"I was kidnapped."

"Kidnapped?"

"Right. I got wind that something was up through a tip. So I went down to the safety vault myself for a look-see. The bonds were gone. But I came up with something that could've been a clue."

"And instead of yelling copper, you followed it up all by your lonesome. Who's gonna buy that?"

"Why not? The publicity would ruin us. Hushing it up'd be the most natural thing in the world."

"Says you."

"Yeah, me. After all, I run the outfit. Who should know if not me, eh, Gripus? Anyway, I follow up my lead, turn up the bad guys and get kidnapped for my trouble."

"Your story stinks. It's got so many holes, you could run a truck through it."

"Name one."

"The fall guy. The one you're gonna frame for the job. Where you gonna find him?"

"I thought maybe you'd lend a hand."

"*Me?*"

"Sure. I've got a deal."

"Deal? *You've* got a deal for *me?* Listen, punk. These bonds you stole. This big haul. That's nothing to me. That's just pocket money, small change. I don't waste my time playing for pennies."

I grinned. "Yeah. But even pennies add up, eh? This job I pulled, Gripus, was just act one."

"What's act two, shamus—your getting pinched?"

"Our cleaning up."

"You've got a screw loose, buster."

"Look. You're big, Gripus. But you could be bigger. You run crime in this burg. But you let the legit end go begging."

"Wise guy. I've muzzled in plenty. I've got my finger in lotsa pies. Take it from me."

"Now look who's talking small time," I complained. "I don't mean a kickback here, a percentage there. That's for the birds. Ever hear of high finance?"

Gripus chuckled. "Waddya want me to do, play the market?"

"Uh-uh. That's no better than the ponies. But how about *owning* the market?"

Gripus tapped my chest with a stubby finger. "Listen. It's one thing to push around some dumb storekeep. It's another to take on big business. They got cops and politicians on the take. They got laws. And they *know* about me."

"Sure. But they don't know about Cyrus Whitney. Not yet."

"Whitney? What's he got to do with anything?"

I smiled knowingly, seated myself in an armchair. Gripus plunked down in its twin, eyed me suspiciously. I said, "If I can show you how to cash in big, how to really rake in the chips, what's in it for me?"

Gripus made a face, as if remembering a taste that didn't quite agree with him. "Listen. I ain't never palled around with no flatfoot."

"What flatfoot? I've just run off with a satchel full of loot. Every cop in town is gunning for me. If I ever queered your play, it was strictly business, nothing personal. This is business, too, only much bigger. Let's say we bury the hatchet, start clean. We can both do ourselves a lot of good. What've you got to lose?"

Gripus thought it over. "I ain't got nothin' to lose," he finally said, "because if you step outta line, I swat you like a bug."

"That's the spirit," I said cheerfully.

"Okay," Gripus said. "Let's hear this great inside dope you got. I hope it's as good as your spiel."

"You know what happened to Whitney the other night?"

"Yeah. I heard a little something about it."

"Know who pulled the job?"

"Could be."

"That's what I figured. There were some papers along with the cash. In the right hands those papers are worth plenty."

"How?"

"That would be telling," I grinned. "You've got to leave me an ace or two."

"Looks more like you want the whole deck."

"Look," I said. "Without you I'm a sitting duck. I need you to cover me in the vault heist. I even need you to help me market the bonds, right? What would

I be doing here if I wasn't on the up-and-up? No one made me come, right? I tell you, Gripus, I'm after the buck now. And being here is the best way to get it. For both of us. Those papers won't mean beans to you. Or anyone else, either. You've got to remember this: as Security Plus chief I got an earful of things no one knows. We can get Whitney to play ball with us— if we get those papers. He won't have any choice. Whitney's the cash baron of Happy City. Get him on your string and you're set for life."

"So what do I gotta do, shamus, to get this king-size meal ticket?"

"Find out who popped the Whitney job. Then buy the papers from em."

"How do I know this stuff when I see it?"

"You don't. I'll have to check it out. If it's the straight goods, I'll give you the high sign."

"I ain't puttin' out dough till I know what's what," Gripus said.

"Yeah, that sounds reasonable." I sat there and thought it over, admiration for Gripus' reasonableness plainly on my face; at least I hoped so. After an appropriate time I said, "Look. You set up the meet, let me get a quick gander at these items. That's just to look over the merchandise, not to buy. This stuff may be the bunk. If it is, that's that. I hang onto my little secret, and we concentrate on turning the bonds into cash."

"Let's hear the other part."

"Sure. That's where we hit the jackpot. We huddle, see? If it's the straight goods, I come clean, spill what I know. If you go for the deal, you buy the stuff. We brace Whitney. Whatever comes out of it we split fifty-fifty. What could be neater?"

"Sixty-forty could be neater. It's my dough that goes on the line. That buys something. And like you said, I got the outfit. What are you without me, shamus? A number in the city pen. Think it over."

"I don't have to," I said earnestly. "You're right. I'm set to play it your way, Gripus."

"My way is the best way," Oswald Gripus said. "Okay, we'll give it a try."

I lay in bed, back in Fingers' hideout, tossing and turning. I was all alone, Fingers having long departed. I listened for the familiar sounds of my own flat. Nothing doing. There was only silence. It gave me the heeby-jeebies. So did just about everything else. I knew what I had to do. But I didn't know if I'd get the chance to do it. When I met the crooks, I'd simply offer them a staggering sum to return the photostats to Whitney. Then I'd tell Gripus that they had the wrong goods. I'd have Hennessy put back the missing bonds. But somewhere else. Maybe behind a crate. So it'd look like they'd been in the safety vault all along, only in the wrong place. Then I'd have to plead amnesia or something. Something *innocent* to account for my absence. Since I hadn't actually committed any crime, I'd be in the clear with the law. Gripus would be another story. I'd have to tell him I'd gotten cold feet, put back the bonds, and called a halt to my burgeoning life of evil. He might not like it, but he probably wouldn't kill me. Provided he bought my yarn about Whitney's papers being wrong. Of course, before any of these very chancy things even happened, I'd have to sell the crooks my scheme. Which meant getting 'em alone out of earshot of Gripus and his stooges. I wondered how I was going to manage that.

The guys that'd cracked Whitney's safe weren't just crooks, they were killers. I could still see the butler flopping down the stairs with part of his head gone. The more I thought about it, the worse it became. I stopped thinking about it and went to sleep.

Chapter 15

It rained again the next day.

I hustled out of bed at seven thirty sharp, as if an invisible alarm clock had gone off in my noggin. I shaved, showered and got dressed as though I really had someplace to go. Some laugh. For all the roaming I could do, I might've been up the river in the big house already. Just to show I could still exercise my freedom, I went and made breakfast: a large orange juice, a couple of fried eggs sunny-side up and three cups of coffee. Then I stood looking out the window at the rain. I hadn't been awake an hour and already I'd used up all the things I could do. Except one.

I turned on the Tele-vista and that made it a clean sweep. The early morning news was full of commercials, politicians, crime waves and sob stories. I was beginning to feel neglected when the Security Plus building sprang into view. The voice-over explained how the cops were still hunting for me. The Board of Directors had authorized an inventory of the whole security vault; it was felt I might've run off with a carload of other items. They were checking. Rumor had me crossing over into foreign turf with my pile of loot, but the cops figured I was still holed up in Happy City. They said it was only a matter of time till they bagged me.

My picture flashed on the screen: an old one, taken off an expired license. We eyed each other commiseratingly for a couple seconds. The voice-over urged all citizens to be on the lookout for slippery Tom Dunjer.

Fortunately things had changed a bit since that snapshot—mainly me. I wondered how long it'd take em to come up with something more recent. A day or two, maybe. I was running out of time and I'd hardly begun. My face vanished off the round screen, was replaced by two pugs beating each other up in the local fight club. I flicked off the Tele-vista and went back to see if the rain had become more interesting. It hadn't.

The call came sometime after three o'clock. I'd been dozing on the couch and almost crawled under it when the phone started jingling. I got hold of myself and picked up the receiver.

"Dunjer, this is Gripus."

"Yeah."

"I turned up your unknown parties."

"No kidding. So soon?"

"You bet, shamus. Them jokers who cracked that job ain't so unknown now."

"Great. They willing to do business?"

"That depends on the price."

"Uh-huh."

"I couldn't tell them the price on account of I don't know what I'm buying."

"I get the picture. You set up the meet?"

"Tonight. At nine thirty. Sound okay?"

"Yeah. I don't seem to have any other pressing engagements."

"That's what I figured. The where is 1050 Clark Street. That's a couple blocks east of skid row. Even the cops steer clear of Clark Street."

"It probably depresses em."

"Sure. But it's perfect for us."

"Us, eh? You going to be there too?"

"Gotta protect my investment. What're pals for?

There ain't no name on the door. It's the last one on the left. Got that?"

"Yeah."

"Okay. Don't get spotted by the cops, shamus. We need you."

"Don't worry."

The line went click.

I sat there trying to work out some strategy. With Gripus in on the act, I couldn't just lay it on the line for the bad guys. I'd have to use stealth. I'd have to size up the layout when I got there, play it by ear. A voice said, "You're in over your head, Dunjer." The voice was mine. It seemed to know what it was talking about.

Parking Fingers' jalopy by a bent fire hydrant, I climbed out onto the curb, stood looking around. The air was damp. The rain had stopped, and large puddles filled the cracked and pitted asphalt like tiny polluted lakes. They'd sure picked one hell of a spot. There were no cars, no people, no streetlamps, even. The two- and three-story frame houses which lined both sides of the block had been spiffy once, probably around the turn of the century. Now they were lopsided, ramshackled structures with boarded-up windows and broken-in doors. The quicker I finished my stint here, the better I'd like it. I glanced at my wrist watch: 9:30 sharp.

I moved across the street hunting for the right house. I wondered where the rest of the crew had parked. Maybe they were late? Maybe there'd been some change in plan? I almost missed 1050 when I got to it. The numbers were hardly visible on the weathered porch front. I got up close and used a match. Pay dirt. I went to the door, tried the knob. Rusty hinges squeaked as the door slid open. Not a glimmer of light from inside. I stared into the darkness. I listened for sounds. There was nothing at all.

I took a couple of hesitant steps into the blackness, fished my match pack out again, struck one. Shadows leaned across the wall. I was in a hallway. I could see the last door on the left. I moved toward it. The door swung in at my touch. I groped for the lightswitch, clicked it on. Nothing happened. I lighted a third match. The room was empty. Paint peeled off the cracked walls. Plaster lay on the floor. This joint had given up the ghost long ago. Maybe Gripus had decided to check out the goods on his own, sent me over here on a wild-goose chase. But why bother in the first place? I could've spent the next month holed up in Fingers' joint, none the wiser that *anything* had happened. I started to get that cold, creepy feeling that comes just before terrible trouble. My match went out. I lighted another, went slowly into the next room. Terrible trouble was lying on the floor, its mouth open and staring up at the ceiling. "It" was Oswald Gripus. He was lying in a puddle of blood. I bent down to touch the body. Still warm. Part of his jacket was singed and burned through. A laser wound. And why not? Bullets could be traced to specific guns. But lasers were all alike. Find a guy with a laser, or plant one near him and you had a potential fall guy.

Like me.

The match died.

I didn't waste time thinking over my next move. I just straightened up and moved.

I didn't need any light to show me where to go, either. Any direction which led out would do.

Except maybe for the front and back doors.

They'd be watched.

What wouldn't?

I got to a side window, peered out. I was looking into a dark, narrow alley. No one there. The house across the alley was only a few feet away, but for all the good that did me, it could've been miles. The windows—what I could see of em in the blackness— were boarded up tight.

I tried the other side of the house.

Another alley which led nowhere; another boarded-up tenement.

I stood there wondering what to do next.

Maybe I was wrong.

Maybe there was no one waiting outside. Gripus could've been followed here and done in by someone who had nothing to do with me. The others would've turned tail at the bloodletting and that might account for my lack of company.

Maybe.

Only I didn't believe it.

Years of sleuthing had taught me to trust my nose.

And my nose smelled setup.

I started up the stairs.

I'd reached the second floor when I heard the sirens. They came from a long way off. But they were growing louder.

The cops were in a big hurry to get somewhere.

I lighted another match, shielded it with my palm. The door to the attic was to my right. At first it wouldn't budge. I put my shoulder to it. The door popped open.

The sirens were still wailing. They seemed very close now; too close. I shut the door behind me, felt my way up the last staircase. I only had a couple of matches left; I didn't want to waste em.

I lighted my second-to-last one at the top of the stairs and took a quick look-see. Empty. There was no place to hide. But then I wasn't looking for a hiding place.

A ladder led up to a trap door.

Nothing happened when I reached the top—the door was stuck or locked. I dug the laser out of my pocket and fried a couple of holes in the wood. I shoved. The door came open.

I crawled out onto the roof, let the door drop quietly back into place.

I was alone under a dark overcast sky. Wind blew in from the waterfront. The rain had left puddles on the roof. I didn't hear the sirens anymore. I had a pretty good idea why.

I crawled through a couple of puddles, got to the edge of the roof, cautiously peered over the side. There were three squad cars down below. Four cops were piling out of the last one. The other two cars were empty; that meant their cargo had spilled into the house. The body would keep em busy for a very short while; then all hell'd break loose. I wanted to be long gone by then.

I chanced one last peek.

The cops weren't the only addition to the neighborhood. The rats had crawled out of the woodwork too. There was a guy loitering across the street. Another one further down the block. They were just barely visible in the glow of the prowl-cars' headlights. There'd be more, I knew, way back in the darkness. And out back, too. Just to make sure I didn't leave before the law showed up. A frame, plain and simple. Only by whom and why? I didn't know. At least I could scratch Gripus. Somehow that failed to give me the deep down satisfied feeling one might expect. Gripus had been axed by the same parties who were after my skin. In a way that made us buddies. It was nothing to cheer about.

Leaving my vantage point, I crawled away toward the middle of the roof. I peered into the darkness. The houses were only about four feet apart. I wouldn't need wings to make the jump, just a little luck. If I landed on a weak spot, I might go sailing right through the roof. And if someone saw me, I'd probably become a target for all kinds of weapons—all of em lethal. On the other hand, if I hung around here, I'd be finished no matter what.

I got up crouching like a runner waiting for the starting gun. I got my legs moving under me and made the leap.

I came down hard on hands and knees on the rooftop of the next house. I felt as if someone had been using me for a ping-pong ball. I'd made plenty of noise. The house I'd landed on was identical to the one I'd just left. There was no percentage in taking it easy. I scrambled up back into my runner's stance and headed for the next house.

Twelve houses down I'd reached the end of the line. I was sweating up a storm. My breath came in short unpleasant gasps. I'd also used up all the houses; this was the end of the block. The only way left now was down.

I used the rear fire escape. It shook with each step I took, but not as much as I was shaking. I could hear sirens again. Reinforcements on the way.

I stepped down into an almost pitch-black alley. Suddenly I had company.

Three gray shapes detached themselves from the darkness, lunged at me.

I twisted sideways, bent double. A fist went flying over my head. I used my foot to trip the first one, grappled with the second, a stout party, sent him crashing into the wall. The first guy was getting off the floor. The third one came right at me. Enough was enough.

I ducked out of the way, and ran out onto the street, groping for my laser. Behind me the three guys came charging out of the alley.

I sent a laser beam over their heads, turned a corner.

I heard shouts:

"Stop him!"

"There he goes."

"It's Tom Dunjer."

Well, that did it—now everyone knew! Or would, as soon as the cops caught up with these birds. Or me.

This block was just like the one I'd left. Except for one small difference. A streetlamp still in working order. Here was one streetlamp too many.

I turned in between two houses, dashed along a black alley, collided with some trash cans, righted myself and kept going.

I was in a backyard.

A wooden fence blocked my way. I didn't hesitate. A guy who's jumped across rooftops isn't going to be stopped by any wooden fence.

My fingers just reached the top. I pulled myself up like an old bag of potatoes, hoisted myself over, dropped to the ground.

There was more yelling going on. The name Dunjer was getting a big play. It sounded like more than three guys. The cops had probably joined the hunt.

I dashed out onto another street, turned another corner and kept going.

I could hear sirens starting up again.

I was one jump ahead of the law, but I knew it couldn't last. All of this racing around might've been just the thing for a well-oiled mech. As far as humans went, it was murder. I'd run out of steam long ago. Another couple of minutes and I'd be helpless. What

216

I needed was a good hiding place. Almost any house would do.

I chose the nearest. I didn't use the front door. I made my way around back. The door and windows were boarded up. So were the two cellar windows. But the boards were old and weathered. I pulled three away from one of the cellar windows, managed to crawl through. From inside I replaced em as best I could.

I had only one match left. I decided not to inspect the premises. It was no time to be choosy. Curling up in a corner, I went to sleep.

Chapter 17

I didn't wake up all at once. Sounds came to me. A dog was barking somewhere. I could hear traffic. That wasn't right. Even if I'd left my bedroom window open, street noises couldn't drift up this far. My bed seemed hard as a board. I shifted positions and drifted off back to slumberland.

I was running a race. I was out in front and winning. I had on shorts and track shoes. The fans in the bleachers were cheering me on. I gave it all I had. All wasn't enough. The pack of runners behind me was gaining. I could feel them breathing down my neck. I tried to go faster. My legs ached, my back ached, my arms ached. I knew then I was going to lose. The crowd began to boo.

I opened my eyes. I was lying on a hard wooden floor. Gray light came through cracks in the boarded-up windows. I seemed to hurt all over. My mouth tasted funny, as if I'd been chewing on old rags. I closed my eyes and then, very slowly, opened them again. The disgusting scene wouldn't go away.

I got my legs under me and stood up like a man who had suffered a long and debilitating illness learning to walk again. I remembered it all now, down to the last grisly detail, and wished I hadn't.

Now what?

First things first, Dunjer, I told myself; if you starve to death, brother, you've blown it. I dug into my pocket, fished out my wallet. I'd prudently stashed two grand in it. For the time being I'd be able to pay my way, even buy breakfast, maybe. My clothes were a mess. Sleeping in em had done nothing to get me on the ten-best-dressed list. I looked as if I was just coming off a six-day drunk. I felt my chin; it was coated with stubble. I got my comb out to comb my hair down— uncharacteristically—over my forehead but decided against it. I didn't want to disturb the natural grimy and tangled effect. I was all set—or as set as I was ever going to be.

Shoving the boards out of the way, I pulled myself up through the basement window.

I was in a backyard. The sky was gray, overcast. The houses around me looked even worse than they had the night before, like structures too rotten even to be condemned. I got out of there.

The streets were still deserted for a few blocks; then they started to fill up. I put my jacket collar up, jammed my hands into pockets and broke into a slow shuffle. Nobody gave me a second glance.

A tired collection of run-down bars and dingy flop-houses was on both sides of the street. A blinking neon sign over the corner movie house spelled out Nudies in bright red letters. The potential customers, as far as I could see, looked too far gone to be inter-ested in nudies. The bums who weren't guzzling whiskey in the bars overflowed onto the streets, sat on the curb, stood in doorways, lay singly and in pairs in the gutter.

I hobbled along for a couple of more blocks, shielded—I hoped—by my newfound anonymity. I stopped at a newsstand, glanced at the headlines. I stood there staring at em like a man who's just found his name posted in the death-notice column. My mouth slowly fell open as if it were being operated by two rusty jaw springs. I wanted to get away fast, but I couldn't move my legs, as though they had secretly been riveted to the pavement.

The name Dunjer had made the headlines on every sheet on the stand. I'd gone to sleep a mere safecracker and overnight been promoted to Grade-A killer. FORMER SLEUTH SLAYS CRIME KINGPIN IN UNDERWORLD SHOOTOUT, a subheadline reported. POLICE SEEK OUTLAW DICK, another one explained. My picture was on every front page. At that it could've been worse. Only one had been snapped during the last five years. The rest all belonged to yesteryear. With some luck no one would associate the trimmer, spiffier me of long ago with the deadbeat derelict I'd just become.

The newsie—an old wizened party—glanced up at me indifferently and went back to reading his scratch sheet. I got my legs moving and shuffled off. It was no act this time; I had all the pep of a ninety-year-old at the end of a very long day. Too bad my day was just beginning.

I forgot about breakfast. My appetite had flown the coop. I had to get to a phone. Any second now, someone might spot me. Dunjer the thief could've always given himself up. A pair of raised hands and a friendly grin would've done the trick. But Mad Dog Dunjer was another story. I'd be fair game for every gun-happy cop in town.

My Whitney mission was a washout, and now that I'd become Happy City's number-one fugitive, my chances of working some deal for him were reduced to absolute zero. The question was could I work some deal for myself?

I turned in at a cigar store, dialed Whitney's private

number. It rang and rang. I hung up and tried his other one with the same results. That wouldn't do. Cyrus Whitney was my ace in the hole. I needed him now. Whitney could call a press conference, explain that I was on an undercover job for him. I'd show up in the middle of the shindig, give em the rest of it. I'd return the dough to the safety vault. With my criminal career exposed as a hoax, whatever crooked motive I might've had for doing in poor Gripus would evaporate; at least I hoped so. If not, I could always hire some legal advice, a darn sight better than dodging cops' bullets any day.

But to do all that I first had to reach Whitney. I put the coin back into the slot, dialed his office. The girl at the switchboard gave me his secretary.

"I'd like to speak to Cyrus Whitney," I told her.

"Who is calling please?"

I gave her the name we'd settled on. "Mr. Dant."

"Does Mr. Whitney know you?"

"Yeah. He's in, eh?"

"Yes, Mr. Dant. If you will hold on for just one moment."

I held on.

The secretary came back on the line. "I am sorry, Mr. Dant, Mr. Whitney is in conference. If you will leave your number, he will call you back."

"Back? When?"

"I really don't know, Mr. Dant. Mr. Whitney may be tied up for the afternoon."

"You *did* give him my name?"

"Of course."

"Thanks."

I hung up. Either Whitney had forgotten who Dant was, or he was trying to pull a fast one. Either way it didn't look as if he were going to be much use to me now. What the hell. If worse came to worse, I could hold my own press conference. Right at Security Plus. After all, I had the tape of my chat with Whitney to back me up. It'd spill the beans about everything, but those were the breaks. What choice did I have?

I put another coin in the slot, dialed my office.

"Yes?" a voice answered; one of the mech operators.

"Miss Follsom, please."

The voice hesitated. "Miss Follsom is not available."

"Listen," I said, "this is an emergency."

"I am *very* sorry."

"Not as sorry as you'll be if you don't put me through to Miss Follsom on the double!"

"I beg your pardon. . . ." The voice was all ice.

"Have a heart, chum; this really *is* an emergency. Scout up Miss Follsom, eh? I know she's there."

"Well," the metallic voice said petulantly, "that's where you're dead wrong. She *isn't* here. She's gone."

"Gone where?"

"How should I know? She took a leave of absence yesterday. There, now I've told you. I'm sure it was none of your business."

"Don't be so sure. Let me speak to Hennessy."

"My goodness, you certainly can pick them."

"What is it?" I asked. "Hennessy's on his coffee break?"

"Don't be inane," the voice said.

"Hennessy's gone too?"

"Exactly."

"You're kidding."

"Why don't you speak to someone else?" the mech urged.

"Because I don't want to. When did Hennessy go."

"Yesterday."

"Another leave of absence?"

"Of course."

"You wouldn't know where *he* went, eh?"

"Naturally not. What do you take me for, a busy-body?"

"Perish the thought."

I hung up. A fine kettle of fish. Both gone. I couldn't believe it. What had they done, run off with each other? Miss Follsom was the keeper of my telltale spool, the one that blew the whistle on the whole Whitney operation. Without it I was a lost cause. There went the only proof I had. I could already hear the cell door slamming shut behind me—provided I lasted that long.

I looked up both Hennessy and Miss Follsom in the city phone directory. Anything was worth a try. I dialed one, then the other. Both rang long and earnestly. Neither answered.

Chapter 18

My first thought was to go and bushwhack Whitney. Like a lot of first thoughts, it wouldn't wash. Maybe I could twist his arm and sit on him, but when I finally dragged him off to the cops, there was no guarantee he'd come clean. He could sing any song he wanted, and I was willing to lay odds I'd hate the words no matter what they were.

There was no one left to call. I shuffled out of the cigar store, went back to the street. It hadn't changed any in the fifteen minutes I'd been away. Derelicts, bums, hobos and panhandlers littered the pavement. The bars and junk shops still looked sour. Crumbly tenements rose on the adjoining streets like monuments to decay. What had changed was me. I'd gone into that phone booth with at least a fighting chance of pulling through this thing, of being ruined, maybe, but staying out of the clink. All that was gone. Just staying alive was going to prove a hardship.

I hobbled along wondering what had happened. Hennessy and Miss Follsom skipping was plain inexplicable. Whitney was easier to figure. Maybe he'd gotten wind of the foul-up. And instead of owning up to his end in the deal—and landing in the hoosegow—was sitting it out, waiting for things to develop. Maybe sooner or later he'd have to own up, but maybe not. The crooks might even contact him, strike a bargain. Meanwhile he was letting me go to the dogs. Why not —what did he have to lose?

So what was I going to do about it?

Not a damn thing. Unless I got hold of that tape spool.

I couldn't leave the district till dark; I'd attract too much attention in my current getup. And if I got spruced up, I'd attract even more. Too many cops were on the prowl for me. At least here I was all but invisible. Who would look twice at a bum?

I had time to kill. I ambled along for a couple of blocks, came across a two-bit eatery that looked crowded enough, went in, ordered coffee, rolls, ham and eggs at the counter, carted em off to a far table in the corner and ate undisturbed.

Outside again, I took in some more sights, found a crummy park near the edge of skid row, parked myself on a peeling bench and let the hours slip by. I got up to grab another bite once, considered taking in the nudie show but decided against it, bought an afternoon tabloid and read how the cops were scouring the city for me. After awhile it began getting dark. I got up and started walking. Soon I'd left skid row far behind.

The Security Plus building was closed down for the night. I stood in a doorway across the street staring at it. So much had happened to me since I'd last been there that it seemed like another world.

I got my legs moving and crossed the street. I stuck to the shadows on the other side. Sticking to em had got me this far, and I wasn't going to give up a good thing now; I had so few left.

I could see the mech doorman standing by the front entrance. I'd been his boss once, but what can you expect from a mech; if he spotted me now, it'd mean a one-way ticket to the lockup. I still had the master control cube in my pocket. But monkeying with a mech in public view spelled trouble. And I had enough trouble as it was.

I went around the next building, cut through a side alley, made my way between some large trash bins and found myself at one of the back doors of the Security Plus building.

Naturally enough, Security Plus guarded its own building. No mech watchman blocked my progress. But an intricate system of wires, relays and alarms did just as well. I got out my master control cube and put em out of commission.

I pushed open the door, stepped into a dim corridor. At least I was no stranger here. I knew this place like the back of my hand.

I got to the door I wanted, opened it just like the other and went down a long flight of metal stairs. I repeated this simple operation two more times and found myself in the subbasement. No mechs were scattered along this route. I'd never assigned any.

A direct speed lift went from the subbasement to the Security Plus floor. I boarded it and was whisked up to the former scene of my employment. No time to shed a nostalgic tear. I had a job to do.

Going straight to Miss Follsom's office, I set to work on her desk.

It didn't take long. No spools. No notes or memos indicating where one might be. Nor was there any hint of where Miss Follsom might be. Searching the rest of her office got me nowhere.

My heart wasn't in it, but I tried Hennessy's office next. I could've saved myself the time. Hennessy too had failed to leave any enlightening missives behind; they usually do when they powder out.

Only why now?

One hell of a time for both of em to take off—especially since they were the only ones who knew what I was up to. In fact it had to be more than coincidence. Maybe their guilty knowledge brought em together and they decided to elope? I thought it over. It didn't seem likely. Intuition, insight and the fact that Miss Follsom once told me Hennessy wasn't her type all but ruled that out.

"All but" of course was the rub. How could I be sure? Easy. They wouldn't choose this particular time when I was in such a terrible pickle—would they? For the sake of long years of friendship, I had to assume not.

Leaving what?

The possibility that maybe their hurried departure had something to do with *me*.

I stood there in Hennessy's office and let that sink in. Then I turned off the light, shut the door behind me and went down the corridor to my own office. Since it faced out on the main drag, I pulled the blinds before clicking on the light.

Nothing had changed—yet. Give em time, I knew, and they'd turn the whole place upside down. I had an almost overpowering urge to sit down at my desk, close my eyes and wait for the stinking mess to go away. If nothing else, it'd feel normal. Not much had for a while.

I chucked the notion, went to the master control board and switched on the talkie tube.

There was dead silence.

"Well, say something," I said.

"You certainly look a mess."

"Thanks."

"I gather things have not worked out entirely to your satisfaction?"

"Put mildly, that's about right. You didn't make a copy of that tape you gave me by any chance?"

"Of course not."

"That figures. You wouldn't know what became of Miss Follsom, Hennessy or the tape itself, would you?"

"Not the tape. Miss Follsom and Hennessy left together. Prior to their departure Mr. Hennessy phoned one Spike McGraw. Does the name mean anything to you?"

"McGraw? Vaguely."

"Your two colleagues arranged to meet him."

"And?"

"And what? That's all. There isn't any more. They left an hour later. Who can tell what happened after that?"

I sighed. "I guess you'd better give me a printout on this McGraw character."

A sheet of paper instantly rolled through the slot.

The master control board said, "I hope you understand that I'm really not supposed to do this. However, in view of our long association . . ."

"Thanks loads."

I snapped off the talkie switch, glanced over McGraw's printout. He was some cookie. There wasn't much that McGraw had done in his life that wasn't crooked. All penny ante as far as I could see. A pork-and-beaner from the word go. Not exactly the type of guy either Hennessy or Miss Follsom would choose to pal around with. But then nothing was going the way it was supposed to anymore. Time to do something decisive.

I used the bathroom to wash up; I shaved with an electric razor I kept around the office, took a swig out of my spare whisky bottle and went down the hall to the mechs' costume room. The mechs often went out in disguise and while I couldn't use their more esoteric getups, which usually consisted of something made up of nuts and bolts, I found plenty that I could use. By the time I was done, some twenty minutes later, my own mother wouldn't've recognized me. My nose was long, I wore wire-frame glasses, my hair was parted dead center in the middle and flattened back with stickum. I had a small beard and moustache. I picked out a spiffy pinstripe vested suit. I looked like a visiting college professor. That's how I wanted to look.

I doused the lights, locked up behind me, and used the speed lift to carry me to the basement. The control cube shorted the mech guard. I went to my locker, got it open and started counting money. When I hit two hundred grand I stopped. I stuffed bills in all the pockets of my pants and jacket. I didn't know what I'd need em for. But a guy who's well-heeled is always better off than a bum. For all I knew, I wouldn't be coming back this way very soon—if ever.

I closed the locker, retraced my steps and went away the way I'd come.

Chapter 19

Decator Street was a low-rent district. It was three miles and a couple of cuts removed from skid row. Small grocery stores, a couple of quiet bars, a filling station squatted under the five- and six-story tenements. I paid the cabby and he drove away. I was seeing more of the town than I had in years—and liking it less by the minute.

I crossed to 1201 Decator, pushed open the wooden door. A small light glowed in the dusty hallway. S. McGraw was in 4B. I didn't ring the bell. The inner door was locked; my picklock opened it. I went up the staircase. I didn't make any noise. I used the picklock a second time on 4B. I opened the door very quietly, stepped in. Darkness. Digging a pencil flashlight out of my pocket, I took inventory. No one in the small, sparse living room. Two doors faced me. I tried one. The kitchen. I tried the other. A bedroom. The bed was unmade but no one was in it. I could've saved myself the trouble of tiptoeing around. I went to work frisking the joint. Twenty minutes later I'd come up with empty hands. I had nowhere to go anyway. I plunked down in one of the worn living-room chairs, turned off my flash and waited.

It was two twenty before I heard the steps in the hallway. The front door opened and the overhead lights snapped on.

A medium-sized, balding man with a thin moustache and wrinkled suit stood staring at me by the open door.

231

I waved my laser at him. "Shut it," I said.

He shut it.

"Come here," I said.

He stepped over slowly. "Listen, mister, if this is a heist . . ."

"It's not. Sit down," I said.

He sat down.

"You're McGraw?"

"That's right, mister. Mind if I smoke?"

I leveled the laser at him. "Sure. Go ahead. Only watch those hands."

Very slowly McGraw pulled a pack of smokes out of his jacket pocket, lighted one. He blew smoke at the ceiling, fixed his gaze on me. "That's better. You startled me, mister. So if this ain't no heist, what is it?"

"Business," I said, using the magic word.

"Yeah," McGraw said meditatively. "I can feature that. Only why the hardware?"

"That's in case we don't see eye to eye."

"I'm very reasonable when it comes to business," McGraw assured me.

"I hope so. You were contacted by two pals of mine, McGraw."

"Yeah? What about?"

"That's what I want to know."

McGraw shrugged. "Who were they?"

"Mike Hennessy and a girl."

"Ah. That pair."

"You know them, eh?"

"Sure. You mentioned something about business."

"Uh-huh."

"How much business?"

"A C-note."

"And you want to know what?"

"Everything."

"Everything ain't so much, mister."

"I'll settle for what you give me—if it seems on the up-and-up."

"You say you're a pal of theirs?"

"Yeah. And I want to get hold of em."

"Well, that's gonna be kinda tough." Spike McGraw wagged his head good-naturedly. "But a deal's a deal. I get the C-note no matter what?"

"No matter what. In advance." I put the laser back in my coat pocket, got my wallet out and peeled off a C. I gave it to McGraw. "Shoot."

"Well, okay. You ain't a cop, are you?"

"Do I look like a cop?"

"Okay, you paid your dough, so I'll level with you. There ain't no way you can see them because they ain't here no more."

"Where's here?"

"Happy City."

"What're you talking about?" I knew I'd gotten something wrong. Happy City was surrounded by a swarm of hostile City-States. No one in his right mind would want to cross borders. It meant either the firing squad or the pen.

"Yeah, mister, I know there ain't a lotta candidates for that kinda travel. But we always get a few. And your couple turned out to be one of them."

"Where'd they go?"

"Labor City."

"Jeezus."

"Yeah. That's some dump, ain't it?"

"Just like that, they upped and took off for Labor City?"

"Who knows? Maybe they been planning it for

years. You can never tell with folks who go in for crazy stunts like that. Maybe they got some hidden gripe, maybe they hanker for good old honest manual labor? Maybe they just got a screw loose. Anyway, your friends are long gone."

"How'd you get em out?"

"Me? I don't get no one out. I just send them to the Inter-City Escape League. For a fee."

"Those crackpots?"

"Who else? It takes all kinds."

I sighed. "I've got to get in touch with em."

"The League?"

"Yeah. Can you take me?"

"Look, mister, if I can take *them*, I can take *you*. But that costs another C-note. Right?"

"Right."

"Okay, mister. You follow me."

McGraw drove. Streetlamps, traffic lights sent brief flickers through the car windows, as if the city were beaming a secret message at us. Once McGraw parked, got out to use a pay phone. I could understand his problem: the Escape League was about as legal as bludgeoning citizens in broad daylight. McGraw couldn't bring just anyone around for a visit. And as far as he knew, I was just anyone—maybe even worse, like a cop. I'd let McGraw worry about it; he'd come up with something.

I didn't even bother paying attention to where we were going. As head of Security Plus I would've been busy trying to memorize every inch of the way. As Dunjer, the fugitive, I couldn't care less. I had other concerns. Trying to make sense of what Hennessy and Miss Follsom were up to was more than I could manage. For all I knew, they'd come up with some case that meant getting the goods on the League or contacting someone in Labor City. It was possible—about as possible as my running for mayor. Hennessy might go for a job like that—if he were the last man or mech left in the office and someone held a gun to his head. But Miss Follsom, never. She was an exec, not a field operative. She'd had no training in the rough and tumble of undercover work. Only pure madness could account for her taking on a field assignment.

Not to mention the fact that both she and Hennessy were leaving me in the lurch.

I sat back and closed my eyes. What a mess. Getting

from one city to another was a major undertaking all by itself. No doubt things'd been smoother in the old days when the Federal Government ran the show. But the old days were long gone. Everyone had worked for the Feds then. And when the Feds went broke, so did everyone else. Caused a lot of bad feeling. Bad Feeling Village sprang up that very year, in fact. Followed by Privateville and Hands-Offberg. The foreign markets crashed too. Cities took over everywhere. At first folks could move around some. But after a while things became sort of fixed. Yeah, things might've been smoother in the old days, but had they been any better? Would they *ever* be better?

The car came to a stop. I looked around to see where I was. Large, dark buildings loomed on both sides of the street. Somewhere in the warehouse district, by all appearances. I didn't know where.

"We're here, mister."

We climbed out of the car.

"This way," McGraw said, starting for the largest of the buildings.

"Your friend's in there, eh?"

"Now they are. Next time, they'll be someplace else. They move around lots."

A side door let us into a dimly lit interior. Crates and boxes were neatly stacked on the floor. We worked our way around em, came to a door; it led into an office.

A small man sat behind a desk; his arms were folded. He had on a dark blue suit, white shirt and narrow black tie. He wore a black hood over his head, with two cutouts for the eyes.

"This is the guy," McGraw said.

The small man nodded. "What can we do for you, pal?"

I stood very still and looked at the little guy. I almost laughed. I raised my voice a notch and said, "Am seeking old friendships, is feeling deserted without them."

McGraw raised his eyebrows, stared at me.

The little guy said, "Is that so?"

I wagged my head. "Is so," I assured him. "Only is needing to chat with you alone."

McGraw looked at the little guy; the little guy looked at McGraw, shrugged. "Why not?"

"He's got a laser," McGraw said.

"Who hasn't these days?" the hooded guy asked. "He have any dough?"

"He's carrying a roll."

"Well, that's the important part, ain't it?"

McGraw shrugged both shoulders as though trying to brush away everything that was happening. "You're the boss," he said.

McGraw turned on his heel, left closing the door behind him. I listened to his fading footsteps, heard the street door shut. I pulled at my moustache; it came away in my hand. I did the same for my beard. I turned to the little man at the desk. "Okay, Sampson, let's cut the crap."

The small man pulled off his head mask, grinned at me. "You didn't have me fooled for a second, Dunjer," Lionel, Baby Face Sampson, said.

Sampson poured me another drink, said, "I figure you can use this."

"You figure right."

I was seated in a straight-backed chair next to Sampson's desk. He poured himself a second drink, too, said, "Cheers."

"Listen, Sampson," I said. "What gives with this setup?"

"Just what you'd imagine. Some wants in, some wants out. We help them get what they want. There's money in it."

"But Jeezus, Sampson, the Inter-City Escape League!"

"It's better than pushing dope, no?"

"The League's supposed to be a bunch of loonies," I complained.

"You ever get a load of the screwballs who sign up for the tour?" Sampson chuckled. "The management, though, is something else. But we don't mind the loony tag. It keeps the cops hunting in the wrong places."

"You in this alone?"

"Me and some of the boys. That's only in Happy City, of course. The guys in the other burgs run their end of the show."

"You could've fooled me."

"We *did* fool you. We fooled everyone. We expect to go on fooling everyone."

"But now I know."

Sampson laughed. "Look who knows. You're number one on everybody's wanted list. Now what can I do for you?"

"More than last time, I hope. I'm trying to track down two of my ops. I hear they passed this way."

"If you mean Hennessy and the Follsom dame, you hear okay."

"They really went to Labor City?"

"The very place."

"Why, for heaven's sake?"

Sampson grinned, shrugged. "That's an interesting question. You figure we ask that question of everyone who comes through here?"

"No."

"Well, we didn't ask them either."

I sat back in the chair, took a last swallow of my drink. "I've got to find em."

"That's going to be tough."

"Can you get me to Labor City?"

"Sure. If you got the bread."

"I got it."

"It's two grand, Dunjer."

"I'll pay."

"Yeah, I almost forgot. Now that you're a public enemy, you've come into some dough. How much was in that safety vault?"

"Don't believe everything that's in the papers, Sampson."

"No need for modesty. We're both in the same racket. Your two ops got something you want, is that it?"

"You could say so."

Sampson grinned. "Well, Dunjer, pal, we've been pals a long time. So let me tell you something. You can't cross over cold. The law on the other side'll nab you in nothing flat. You need connections once you get there."

"You tell my ops, too?"

"Yeah. As a matter of fact, I did."

"It costs extra, eh?"

"Another grand, Dunjer."

"Cheap at any price, Sampson."

Chapter 21

It took a day to make arrangements.

I took it easy, cooled my heels in Sampson's warehouse. The Tele-vista kept me company when I wasn't sleeping, brought me news about my favorite person, namely me.

I was making a splash, all right.

The law had finally come up with a suitable photo. I could see myself on the screen just the way I'd looked last year. So could everyone else in Happy City. I was almost glad I was leaving. I could hardly wait for what would happen when I came back. *If* I came back.

The most startling item on the screen had to do with the safety vault. A lot of dough was missing, more than the cops had at first figured. They were still busy adding it up. If the cops were right, I'd probably go down in the books as the Supercrook of the Decade—a distinction I hardly deserved.

This last item had me stumped. It could've been pure baloney, a foul-up in simple addition anywhere along the line. Or maybe a phony story being played up just because it made headlines. The dough I'd swiped was nothing to sneeze at. But not the take the networks were hinting at.

I put this problem at the bottom of my lengthening problem list—one which was beginning to seem endless—and waited for the day to wind down.

* * *

"Good luck," Sampson said.

"Thanks."

We shook hands.

"You know what to do?"

"Uh-huh, I hope so."

"I hope so, too—for your sake."

I was done up in a pair of overalls and a work shirt. I carried a metal lunchbox full of my valuables. "My two ops go out this way?"

"Yep."

"Well, what's good enough for the help ought to be good enough for the boss, eh?"

I climbed into the wooden crate.

I could hear em nailing it shut on the outside.

I don't know how long I slept. My back felt as if I'd been resting in a vise. My legs were tingling and numb as though all the blood had been drained out of em.

I'd been bounced around on a truck till I felt like a pair of dice. Then I'd waited on a loading platform along with a lot of other crates. I could see em out of a peephole. The other crates, unlike me, seemed to take the waiting in stride, which was natural enough, since they were mostly hardware. Specialized mech machinery was about the sole item we exported to Labor City. Labor City was a bit old-fashioned in some ways: they liked their labor done by human hands. But some jobs needed that special touch.

After a while mechs appeared and began loading the crates. The doors were sealed, and the mech-powered train pulled out of the station.

I rattled around like a set of loose teeth.

After hours of rattling—which seemed like days, and maybe even months—the train began to slow down. Probably I was in Labor City. I didn't find out for a couple more hours, even after the train had stopped. No one showed up to unseal the doors and unload the merchandise. That's when I fell asleep. You couldn't blame me. There wasn't a whole lot else to do.

I was awakened by voices—human ones.

I put my eye to the peephole. Two guys had begun to unload. I liked their taste in clothing—it was identical to mine. I sat back and waited my turn.

It came by and by.

I was in a freight yard. I kept my eye glued to the peephole. When the pair of unloaders climbed back into the train car and no one else seemed in hailing distance, I pushed hard on the side of the crate. It opened like a door and I crawled out. Since I was already on my hands and knees, I saw no reason to straighten up. I didn't even know if I could. I crawled along. There were rows of crates and boxes here waiting to be carted off to their destinations. I used em for cover. After I'd gone some distance from the train, I chanced a look-see. Trains. More crates. A depot. Some folks on the move. I could see buildings beyond the station. No one seemed to be looking my way.

I straightened up and, clutching my lunch box, marched out toward civilization. Or at least the version they were practicing in these parts.

Labor City hustled and bustled around me. Bill-boards proclaimed: WORK IS LIFE. Neon lights spelled out: THE COUNCIL PLANS. Signs read: DO IT YOURSELF. Lord knows I was trying to.

Little square-topped cars, scooters and bicycles clogged the streets. I waited my turn, crossed at the light.

A poster read: Groffs' Is an Honest Work Shirt. Ex-change Your Wages for a Groffs. It's Swell. I kept glancing at the map Sampson had given me. A house, somewhere on the other side of town, was marked with an X. That was my destination. I decided to hoof it. I didn't want to mix with the locals unless I had to. I didn't know their folkways well enough to rub shoulders with em. I might give myself away by a wrong word, a misplaced allusion. I thought of hop-ping a hack but didn't know if they even had any in this neck of the woods. Sampson had provided me with a hefty sample of the local dough. It'd cost me plenty, but now I had a lot of change. What I didn't know was what it bought. A couple of buses went by; I looked at em wistfully and kept walking. I seemed to blend in okay with the street crowd. The overalls and work shirt looked like the national uniform. There were other outfits, too. All of em would prob-ably stand up under an honest day's work. I didn't see any briefcases. There were plenty of lunch boxes. The place was getting me down. At least no one had pinched me for being an interloper. On the other hand, there was still lots of time; I hadn't done anything yet.

I hit the center of town. No office buildings, no department stores, no theaters. Factories stretched off into the distance. Large, small, all shapes and sizes. I didn't know what went on in em. Maybe all this was only architecture. Maybe inside was a dreamland. I didn't bother asking.

I stood across the street and looked at the house. It was just a house. Plain, unadorned, identical to all the houses to the right and left of it. I checked the number again against the one Sampson had given me. It matched. "Here goes nothing," I said and crossed the street.

The name on the bell was John Beezer.

I rang, was rewarded by an instant answering buzz. I went into a carpeted hallway, trudged up a flight of stairs. My legs weren't doing any too well; all this walking made em feel old and beat-up—just like their owner.

The door of apartment 2A was open when I reached it. I stepped in. A heavyset man with blond curly hair was waiting for me.

"Sampson sent me," I told him.

"You're Dunjer?"

I said I was.

"This way."

I followed him into a living room. Two men and a woman were there. The woman was tall, angular, in her forties. One of the men was youngish, short. The other was medium sized, in his mid-thirties. All four wore work clothes.

"The committee," the blond man said. "I'm Beezer. That's Blake, Corrigan and Linda Dowland."

"Sit down," Linda Dowland said.

"Yeah, thanks." I sat down in a padded easy chair. Beezer chose a hard-backed wooden chair. The other two plunked down on the couch. They looked at me, I looked at em. It was time to say something smart, or at least pertinent. I said it. "Maybe you folks could hustle up some grub, eh?"

"Food?" Linda Dowland asked.

"Yeah, chow. Is that included on my bill, or does it come extra?"

"On the house," Beezer said. He went off to the kitchen, presently returned with a couple of cold roast beef sandwiches, a salad and beer. I gobbled em up. While I ate, the committee talked at me.

The woman said, "We don't know what you want here, Mr. Dunjer. But within reason, we're prepared to help you adjust."

Blake, the short guy, chimed in. "We're sort of the adjustment committee."

Corrigan said, "If it's an honest day's work you're looking for, Mac, you'll find it here; yes, sir!"

"That's right," Linda Dowland assured me. The joys of hard work: no frills, no bosses over you—"

"Just the Union shop," Beezer broke in.

"It's swell," Blake said. "Swell."

"A man knows his worth by the sweat of his brow," Corrigan said.

"What trade has captured your fancy, Mr. Dunjer?" Linda Dowland smiled at me.

I smiled back, finished my beer, wiped my lips with the back of my hand, and said, "Your names aren't Beezer, Blake, Corrigan and Dowland. That's for a starter. Let's see what else, eh? This house has to be a one-shot deal. You folks handle too many zanies to work out of headquarters. You'd be sitting ducks. Most of your immigrants've got to stand out like sore thumbs. It's only a matter of time till they get nailed by the law. And if you birds stayed put, you'd be out of business in no time.

"Okay, you know my name, so you must have some way of keeping in touch with Happy City. Only you don't know who I am, what I'm here for. That scratches a phone hookup. Radio can't be it, either. How about a telegraph, maybe? Some of these adjustments you folk are going to help me make, I bet they cost a little extra, eh? Well, that's all part of the game, I guess. Thanks for the meal; I needed that. And, yeah, Sampson spilled the beans about you folks. Maybe you're not the con men we got back in Happy City running the show, but you got to be something close or Simpson wouldn't deal with you."

Beezer frowned. "Who are you, Dunjer? What's your angle?"

"I'm head of a security outfit. Or was till I got tangled up with the law. And my angle is to get untangled. That's why I'm here. What my dough bought wasn't help adjusting. It was help tracking down two of my ops who came this way."

"Who?" Linda Dowland asked.

"Hennessy and Follsom."

"You're late," Blake said. "It's a shame."

"Late for *what*?" I heard myself ask.

"They left us," Linda Dowland said.

"When?"

"A couple of hours after they got here," Beezer said. "Hardly got a chance to see the sights."

"Where'd they go?" I asked. "Back to Happy City?"

"Why should they do that?" Corrigan said. "They headed for Capital City."

"Capital City?"

"Sure. Where the capitalists suck the workers' blood," Beezer said. "Only there aren't any workers there, just businessmen."

"Mechs do the work, eh?"

"Nope," said Blake. "Just machines. Automated, computerized machines. All stationary. They don't talk, don't walk. They just produce."

"Sounds okay," I said.

"It stinks," Corrigan said.

"To each his own," Linda Dowland said.

"By the sweat of our brows," Blake said.

"You really buy that guff?" I asked.

Beezer shrugged. "It's a living."

"Yeah. My ops didn't say *why* they were going to Capital City, eh?"

"We never asked," Beezer said. "They said we should fix it so they could get to Capital City."

"H-m-m-m. Look, pals, all this travel wears a man out. Maybe we could just wire ahead or something and ask em to come back, eh?"

"Nix," Beezer said.

"We do have a telegraph to Happy City," Linda Dowland said, "but not to Capital City."

"What do you have?"

"Nothing," Blake said.

"It's like this," Beezer said. "We just send you. You get yourself a hotel room. Lots of suburbs and lots of business in Capital City. So loads of guys stay overnight. No sweat; by the time we're through with a client, no one will be the wiser. There's a drop. The client leaves a note. The note gives his hotel and room number. He's contacted by the Capital City League team. That's the story."

"Some story."

"You don't have to go," Blake said. "But if you want to, we'll take you."

"It will cost plenty," Beezer said. "But what doesn't these days?"

"Worth every penny of it," Corrigan said.

Chapter 23

We drove in a truck a good part of the day. Beezer was at the wheel. I was still in my work clothes. We didn't talk much. What was there to say? We stopped for chow a couple of times, then hit the road again. Night began to settle over the countryside. By now darkness and I were old pals. Darkness, in fact, seemed to've taken over my life.

Sometime around eleven at night we pulled off the highway onto a narrow dirt road. Some ten minutes later the road came to an end. Beezer and I climbed out, continued on foot. I didn't mind stretching a leg. Trees and shrubs were on all sides of us. Beezer shone his flashlight on the ground.

I asked, "Where are we?"

"About two miles from Capital City."

"We just going to keep hiking along till we hit civilization?"

"Capital City isn't my idea of civilization. There's an electric fence and all kinds of mechanized look-outs. Guards, too. The border's crawling with them."

"So what do we do?"

"Go under."

"The fence?"

"Sure. Watch your step," Beezer said.

We had stepped into a tunnel; it curved down. Beezer's flash put a circle of light at our feet.

"You dug your own tunnel?" I asked.

"This place," Beezer said, "is an old mine, dug years ago before the Fed government went under."

"How'd you find it?"

"An old state map. We were looking for a way to get across. We checked out a lot of spots. This was best."

The tunnel began to level off.

I said, "I can't wear these duds into Capital City, can I?"

Beezer waved a hand. "Everything's taken care of, you'll see. Better save your breath, we've got a two mile hike here."

It was a one-room cabin. The paint had peeled off the walls. Years ago. There were no windows. None were needed. We were still in the tunnel.

"Help yourself," Beezer said.

There were suits hanging from metal pipes, shoes on the floor, a variety of shirts neatly stacked. There were even socks and underwear piled on newspaper on the floor.

"Not bad," I said.

"The best," Beezer said. "Anything but the best would be a dead giveaway upstairs."

"Capital City's above us?"

"The outskirts."

"Well, I won't mind getting rid of this denim uniform. Got a mirror around here?"

"We never got around to that."

"Can't have everything."

Beezer stood at the mouth of the tunnel. "Listen, Dunjer, we made an exception with you."

"What kind?"

"No blindfold going in or coming out of here."

"Thanks. Why?"

"Professional courtesy. Only don't get caught. And if you do, don't lead them back to us."

"It's a deal. What profession are we being courteous about?"

"Don't kid me; you're in the rackets, Dunjer—you're hot. So are your pals. You get a nose for racket guys after awhile. Sometimes taking the trip's the only way, right?"

He waved. I turned. A second later I was alone walking through the woods. I didn't have far to go. I could see lights up head, a roadway. The city wouldn't be far away.

I had exchanged my lunch box for a briefcase, a decided improvement. I had on a white shirt, polka-dot tie, black pinstripe suit. My shoes were black and highly polished. My underwear was brand new and so were my socks. I was as spiffy as a newly minted dime. And worth about as much if anyone tumbled I was an outlander.

I stepped out of the bushes, onto the road. I brushed myself off, straightened my tie and trudged off toward the city. A short while ago I was thankful to be using my legs again; now all I could think about was a nice, soft seat. Adversity was making me fickle.

I could see Capital City in the distance. It rose up into the sky, a panorama of brightly lit structures. The town fathers had really done a bang-up job in this neck of the woods.

I checked into the Dorchester Hotel. It was a quarter past two. I used a phony credit card the League had thoughtfully provided me with. I hoped I wasn't going to stay long.

"Room 706," the desk clerk said.

I rode the elevator up, tried out my key in the lock, gave the place the once-over, left my briefcase on the bed, relocked the door and went downstairs again.

About the last thing I needed was more exercise. But one more item needed attending to. I hiked for ten blocks before I came to the right intersection. The streets were deserted at this hour.

I counted five trees from the corner, bent over. A hollow notch was dug deep into the tree. I folded the small piece of paper which bore my hotel and room number, but not my name, squeezed it into the man-made pocket. I straightened up and walked away from there.

Nothing to do now but get some shut-eye. I didn't mind.

Chapter 24

Something was going beep-beep. I put a pillow over my head and hoped it'd go away. It didn't. I got an eyelid open with about as much effort as if I'd been using a crowbar. I looked around for the irritating sound. It seemed to be coming from the phone on the nightstand. I picked up the phone and the sound stopped. I was making progress. Now if I could only remember where I was.

"Beezer," a woman's voice said.

Suddenly I remembered and wished I hadn't. "Yeah," I said into the phone. "You've got the right party."

"Meet me in the hotel dining room in twenty minutes. The last table by the west wall. I'll be wearing a red carnation."

"How about half an hour?"

"Twenty minutes."

"Uh-huh. You drive a hard bargain, lady."

The waiter was dressed in a business suit. He brought ham and eggs, coffee and orange juice. I half expected the food to be wrapped in dollar bills. I turned to my companion. "You've got a name?"

"Call me Janet." She was a short, pert brunette somewhere in her twenties. She had on a matching blue jacket and skirt. A business suit, I supposed. Why not? Everyone seemed to be wearing one.

"Okay, Janet. Let's save a little time. My name's

Dunjer. I come from Happy City. I'm a security exec there. Got that?"

Janet nodded, took a sip of her coffee. "Actually," she said, "this is most unusual. *I'm* supposed to be doing the orientation."

"Where's the rest of the committee?"

"I *am* the committee, Mr. Dunjer. We in Capital City don't believe in collectivism."

"Uh-huh. Unusual or not, we skip your orientation, eh? I don't want dough, stocks, bonds, a little cottage in this burg where I can settle down and watch my securities draw dividends. I don't even want a tour of your stock exchange."

"What in heaven's name *do* you want, Mr. Dunjer?"

"Two people who should be somewhere in Capital City. They went the same route I did, turned up here a couple of days ago."

"Who are they?"

"Hennessy and Follsom."

Janet looked at me blankly. "I don't know them."

"Jeezus!"

Janet held up her hand. "Don't jump to conclusions, Mr. Dunjer. I'm not the only contact. There are many of us. And for security reasons we are not aware of each other's activities."

"Sorry," I said. "The thing is I just got to get hold of those two. Every minute counts."

Janet finished her coffee. "I understand. I am about to do something that is rarely done. I will take you to our offices. Call it professional courtesy."

"It's been called that before. Thanks. What profession is it?"

"You're obviously a man of substance, Mr. Dunjer. You mentioned executive. I'll take the chance."

"Yeah," I said. "I guess you can't hide quality, eh?"

It was an office building. What wasn't? A thin man sat at a desk in shirtsleeves. Janet stood looking out the window. I said, "Are you sure?"

"Positive," the man said in a dry voice.

"That doesn't make sense," I insisted.

"I'm sorry," the man said. He was shuffling some index cards around. "No one bearing those names used our services."

"What about the descriptions?"

The thin man shrugged. "What descriptions? These cards contain only names."

"How many folks did you get from Labor City the day before yesterday?"

"Thirty-three."

"No kidding, that many?"

Janet said, "You've seen Labor City?"

"Yeah."

"Then you shouldn't be surprised."

"I guess not. Were there any couples in this bunch?"

"Eight," the man said.

"They all stay here?"

The man consulted his cards. "Yes. All but one."

"Who was the one?"

"A Mrs. and Mr. Josiah Bronson."

"Where'd they take off for?"

"Hatesville."

I whistled. "Why'd anyone want to go *there*?"

"We don't ask, Mr. Dunjer," the man said. "We just take."

"Nuts. Can I get a description of the pair?"

"We can try," the man said. He reached for the phone, dialed a number. "Hello. Nick there? Put him on. Nick. Jerry here. We need a description. Your friends of two days ago." The man listened, turned to me. "Old folks. White-haired. Seemed like a very devoted couple."

"Ask him how tall they were."

The man did. "The woman was about five five; her husband around five nine."

"Did Nick help em get to Hatesville?"

"Yes."

"Anything special about the trip—something a bit out of the way or different?"

The man asked. "No. Doesn't look that way. Except their going to Hatesville. Almost no one goes there. This couple did want a lot of precautions taken— were afraid of being stopped in town. No chance of that, of course. But they were old. Caution was to be expected. Anything else?"

"No. Thank Nick for me."

The man did and hung up the phone. "I'm sorry, Mr. Dunjer."

I shrugged. "They're the right height for my pair. And what would an old couple be doing in Hatesville? A cautious one, yet?"

"What would your friends be doing there?"

From the window Janet called, "Jerry."

The man at the desk was suddenly alert. "Trouble?"

"I don't know. There's a man down there. By the apartment building. Just standing. He's looked up this way more than once."

Jerry got to his feet, went to the window. "The one in the dark coat?"

"Yes."

"Don't recognize him. Could be a new man on the vice squad."

"Your outfit's considered a vice here?"

The thin man nodded. I strolled to the window, peered out over Janet's shoulder.

The man across the street was tall, slender. He had a pointed moustache and dark, suntanned skin. He looked to be in his thirties. I couldn't see his teeth, but I knew they'd be very white. His handle was Paul Regan. The last time I'd seen him we'd swapped hellos in an underworld dive called the Happy Hour. He'd been with a dame named Lulu. I was busy spreading the word about the Whitney heist. He'd suggested I see Gripus. And now here he was, almost sitting in my lap. It sure was a small world.

I cleared my throat. "You may not believe this, but *I* know that guy. He's from *my* burg—Happy City. The mug's name is Paul Regan."

"And he took the trip before you?" Jerry said.

I shrugged. "I spoke to him less than a week ago. In the old hometown."

"Well, he didn't take it after," Janet said. "You were the last one to come through. He might have been at your heels, an hour or two behind. But he'd never have found your hotel. And unless he followed us from the Dorchester, there's simply no way he could have discovered this office."

I asked, "Could he've come over with that crowd a couple days ago?"

"Possibly." Jerry went back to his desk, skimmed through his index cards. "No Regan here."

"He might've used a phony name," I pointed out. "Only Lord knows why he'd come here two days ago.

Even *I* didn't know I'd be here then. And odds have it he's hunting for me."

"Maybe," Jerry said. "But he could be after the League in some way."

"Well, you can ask him. After I beat it. You folks got a back way outta here?"

"More than one," Janet said. "That's why we chose this building."

"Okay. And book me on a trip to Hatesville."

"You're going after the Bronsons?" Janet asked.

"Yeah. The thought of two old parties like that taking off for Hatesville strikes me as *unnatural*. Besides, what else can I do?"

Chapter 25

"This is the worst yet," I complained in a whisper.

"You're telling me," Jerry whispered back. "I hate these rush jobs. I shouldn't even be here. It's not my turn in the field."

"You were paid enough."

"What's money if this gets me killed?"

We were flat on our bellies in the dirt; no worm was ever flatter. This really *was* the worst trip yet. I had half a mind to get a refund and go home. Too bad home was apt to be a bit uncomfortable just now.

We were waiting for the moon to duck under a cloud. It did a moment later.

"Let's go!" Jerry hissed.

"After you, chum," I said. "The customer gets to go last."

We crawled up the hill. I had no trouble keeping tabs on my guide: all I had to do was follow his string of whispered curses.

We reached the top, slithered over, kept going. Both the thin man and I were dressed in black from head to toe. But I was the one lugging the knapsack on my back. I had to—it contained my gear for Hatesville, a real necessity. Without it I'd've been a goner. I was probably a goner anyway.

The dirt turned to grass. We pulled up behind a clump of bushes.

"Now what?" I whispered.

"We wait for the moon to come out again."

"I could do without this game," I said.

Presently the moon peeked out. Now I could see the pair of sentries across the clearing. They seemed to be carrying plenty of hardware. Their presence certainly didn't cheer me. "Where's the barbed wire?" I wanted to know.

"Isn't any. The field's mined." Jerry reached for a pair of binoculars on his belt. "If our boys are on the job, we've got it made."

"Jeezus! You mean you don't know?"

Jerry focused his glasses. "This isn't our regular day for crossing over. It's an extra. You might call it overtime. That's why it costs so much."

"I might call it extortion, too. What happens if they're not there?"

"We wait for the moon to go away. Head back over the hill and hike five miles. That's where we got some more of our boys."

"A lot of traffic here, eh?"

"Yep. But it's mostly in the other direction. The sentries are stationed to keep the Hatesville population *in*, not our folks out."

"I can believe it," I said.

"The old folks? Sure I remember them," the larger of the two sentries said. "Don't get many comin' our way from Capital City, you know. Goin' to make the sneak myself some day. You bet."

The three of us were in the sentry shack. The other guard had gone back to his post. I was busy climbing out of my black night-crawler's outfit.

"Who's their contact in the city?" Jerry asked.

"I sent them to Morris," the guard said.

"Then that's where I want to go," I said.

"You must really be hard up for somethin', fella,"

the guard said. "Goin' into Hatesville's like putting
your neck in a noose."

"It's already in a noose," I told him. "Or I wouldn't
be taking this trip."

By now I had my soiled black garments off and
was putting on the coarse gray uniform of a prol.
It was no improvement at all.

Jerry turned to me. "There's a map of the city in
your knapsack. Memorize as much as you can and
destroy it."

"Are you kidding? If I could do that, I'd be doing
stunts on the Tele-vista for a living."

"The key points are marked. You don't understand,
Dunjer. They find that map on you, you're shot on
the spot."

"On what grounds?"

"They don't need any grounds. Not in Hatesville,"
Jerry said. "Hatesville isn't like other cities."

"Hatesville is Hell," the guard said.

"Who's dictator these days?" I asked.

"Fella named Shatz," the guard said.

"Used to be police chief," Jerry said.

"This Shatz knocked off our old president, Kempfer,
about three months ago," the guard said. "Kempfer
useta be head of the secret police. Shatz won't last
long either."

"No one lasts very long," Jerry said.

Chapter 26

I got rid of the map before entering town. I buried my briefcase near a giant tree across from a curve sign on the highway. It wouldn't do to lug a new, shiny briefcase into Hatesville—especially one which contained loads of money and a laser. Not to mention a couple of other items I figured might come in handy. Nothing would ever come in handy again if I were stopped and searched and any of this stuff turned up. And in Hatesville a guy on the prowl at night was apt to be stopped.

I moved from shadow to shadow until the highway was far behind me. Drab, colorless buildings stretched down the block; an occasional streetlamp sent yellow light into the darkness. I saw no one else on the streets. A curfew'd been in effect last week. According to the border guard it was lifted now.

I kept close to the buildings. Twice I caught sight of a patrol. Both times I froze and tried to look like part of the brick wall. Neither patrol turned down my block.

I got lost more than a couple of times. The streets I was supposed to follow were clearly marked on the map. But in my mind the street names began to fade, get scrambled, disappear altogether. I stumbled along, hugging my brick walls, tring to keep a lookout for more patrols.

After a while the sights began to change. More people were on the streets. There were more lights. The drab buildings began to drop away, to be replaced by restaurants, bars, movie theaters. A street sign said: Remling Road. I remembered it from the map. Remling Road led to the downtown district. That's where I wanted to go.

The further I went, the more lively things became. Cars were in the streets now. More people crowded the pavements. A lot of em were wearing the identical outfit I had on. Some weren't. Blue or brown uniforms popped up. A couple were decked out in yellow. I saw red once. And a group of soldiers in black. I stopped worrying about being spotted. For the time being I was one of the crowd, a tried-and-true denizen of Hatesville; some guys get all the luck.

A lot of posters and billboards kept me company as I hiked. They all had the same subject. Ludvig Shatz, a bony-faced bird with a moustache, glowered from some posters, grinned from others. A DUTY FIRST caption got the glower. A grinning one read: PRESIDENT SHATZ PROTECTS THE DECENT. *What the hell am I doing here?* I kept wondering. Happy City and its problems seemed very far away.

I should've been huffing and puffing by the time I reached the Silver Dollar Café, but I wasn't. Too tensed up to feel anything but the adrenalin pumping through my body. The shakes'd come next. I wondered if I could avoid the screaming mimis? This place reminded me of an old film I'd seen about Nazi Germany. But it was just a police state. Police states were all alike.

Pushing open the double doors, I stepped into the café.

The joint was packed.

I stood there trying to remember my instructions. They weren't all that hard, but my brain had sprung a leak. Three hours trudging through Hatesville and I was ready to toss in the sponge. I could hardly wait till things got really tough.

I squeezed my way through the crush, got to the end of the bar. That's where I was supposed to be, I recalled. I fished a black pin out of my pocket, one that Jerry had given me, stuck it into my collar. Now all I had to do was wait till someone contacted me. If they didn't I could always spend the night in a flophouse and come back tomorrow. Provided I lasted that long.

I signalled the barkeep. He was a fat, burly character.

"What's it gonna be, Mac?"

"A beer."

The barkeep returned with a mug, put it down in front of me and went away.

I sat slurping my beer. The gray uniform chafed my skin. I wondered how the locals could stand it.

Presently the barkeep waddled over, began wiping the bar in front of me. "See that door over in back, Mac?"

I turned, looked. "Uh-huh."

"Go through it. There's a phone on the other side. There's a guy wants to talk with you. He's on the line. Name's Morris."

I didn't have to be told twice. I got up, elbowed my way toward the door, went through it. A wall phone, its earpiece off the hook, was waiting for me.

"Hello?"

"Listen," a voice said. "Do not speak. Do not ask questions. Do precisely as I tell you. There is a back door in the place you are now at. Use it as soon as we are done. You will find yourself in an alley. Turn right. You will come to a wooden fence. An unlocked door in the fence will lead into another alley. Continue walking right. You will emerge on Grant Street, Cross over and head west on Grant for three blocks. You will see a trolley stop. Wait there. Board the first trolley that comes along. Continue to wear your pin. A man wearing a similar pin will board the trolley. Do not speak to him or signal him in any way. Leave when he does—"

I interrupted him. "Look, pal, I know you've got this down to a fine art, but you're forgetting one small item."

"And what is that?" The voice sounded skeptical.

"When I get in this trolley car, what do I put in the fare box. I haven't the faintest idea."

"H-m-m-m. A dime."

"Thanks, pal; anything else?"

"Yes. Do not approach the man after he leaves the trolley. Follow him. We shall handle the rest."

The phone went click. I was holding a dead line.

The guy got on at the third stop—a medium-sized man in gray cap and uniform. The pin was stuck in his cap. He sat down three seats in front of me. The trolley rattled along. The downtown section faded behind me into the darkness. The car twisted and turned like a rattlesnake with indigestion. Drab buildings again sprang up outside the trolley windows. I didn't know where we were and I didn't care. Some twenty minutes later the man with the pin left the car. I followed at his heels.

I sat on a hard-backed wooden chair by the kitchen table. A pot of coffee was perking on the burner.

A. G. Frisbee, a stout man in his late forties, in shirtsleeves and suspenders, sat facing me. The man who had brought me to this place lay sleeping in the living room on a couch.

A. G. Frisbee said, "My apologies for any inconvenience you might have suffered, Mr.—?"

"Dunjer."

"Dunjer. You see, Shatzville—that's our new name—isn't quite like most other cities. We must take precautions."

"*What* precautions?" I asked. All this runaround had made me irritable.

"Once you left the alley, Mr. Dunjer, you were under constant observation."

"So?"

"We had to make certain you weren't being followed."

"And if I was?"

"Frankly, we would have broken contact."

"You mean thrown me to the wolves."

A. G. Frisbee shrugged. "As you wish."

"Some outfit you folks run."

"Hatesville, Mr. Dunjer. That's what our city is known as."

"Yeah. But you don't have to live up to the name."

"We are not trying to. But if our group were to be exposed, the consequences would be frightful."

"I get the point, Mr. Frisbee."

A. G. Frisbee rose, poured two cups of steaming coffee, seated himself again. I put sugar and cream in mine, took a swallow. Frisbee was looking at me.

"Forgive me for prying, but since you did request aid, I must ask: why did you come to Shatzville? What do you hope to accomplish here?"

"Accomplish? Nothing. The quicker I blow this burg, the better. I haven't been here a day and already it feels like years."

"I don't believe I understand."

"I'm hunting a couple. I think they came here disguised as old folks."

"Ah! The Bronsons."

"Know em, eh?"

"Of course. We get so few here."

"What happened to em? They still in town?"

"Mrs. Bronson is."

"Just her?"

Frisbee nodded. "Mr. Bronson moved on. He took the trip again. He paid good money so we did what he requested."

"I almost hate to ask. What did he request?"

"To be taken to Puritanburg."

"And he's there now?"

"That is where we deposited him. What has happened to him since then is anyone's guess."

"You said his wife is still here?"

"I'm afraid so."

"Afraid?"

"Mrs. Bronson was to be taken home. I assume the rigors of the journey proved too great for one her age."

"Where's home?"

"Well, the ultimate destination was Happy City."

"You don't say? What happened?"

"She was compromised. Don't ask me how."

"What do you mean 'compromised,' for God's sake?"

"Pointed out in the street. Denounced as an illegal."

"In the street, yet. What was your boy doing while all this was going on?"

268

"Our agent fled. He was barely able to save himself."

"Like that, eh?"

"This is Hatesville, Mr. Dunjer."

"You're telling me. So where is she now?"

"Why, the city prison. Where else?"

Chapter 27

A. G. Frisbee was at the wheel.

"I realize I offered you aid, Mr. Dunjer, but that was aid in adjusting to Shatzville—"

"I *am* adjusting, pal. This place feels just like home, and I owe it all to you. Unfortunately home hasn't been feeling too great lately."

"I meant, Mr. Dunjer, that I did not hire out to be your chauffeur."

"For what I'm paying you, Frisbee, you'll hire out for anything I want."

Three A.M. Almost no other cars on the roadway. Any second a squad car might happen along and pull us over. It was a bit chancy. Frisbee had rummaged through his war chest, dug some cop uniforms out of mothballs. We were both decked out in coarse dark blue suits replete with black belt and boots—not unlike the outfit worn by our sanitation crews back in Happy City—just the thing if we ran into some nearsighted lawmen. Frisbee had fixed us both up with phony IDs, too. Those and a lot of luck might just see us through the night.

Our car headlights caught the curve sign by the highway's edge.

"Okay," I said. "We pull up here."

I climbed out of my car and hunted around for my giant tree. It was where I'd left it across the road. The way things were going, I should've been thankful that it hadn't been cut down in my absence. I went over, used a dead branch to dig up my briefcase and hustled back to the car.

The clock was pushing three thirty, but as far as I was concerned, the night was still young.

The Hatesville City Prison was a large hundred-story building with no windows which took up an entire city block and then some.

"The little one over there," Frisbee said.

I peered through the car window, saw a three-story brick building. The windows were barred. A green sign over the door read: Interrogation Center.

"You sure that's the right place?" I asked. "I'm not going to get a second chance. For all I know, I won't even get a first chance."

"She's there all right," Frisbee assured me. "That's where they go the first few nights. Listen to reason, Mr. Dunjer; there's no way you can get that woman out. It's never been done before and dozens have tried—hundreds, perhaps, through the years. It would take a small army."

"We don't have a small army, just you and me."

"Not *me*, Mr. Dunjer. As soon as those sirens start to ring—and I assure you they will—I'm going to run for my life. You'll talk, of course. They all talk in the end. But Frisbee isn't my real name, you know. We'll cover our tracks. It will be costly, but you leave us no choice. What you don't understand, Mr. Dunjer, is that you're not going up against mere flesh and blood. Oh, no. The prison system is unique in Shatzville, and that's what makes your task so hopeless: that building is totally automated, you know."

"Actually I do know." I climbed out of the car. "Wait for me. There won't be any alarms."

"You're a madman."

"Uh-huh. This may take awhile. Don't get jumpy, Frisbee. Sit tight. Just remember—if you don't hear an alarm, everything's aces."

Frisbee looked too scared to come up with a snappy answer. I went off into the night. I didn't go directly up to the Interrogation Center and knock on the door. That rarely works. Instead I went around the block and kept walking. The main prison was an island unto itself, but the Center shared its block with a number of other structures. I hiked past a grocery store, a storefront lawyer's office, a stationery store. I found the opening I was looking for between buildings and squeezed my way through. I had to climb over a garbage can and almost stepped on a very irate cat, but I made it to the back alley behind the Interrogation Center.

The view was lousy.

There were windows here, but they were all barred. There was a back door, but it was made of solid metal. I wasn't discouraged.

I liked the back door.

No guards were hanging around it with carbines slung over their shoulders. The prison authorities were relying entirely on their foolproof automated guard system. Who could blame them? It cost a bundle and it really was foolproof. I ought to know —it'd come from Happy City. And twelve years ago, as a junior security op, I'd helped test it out. They were blood brothers to the mechs we had scooting around at Security Plus but a lot less complicated.

I dug the master control cube out of my pocket. I pressed override. I went to the door. And pushed it open.

I was in a long empty corridor. I started walking.

I reached a second door—one made of bright, shiny metal. An electric eye in the far right corner winked at me. A flat metallic voice intoned: "Identify yourself." I used the override button. The voice shut up. The door swung open to my touch. There was no alarm.

I stepped through.

I was in a brightly lit wider corridor now. Closed doors on either side of me—an office section. No one seemed to be working overtime.

I moved along.

I had on my blue cop's getup—perfect attire, according to Frisbee, for the Interrogation Center. There were hundreds of lawmen working the prisons. No one'd know me from a hole in the wall. Better yet, the master control cube and its override properties were completely unknown in Hatesville. The company brochure always kept mum on that one very minor point. Only top Happy City security outfits rated a cube.

But a cube wouldn't help me find my way.

Unfortunately Frisbee had failed to supply me with a map of the joint. I didn't know one hallway from the next. And what I knew even less was where they kept the lockup. Or where in the lockup they stashed the illegals.

I'd have to go hunting, plain and simple.

I went along—past the closed offices—to the hallway's end. The door I came to wasn't locked. I opened it cautiously and peeked through.

A pair of hallways faced me, branching off to the left and right. Noises came from the left one. I headed that way.

I didn't have far to go.

A domed archway led into a huge hall. Desks and chairs covered the floors. Charts and graphs were strung up along the walls. Men and women, all dressed in my blue uniform, no less, either sat at the desks or bustled along between em.

I didn't waste time gawking; I moved out to join the throng.

In less than thirty seconds I was surrounded by tumult. I was all but invisible in the crush. I stopped at a desk, leaned over to bawl at a middle-aged, blue-clad woman at a typewriter, "I'm new here. Which way to the pens?"

Her gray eyes held no interest as she yelled back, "New internees or processed internees?"

"New."

"Third floor rear. Elevator banks on the left." She pointed vaguely down the hall, went back to her work.

I moved off at a fast clip.

The elevators were at the far end of the hall. Stepping in, I punched three and was carried up.

The doors opened on a third floor which was all metal and cells.

A guard—the first live one I'd seen—detached himself from a hard-backed wooden chair, ambled my way. I hadn't expected a guard. But by now I should've been used to things I didn't expect.

The guard was a pudgy white-haired guy in his sixties. He wore a gun on his belt.

"What is it?" he asked. A reasonable enough question. I wondered what I was going to say. I didn't seem to have too many choices.

"I'm looking for a Mrs. Bronson."

"Bronson, huh? Well, let's see, son." I followed him back to his chair. A clipboard was lying next to it. The guard began turning pages. He glanced up, a stubby finger resting on a name. "A Mrs. Josiah Bronson?"

"Uh-huh."

"Here she is. What is it?"

"She's wanted downstairs."

The guard squinted at me in the dim light. "Now?" I shrugged. "Orders."

"Well, that's a dandy, all right. Couldn't get the cells open even if I wanted to. Got to call down to control central, have them issue a computer directive. You new here?"

"Yeah."

"Well, you always go through control central first, see? They call up through that phone." He jerked a thumb toward a call box on the wall. "Then I go over, give the password, so to speak, the door goes pop, and I fetch the prisoner."

"Right," I said. "What cell's the Bronson woman in?"

"One hundred and sixty."

"Take me to it. I'll show you something you don't know."

"And what would that be?" the guard grinned good-naturedly.

"I'll open the door myself."

The guard slapped his knee and laughed. "That's a good one."

"Nope, I'm not kidding. I'll open the door. No computer directive, no nothing. Just a little moxie."

"Can't be done, son."

"Bet you twenty bucks it can."

The guard shook his head. "You're new here; that's why you got such damn fool notions in your noodle. I don't want to take your money."

"What's money if you can't have fun with it, eh?" I reached into my pocket, found my wallet, pulled out a twenty-dollar bill. Folding it lengthwise, I put it in the guard's palm.

The guard looked at the dough, got to his feet. "Silliest thing I ever heard of."

I followed him down one corridor, then the next. We reached 160.

"Here it is, son; go ahead."

I went to the peephole, looked in. The cell was pitch-dark. I couldn't see a thing. It didn't much matter. If the lady in there actually *was* a Mrs. Bronson, my name was mud.

I got the master control cube out of my pocket, pressed the override button. I turned to the guard. "Go on, try the door."

"Look, son, a joke's a joke. I'll give you back your twenty. Hell, you didn't even touch that door."

"Didn't have to. We've come this far, you might as well humor me one last time, eh?"

The guard, a grin on his face, slowly stepped over to the door. I was behind him now, over to one side. I reached for my laser as his hand stretched out for the door, touched it gently.

The door swung in on silent hinges.

The guard's mouth opened wide, as if he were going to show the dentist which tooth hurt. His forehead wrinkled like a washboard. His eyes looked like they were about to pop out of his skull and roll off down the hallway. His hand began to move toward his holster. He was a bit late.

I said, "Uh-uh."

The guard's hand stopped moving. His head swiveled in my direction. He saw the laser. "What is this?" he asked.

"Trouble, what else?" I raised my voice. "Mrs. Bronson, will you kindly step out here for a moment."

A bewildered-looking figure came out of the cell —an old, white-haired lady rubbing sleep from her eyes.

I peered at her. "Miss Follsom, that *is* you?"

"I think I'm going to faint, boss," the elderly lady said in a youngish voice.

"Not now, Miss Follsom; save it for later. We've got to make tracks." To the guard I said, "Unstrap your holster. Let it fall to the floor. Then pull off your uniform, boots and all, and step into the cell."

"I really don't understand this," the guard said.

"You're not supposed to," I explained.

"The fit's not too good, boss," Miss Follsom said as we rode down the elevator. She had on the portly guard's uniform.

"Yeah, they don't make em like they used to."

We hit the ground floor.

"Try not to look like a prisoner, Miss Follsom; it excites the natives. Just stick close to me and move fast."

I headed down the main aisle, Miss Follsom at my side. Noise and bustle rolled over us like a huge wave. We'd made it halfway toward the back of the joint—a direction I'd at least traveled before—when we hit a snag.

"You there," a burly character in a blue suit with a captain's badge shouted. "You there" was Miss

Follsom. The guy was planted smack in front of us. "Where did you get that uniform?" he roared. "It's three sizes too large. Let's see your badge number, officer."

"What do I do, Mr. Dunjer?"

"It's too late to ask for a lawyer; we'd better run for it."

My hand was on the control cube. My thumb pressed down on the override button. I clicked it over four notches to total.

The Interrogation Center winked out.

The large hall plunged into darkness.

Everything in the building had gone on the fritz.

I grabbed Miss Follsom by the hand, trotted off in the direction of the back door.

People, desks, chairs got in our way. We went over or around em.

Voices were shouting. They weren't about us. Only a lunatic could associate this unheard-of catastrophe with the female cop in the baggy uniform.

Matches, cigarette lighters, small pocket flashlights lighted up the large hall like lost fireflies. The feeble lights didn't help much. Just enough to keep us from landing in someone's arms.

"There's a wall up ahead, Mr. Dunjer."

"Yeah. Look for a door somewhere to the right."

No one stopped us when we reached the door. In fact, we had company. The building just now must've seemed like a great place not to be.

We ran down the first hallway, then the second. The metal door which led outside swung open against my palm.

A. G. Frisbee was where I'd left him, behind the

wheel of his car. He was staring at the darkened Interrogation Center as we piled into the backseat.

"Step on it, Frisbee," I said.

He didn't have to be told twice.

"See," I told Frisbee. "No alarms, no shooting, no pursuit, even. At least for the time being."

"Where do you want to go, Mr. Dunjer?" Frisbee seemed awed.

"Back to the hideout, Frisbee. Try not to get a speeding ticket, eh? We're still in the clear."

"How did you ever find me, boss?"

"Years of tracking crooks has given me that special knack. Besides, you left a trail a mile wide. What in heaven's name is going on, Miss Follsom?"

"Don't ask." Miss Follsom was busy plucking a thin layer of plastic from her face, a considerable improvement.

"Dye your hair?"

"It's a wig. They hadn't searched me yet or anything." She removed it, fluffed out her blond hair.

"Must've been terrible, eh?"

"It was the pits."

I put a reassuring arm around her. It seemed the right place for the arm to be. Miss Follsom snuggled against me. Outside, the grim anonymous buildings of Hatesville whisked by. Somehow they didn't seem quite as hateful now.

"So tell me," I said.

"Kreeg," Miss Follsom said.

"Gimpy Kreeg?"

"You know him, uh, boss?"

"Yeah. What's he done?"

"Ran off with the spool."

"Jeezus!"

"And money from the security vault; a bunch of it."

"Double Jeezus! That's *absolutely impossible*. Why are you spinning such wild and woolly yarns, Miss Follsom?"

"I wish they were, boss."

"How did he get into the security vault?"

"We don't know. But there's two million gone. We think he has it."

"Okay, how did you pin it on Kreeg?"

"Hennessy caught Kreeg rifling our offices. He was working late. He heard sounds coming from your office—"

"And figured it was me."

"A logical conclusion, boss. He dropped over to chat and found Kreeg."

"With a gun, no doubt."

"Precisely. A gun and the spool he'd taken out of my desk."

"He knew it was there?"

"So it seems. Later we found out how he got in the building."

"Lemme guess. A phony ID."

"Right you are."

"Uh-huh. And he must've had a couple of gadgets to douse the alarms and know where the spotter-eyes were so he could avoid em. Then what?"

"He locked Hennessy in a closet and made his getaway."

"But Hennessy recognized him, eh?"

"He'd run into Kreeg a couple of times, Mr. Dunjer, in the line of duty."

"What about that two million?"

"The police audit discovered it gone. By then Hennessy had traced Kreeg through the grapevine. He hadn't tried to cover his movements. He was boasting he had come into two million. But it didn't matter. He was going to leave Happy City. And he did."

"And you and Hennessy went after him," I said in some wonder, giving her a gentle hug. "Thank you, Miss Follsom."

"What else could we do? We thought Kreeg was just going from one city to the next. Hennessy borrowed some money from the safety vault so we could pay our way."

"Damn vault's busier than the city bank."

"Well, Kreeg kept right on going. He was using the name Flink. We checked over the League's client list at each City-State. That's how we kept tabs on him. But he was always one jump ahead. I guess he still is."

I sighed. "And when you saw Paul Regan's name on one of those lists—saw he was going to be a fellow passenger—you two disguised yourselves."

"Right, boss. We never figured out how he fit into things. But we didn't want to take any chances. Anyway, when we saw that Kreeg had left Hatesville, too, we decided that I should go back to Happy City and tell you what's what, while Hennessy continued after Kreeg. But I got pinched and you saved me, boss."

"Uh-huh. Kreeg and Hennessy headed for Puritanburg, eh?"

"That's the place, boss."

"Care to take in the sights with me, Miss Follsom?"

"I wouldn't miss it for the world."

Chapter 28

A strong wind was blowing. The sky was a cloudless blue. Mountain peaks towered on all sides of us.

"Actually, boss," Miss Follsom said, "I may not exactly be cut out for this type of life."

"You're not the only one," I said. I used whatever breath I had left to call to our guide up ahead, "Hey, buddy, rest time!"

The guide, a pale-faced young man, came to a halt.

The three of us huddled, our backs to the mountainside. We were on a wide ledge. Below us we could see a green, fertile valley.

"Listen, mister," the guide said, "we ain't got all day. We got miles to cover before nighttime. We gotta reach the shelter or we'll freeze out here."

"Freeze, eh? That's about all that hasn't happened yet."

"It's a tough, hard climb. We warned you before you signed up."

"Uh-huh," I said. "Look, tell me something."

The guide shrugged.

I pointed a finger across the valley to low hills on the other side. "We've got to get beyond those hills, eh?"

"That's where we're headed."

"Yeah. But instead of going across the valley, which looks easy as pie, we're slugging around these mountains on a three-day trek. How come?"

"Ever hear of Time-warp Valley, mister?"

"Uh-uh. What is it, an amusement park?"

"It's that place down there. Forbidden."

"No kidding. I don't see any fences or guards."

"Don't need any. No one in his right mind would go down there. Ever hear of the M-bomb explosions a century ago?"

"Can't say I have," I said. "Were they something awful?"

"Bad enough. But it's worse in that valley now."

"So tell us how, already," Miss Follsom said.

"People vanish. Some never return. Others do and tell strange tales."

"Like what?"

"They come out on the other side; they've skipped days, weeks, maybe even years."

"Look, I don't want to be a spoilsport, but since I'm footing the bill," I said, "I think we ought to take the shortest route. Beginning now."

Our guide shook his head. "Not me, mister. Listen, you want to go, go. There's nothing to it. See that pinkish hill over there? Well, what you're looking for is right over the hill. You can see it from the valley. Just keep walking in a straight line. Of course there's no telling *when* you'll end up. But that's your lookout, isn't it? The folks in Puritanburg are real friendly. If you want, I'll see you down to the base of the cliff."

"Do we want, Miss Follsom?" I asked.

"We want," she said.

"You heard the lady," I said. "Let's shake a leg."

Miss Follsom and I looked back a couple of times. The mountains we'd left had grown smaller; we were covering ground. If there was any time warp lurking in the valley, we failed to notice. No mists or hazes got in our way. There was nothing but green grass and flowing fields. The pinkish mountain in front of us kept growing bigger.

We heard the gunshots before we cleared the hill.

"I thought this place was supposed to be peaceful," I complained.

"Maybe it's a rifle range, boss. Perhaps they're practicing."

"Yeah. Listen to that. Someone seems to be practicing screaming, too."

I helped Miss Follsom around the last bend. The city was less than a half mile away. Something which sounded like machine-gun fire had opened up.

"What do you say, Miss Follsom?" I asked. "We've come this far; we can't very well turn back, can we?"

"Not very well."

Two guards stopped us some twenty minutes later at the town gate. They both had rifles. The rifles were pointed at us.

I kept my hands in plain sight. "We're just tourists," I explained.

"Tourists?" the smaller of the guards sneered. "That's a good one. Haven't been any tourists in years. Whaddya think, Ed?"

The larger of the guards shrugged. "Strumpetville spies, what else."

"What do we do with them?" the small guard asked.

"Let's take them to the Big Boss."

"Yeah. The Big Boss'll fix them."

A Jeep carried us and two other guards through winding streets.

284

I held Miss Follsom's hand. "I'm sorry I got you into this," I said.

"That's okay, boss. We've been in tight spots before and pulled through."

"Yeah. But somehow this feels unique."

We parked before a large domed building, were marched up stone steps, through wide doors, down marble corridors. We halted.

"In here," the guard said.

We stepped through a door; it clanged shut behind us.

"It's a cell, Mr. Dunjer."

"Uh-huh. That's where they usually put prisoners."

We sat down on a hard wooden bench and waited. The guards had taken all my belongings, including the laser. If worse came to worse, I could always try judo. Or prayer.

Some thirty minutes later the door swung in again. Two guards stepped through and smartly stood at attention.

A medium-sized figure in military attire came striding in. He stopped dead in his tracks and stared at us.

I got to my feet slowly as if I weren't too sure they could still move. My lips opened, but no words came through. I heard Miss Follsom gasp.

"Mr. Dunjer!" the military figure said. "Miss Follsom!"

"Hennessy," I said. "*You're* the Big Boss?"

Mike Hennessy blushed. "It didn't happen overnight. It took lots of long, hard work."

"It did?" I asked.

"Two years' worth," Mike Hennessy said.

Chapter 29

The three of us sat in Hennessy's huge office. Through the giant window we could see troops on the move outside. "So you went through the valley, huh? That probably explains it," Hennessy was saying. "There *is* some spooky time twist out there."

"So how did you become Big Boss?" Miss Follsom asked.

"Easy," Hennessy said. "I had enough dough left over to bribe my way. Besides, I used a lot of security stuff they don't know about around here, like bugging, planting false evidence and blackmail."

"H-m-m-m," I said. "Planting false evidence is usually sure fire."

"You're telling me."

"How'd you happen to stop here?" I asked Hennessy.

"Well, frankly, this place looked like a pushover. I was trailing Kreeg, you know."

"I know. And thanks."

"Don't mention it. I was a couple of days behind. Kreeg used the valley, but I went the long way. By the time I'd hit Puritanburg, Kreeg was set up next door in Strumpetville as dictator."

"Fast work," I said.

"Not really. You see, Kreeg had gone *back* six months. He had even more dough than I did; lots more. He *bought* Strumpetville lock, stock and barrel. There wasn't much I could do to get at him, so I set up shop right here."

"And all these soldiers, Hennessy?"

"Oh, that." Hennessy waved em away. "That's just a little war we have every couple of months with Strumpetville. One of these days I'll knock over that burg. We need a bit more room around here."

"One of these days better be soon," I said. "My one chance to clear myself is to get hold of that tape. Although Lord knows why he should've kept it all this time."

"Who can tell?" Hennessy said. "Come along, let me show you something."

The three of us trooped out onto the street again. We walked to a long squarish five-story building two blocks over. I didn't care for it one bit.

"What's this?" I asked.

"Prison," the Big Boss said.

We went through the prison doors, down the usual cellblock corridors. You've seen one; you've seen em all.

We stopped by a light, airy cell with southern exposure.

"Look in there," Hennessy said.

I looked.

"Good God," I said, "Paul Regan!"

"Tell them your story, Regan," Hennessy said. "And I'll knock two days off your sentence."

"Just two days?" Miss Follsom said.

"It gets him out tomorrow," Hennessy said.

"I'll tell you, Dunjer. Why not?" Regan said, "When you came to me in the Happy Hour with that yarn about Whitney's being taken, I got in touch with the man himself."

"Very enterprising," I said.

"He made me an offer. He wanted me to knock off a guy called Kreeg."

"Didn't know that was in your line, Regan."

Regan shrugged. "A little of this, a little of that; it all adds up. Besides, he paid plenty."

"Yeah, he always does."

"I started hunting this Kreeg guy, but he'd skipped Happy City. I checked in with Whitney; he wanted me to go after him. This time he really made it worth my while. I went. He gave me one last errand, said you'd be going after Kreeg yourself, probably, that you'd be a couple days behind me: what Whitney wanted was that I should kill you, too."

Chapter 30

We huddled in the alley. Trash cans kept us company. Overhead the dark night looked down on us like an inquisitive spectator. "Us" were three black-clad commandos and myself. In the distance we could see a blaze of neon lights—Strumpetville's honky-tonk district; it made up most of the town.

"How much time?" I whispered.

"About thirty seconds," a voice spoke next to my ear.

I settled down by the trash can as if we'd become old friends and waited.

The shelling began right on cue. Artillery fire burst over the city. Alarms went off like a symphony gone loony. The northwest gate, I knew, was being stormed.

"Let's go," a voice said; it didn't mean me.

Three dark shadows slid out of the alley, moved silently toward the two armed sentries standing before the building. The sentries were busy watching the fireworks. That was a mistake; they should've been looking over their shoulders. They never knew what hit em.

I got out of my clothes fast. The taller sentry had been stripped of his. I climbed into his duds. A tight fit, but then I wasn't going to pose in a fashion show.

"I'm set," I said.

One of the commandos spoke into a communo. "Let 'er rip."

"That's it?" I asked.

"The lines are all cut. No phones working. No hookups to GQ. Need any help?"

"Uh-uh. You've risked your necks enough. This one's my baby."

I moved off at a fast clip.

The lights had died in the building when the shelling began, but the speed lift still worked. I went through the darkened lobby, took the speed lift to the penthouse floor.

The hall was in semidarkness. A small emergency lamp sent black shadows flickering across the walls.

A sleepy-eyed guard turned toward me; no curiosity registered in his face as he glanced over my uniform.

I clubbed him down with my carbine.

I used his belt to tie his hands, took his weapons and walked down the hall to the large double doors. I inched em open very quietly.

It took me a moment to see in the gloom. Three candles cast a weak yellow glow which only partially illuminated the huge ornate living room. The drapes were drawn. In the far corner a short stubby man was fiddling with a phone bank; nothing seemed to be happening.

I made no noise moving through the thick carpet. I left the carbines by the door. A laser was in my hand.

I was very close to the short man before I spoke: "The phones don't work, Gimpy."

Gimpy Kreeg whirled around.

"Whaddya mean by—?"

"Look closely, Gimpy. Recognize me?" I put a mean, hard grin on my face without any effort at all. The laser was pointed squarely at Kreeg's chest.

Kreeg stared at me in the weak light. A look of

incredulity crossed his face as if one of the easy chairs had gotten up to serenade him.

"Dunjer," he whispered. "Listen, Dunjer—"

"No. *You* listen, punk. This is it for you—the end of the line. Figured you were on top of the world, eh? Too bad you won't live to enjoy it." I waved the laser at him, just to make sure he got the message. I had to move fast, before his stooges started checking on him. "You ran off with something I needed, punk; you ruined me. I've got nothing to lose now; I'm done. But so are you."

"No! Listen, Dunjer! You've got to listen!" The little guy was sweating up a storm; it did my heart good to see it. "Why's it too late? You mean the tape, right? I've got the tape. I'll give it to you, honest to God! Here—"

"You're lying, punk," I snarled. "You're going to die!"

"No! No! In the drawer, there; see for yourself!"

I followed Kreeg's shaking finger, went to a desk, pulled open the top drawer. A small familiar spool of tape bearing the Security Plus stamp was nestled there on a pile of papers. I let out a deep sigh, felt its comforting weight in the palm of my hand, let it fall into my pocket.

I turned my attention to Kreeg again. "Okay," I said. "Fair's fair. Maybe we'll let you live, eh? It depends on what kind of answers you come up with. Let's try a simple one first. Why'd you take this tape in the first place? What's it to you?"

"Insurance. I figured Whitney'd come after me. I was gonna use that tape to keep him in line."

"I don't get it. Why should he come after you?"

"Because of the dough I took."

"What dough? Talk sense Gimpy." I waved my laser at him to inspire sense.

"Listen. Whitney was in hock to Gripus. Yeah, he'd gone in over his head and Gripus bailed him out, see? Now Gripus owned a big piece of Whitney. Get it?"

I nodded. "You worked for Gripus, didn't you, Gimpy?"

"Sure. Know what my job was? *Bugging*."

"You're a colleague, eh?"

"I'm not in your league, Dunjer. But I get by. Gripus had me bug Whitney. That was a long time ago, see? And then he had me bug you."

"No one gets in my office except me."

Gimpy Kreeg grinned. "Not unless they got a master control cube. Whitney had a lotta ins, right? He got himself a master control cube. He and Gripus used it to loot the safety vault for all it was worth. Wait till the cops get around to *really* checking. All this covers a lotta time. Millions are gone, see?"

"Whitney shouldn't've been able to get that cube," I complained. "It's restricted."

"The deal musta seemed legit to the guys who sold him the gizmo or he wouldn'ta got it. But to get away with the caper, he needed one more thing: a fall guy, someone to take the rap. *You*, Dunjer. Whitney set you up, Gripus staged the stickup at Whitney's place."

"They killed the butler," I pointed out.

"Why not? What's a butler to Gripus or Whitney? It sold you."

"I guess it did."

"The whole idea was for you to loot the safety vault, too. And then powder out. That way they could blame *all* the lost dough on you. And that's what they did, ain't it?"

"Yeah. That's what they did. Who killed Gripus—Whitney?"

"Now you're cookin'. Sure. Gripus had his hooks in Whitney, was takin him for all he was worth. This was Whitney's chance to get out from under. It was a cinch to pin the trick on you."

"And you saw your chance too, didn't you, Gimpy?"

"You bet, Dunjer. I was supposed to make one last haul from the safety vault right after you skipped. They gave me the cube, see? That's all I needed. I nicked the vault for plenty, got the tape and beat it. Listen, with Gripus alive I'd've passed it by; he'd've nailed me for sure. But I figured I could outrun Whitney. And I did."

"But not me, Gimpy."

"Have a heart, Dunjer. You got what you wanted, didn't you? Live and let live. What've I ever done to you?"

"Except ruin me, nothing. You got a nice airy closet around here, one that locks from the outside?"

"Sure. Right over there."

"Why don't you step inside, Gimpy."

"You're not gonna shoot me?"

"Uh-uh."

"I appreciate that, Dunjer."

I shrugged. "Like you said, Gimpy, live and let live, eh? Besides, what I should've done is shoot you *before* all this began. What good would it do now?"

Chapter 31

Miss Follsom and I trudged through Time-warp Valley. We only had a couple of hours to go before we hit the mountains. From there it'd still be a long haul to Hatesville.

"Hennessy looked really happy in his little City-State, didn't he, boss?" Miss Follsom said.

"He's the top of the heap, Miss Follsom."

"We could have stayed."

"I suppose so."

"Why didn't we?"

"I don't know. Did you want to?"

"No."

"Neither did I."

"So what happens when we get back to Happy City?"

"That's anyone's guess. Maybe the firing squad for me, eh? I'll try to clear myself. What else can I do?"

"You've got the tape."

"Uh-huh. And Whitney's got all that dough and a battery of lawyers. It'll be touch and go for a while."

"I'll stick with you no matter what, Mr. Dunjer."

I took her hand, held it. "I'm counting on that, Miss Follsom."

"And you can prove that Mr. Whitney had his own master control cube, can't you?"

"There should be some records. I'm counting on that, too. And Gripus may be gone, but his boys are still around; now that we know what to look for, maybe we can get some of em to talk."

"You've got your work cut out for you."

"Yeah. Beginning now. This Escape League stuff is for the birds. They'll take us for every penny we've got. I know the route. We can get back on our own hook. It'll mean traveling by night and roughing it a bit. But if you're game, Miss Follsom, I'd like to give it a whirl."

"Whirl away, boss. I'm always game."

Chapter 32

"Stop here," I said quietly.

"No one's noticed us yet, have they?"

We were approaching Happy City's business district.

"Not yet, Miss Follsom. But it's only a matter of time. Remember you're rubbing shoulders with public enemy number one. We'll have to split up, I'm afraid. This district is full of cops. They could start shooting at the drop of a hat."

"Maybe they've forgotten about you by now."

"Fat chance. It may seem like a long time to us, but it's only been a couple of weeks. I bet I'm still a front-page item. Lemme take a chance and grab a paper. Wait here."

There was a newsstand on the corner. I went over, trying not to look furtive. I plunked down my nickel, was handed a copy of the *Daily Tattler*. I started to turn away quickly, before the newsie could see my face, my eyes racing over the front page. I stopped dead in my tracks. My feet felt as if they'd been cemented to the pavement. According to the date in the upper right-hand corner, it was now six months *before* I ever went on the lam.

The Security Plus building was down the block.

"What if we meet ourselves, boss?"

"We'll have to choose up to see who does what chores; it'll be some mess, eh, Miss Follsom?"

The mech doorman saluted as we went past. I pulled to a stop.

"Anyone go in this morning who looked like us?"

"Why no, sir."

"Uh-huh. Thanks."

We took the speed lift up. "Stick with me, Miss Follsom; we may need each other."

Mechs nodded to us as we went down the corridor. My office was just as I'd left it. No other Dunjer was sitting in my chair. I looked up at the wall clock: 9:30. Either I was late, or I was here already. Miss Follsom's office was empty, too.

"Follow me," I said. Miss Follsom and I trooped into Hennessy's office. A mech was holding down his desk.

"Where's Hennessy?" I asked.

"I beg your pardon, sir; is this some sort of joke?"

"Uh-uh. Just answer the question."

"Hennessy resigned over a year ago, Mr. Dunjer. He left Happy City. He is somewhere out among the City-States. Therefore it is impossible to answer your question precisely. No one can know where he is."

"Thanks," I said.

We went back to my office.

"Did you notice, Miss Follsom, that the corridor walls are painted green, that my floor has a brown rug on it and that the control board has too much chrome?"

"I noticed the green paint. I was too stunned for the rest of it."

"Well, the walls used to be white. I had no rug. It adds up, I'm afraid."

"To what?"

"To us being the only us here."

"But how's that possible, boss?"

298

"Probably because here isn't *quite* the here we left."

"That's crazy."

"What isn't? There may be hundreds of here's, even thousands. Each one a teeny bit different."

"But what happened to our other selves? They must have been here yesterday."

I shrugged. "Maybe they got shifted sideways to another here, or cancelled out."

"Then *everything* might be different!"

"Uh-uh. Look around. Everything is just about the same. The big difference is *us*. And Hennessy. And Gimpy Kreeg, I'll bet. Because we went through Time-warp Valley. There's some kind of adjustment that takes place. Don't ask me how."

"It's *wierd*," Miss Follsom shivered.

"It scares the hell out of me," I admitted.

"At least we know one thing, boss. Why Time-warp Valley is forbidden."

"Damn right."

"So what do we do now?"

"Sweep the whole floor for bugs and then call a general staff meeting. How's that for starters?"

"Sounds promising."

I paused to survey my audience. Thirty-eight mechs nodded in unison. There was something about that simple gesture I could've done without. "That about wraps it up," I continued. "We've got maybe six months to get the goods on Whitney and Gripus. It should be a lock. They don't know we're wise to em. Bug em so we've got every word they say. Set up peep-eye cameras in the safety vault. Gimpy Kreeg used to be Gripus's bugging pro, but he's probably blown town. Find out who's got the slot now and keep tabs on em. Let's hustle, guys; they'll never know what hit em."

My mech crew slowly filed out of the conference room. I turned to Miss Follsom. "Well, that's that. I hope."

"But won't you lose your job, boss, if Mr. Whitney goes to jail?"

"Are you kidding? I'll be a hero. Who knows—they might even make *me* Chairman of the Board."

"How nice."

"Yeah. It wouldn't hurt at all. Miss Follsom, there is one question I've been meaning to ask you."

"Ask anything, Mr. Dunjer."

"You do have a first name, don't you?"

"Why, of course. Laura."

"Ah. Would you mind if I called you Laura, Miss Follsom?"

"No. I'd love it, Mr. Dunjer."

"Great. You think maybe you could call me Tom?"

"Certainly."

"How about joining me for dinner tonight, Laura?"

"I'd be delighted, Tom."

"H-m-m-m. It's only eleven thirty. Let's say we get an early start, eh?"

"That sounds wonderful."

"Yeah. That's what I figure, too."

I put my arm around her.

We got out of there.

AFTERWORD to Outerworld

by Ron Goulart

I was an only child.

Had a room of my own, shared it with nobody. Never needed to worry about a sibling tossing and turning and committing all sorts of annoying acts in a bunk immediately above me. My vast accumulation of comic books, mixed with a tasteful smattering of pulps, was for my eyes only and remained pristine mint until I was fullgrown. If you can consider five feet four inches to be fullgrown. I never had to worry about a brother borrowing my necktie, my car or my girlfriend.

I am used to being a loner.

Even now that I've altered my anchorite state to the extent of taking a wife and producing two strapping sons, I still work in a separate wing of the house. The guy who had this place before us kept his mother-in-law in it, which should give you some idea of how isolated it actually is.

The only time I was ever in a double volume before, I shared it with myself. That was one of those paperbacks of fond memory where no matter which way you held it, half was upside down. And what warmhearted laughter we double authors used to share when our publisher sent us royalty statements showing that one half the volume had sold much better than the other.

The furthest I've gone is to share a byline with Gil Kane on our STAR HAWKS comic strip.

Then they tell me I have to share a book with this Haiblum guy.

What's he going to be like? Is he going to throw a lot of wild orgiastic parties, play his collection of E. Power Biggs albums loudly until near dawn, display an uncontrollable fondness for clog dancing, practice endlessly to get on *Bowling For Dollars*?

Once you're in a book with a guy, it's like a long-term lease. You can't move out.

Well, I read *Outerworld* and I'm happy to report Haiblum is an okay neighbor.

You can't help but like somebody who's obviously been bitten by a lot of the same stuff you have.

I mean, how many other writers you might bump into at Dell's 1 Dag Hammarskjold Plaza offices have ever heard of forgotten tough guy writers such as Paul Cain, Raoul Whitfield, Norbert Davis or Frederick Nebel?

Some of them are not even too sure about Dag Hammarskjold.

But Haiblum is obviously a man who's steeped himself in the pulpwood private eye fiction of yester-year. He has also chuckled over the works of science fiction's handful of true funnymen. I imagine, too, he's familiar with the superior type of television entertainment that can be found only on the late show.

In *Outerworld* he's blended the hardboiled, the screwball and science fiction; making homage to a lot of his idols, but remaining his own man all the while.

The result is a highly entertaining yarn. He has a good ear, he knows how to keep things moving.

Whenever I've encountered Haiblum in real life, which is usually at ceremonial festivities where there are too many writers and too much cigarette smoke, he's been wearing an anticipatory grin on his face. The world he moves through obviously amuses and delights him, he can't seem to wait to see what hilarious thing is going to happen next. He's certainly able to convey this attitude in his writing.

Now if this were a highminded college text instead of a piece of paperback escapist fare, here would be a good place to ask you all to compare and contrast our two novels.

Haiblum and I have obviously been stuffing similar input into our brains. We can't seem to forget one single private eye story we've ever read, we're fascinated with multiple intrigues, shady politics and the wonderful foolishness that tries to pass itself off as sober reality.

Myself, I'd say Haiblum is better able to stick to his narrative line. I'm quite often distracted into odd and quirky byways.

But then, it takes all kinds of clowns to make a circus.